I0746692

A Spark of Magic

By Tabatha Shipley

ISBN 978-1-7376512-0-8 (paperback)
ISBN 978-1-7376512-1-5 (ebook)

Tabatha Shipley Books

Also by Tabatha Shipley

<u>Kingdom of Fraun Series</u>

Breaking Eselda

Redeeming Jordyn

Training Tutor

Empowering Sawchett

30 Days Without Wings

Projection

December 27

Angela

Tucked in a valuable private alcove of the crowded hallway, I swipe my hand in a circle along the beige painted bricks and watch the image spawn in the wake of my hand. In a flash I'm looking at my tiny blond sister, eating a bowl of oatmeal with one hand while she thumbs something on her phone screen with the other. The blue bowl and the wooden table are both instantly familiar to me, but only by sight. I haven't spent enough time there to imagine the feel of the table. My nostalgia is tainted by my years spent here, at the Academy. As I watch, Mom rushes into the room dressed for work in heels and a skirt. Her hands are working at her right ear, fastening an earring. She leans down, kissing Evelyn on the forehead and swiping the phone from her hands in one practiced motion. "Finish up, we have ten minutes."

That's my cue to dial. I swipe the image off the wall and unlock my cell phone. I click on the favorites button with the picture of her dirty blonde hair swept up in a bun and the call starts. It rings only twice before Mom answers, breathless. "Angela, honey, how are you?"

"I'm great, Mom. I don't have a lot of time before class, but I wanted to say good morning."

"We are just having breakfast, getting ready to head out. How's school?"

I look around the hallway, watch kids rush to get where they're going. Third period will start any second now. I don't really have time to chat. Of course, that's why I'm calling right now. With the time difference, Mom is getting ready to head out when I'm getting to my third period. We're both busy, which means there's not a lot of time for questions. You see, most of what my Mom knows about the school I'm standing in is a total lie. I hate lying to her. "Same as always, nothing to worry about," I answer.

"Grades are good?"

"Of course. All passing." Grades wouldn't really tell the whole story right now. I'm in my final year at the Academy of Magic. Everything I am doing now relates directly to learning to control my spark. No more math, no more science. Our focus is on learning the occupations that are out there, because I've got one week left before I may be the person who is controlling all of the Magic in the world.

"It's so odd that you have to be back up there so soon. You were only here for five days. That's basically just a long weekend," Mom says. Her sigh is heavy and I feel my shoulders drop lower with the weight of the guilt.

"It's only because this is my last year, Mom. All the Seniors are here. We are getting a lot done because no underclassmen are here." That part is true. For this final week leading up to the big day, less than ten teachers and thirty students will be at the Academy. But on January 1 anyone in the world with a Magical spark will be in attendance. The entire school is already buzzing with the anticipation of this big event. Already my Christmas holiday at home seems like a distant memory.

Mom's voice drops a little, like maybe she's trying to keep this part of our conversation from my sister Evelyn. "You're okay up there? Safe?" she asks.

"I'm okay, Mom."

"I just worry. I hate being this far away from you. That boarding school is so good for you, but it's so far away."

"I know, Mom. It's almost over. I'm graduating this year. Then I can come home." I almost choke on the lie. My eyes water. If things go the way I want them to go, that's not what will happen at all. In a week, I may be the next Magician. Which means living at the Academy for the next decade.

"True." Her voice returns to a normal volume. "Do you want to say a quick hello to your sister?"

"I can't Mom, I have to go. I'm gonna be late. Talk soon. Love you."

"Oh, I love you too. Call us after school, okay?"

"I'll try. Bye." I hang up quickly and wipe at the residual tears in my eyes even as I step back into the crowded hallway and let the tide carry me toward Dispatch class. I slip inside and drop into a chair at the back of the room. I get my laptop out and booted up before the late bell rings.

At the front of the room, Andres Rodriguez stands up. He is easily the coolest teacher at the Academy with his laid-back rocker style. He dresses like a musician, not like a teacher. Baggy pants, t-shirts, an earring, and Converse are his regular style. His hair is longish and has that intentionally messed up style you'd associate with someone who regularly bangs his head around while playing guitar. He is an amateur musician, something he regularly talks about, but his profession is Magical Dispatch. He teaches morning classes, like mine, and works at the Dispatch center, also on campus, in the afternoons. His wife, Selena, has the opposite schedule. "Buenos días clase," he greets. "Please find the document I have emailed you and connect to the simulation. You may work with partners if you'd prefer. Good luck." He props one leg up on the wall behind him and leans back, crossing his arms in front of his chest. He smiles. Clearly, those are all the directions we're getting today.

I open the document and type into the heading. Name: Angela Terra. Occupation:

The cursor flashes, impatiently waiting. This is a touchy subject. Everyone in The Academy has an occupation already. It's what we train for, what we were chosen for, what we are working toward. Everyone on earth is scanned the day they enter school for the first time. The second they spot Academy potential inside you, that little spark of Magic, they take you up here. If they haven't found you by age ten, you don't have the spark. I've been here since a month before I turned five.

The Academy has a better scan. One that identifies the use for your spark. This scan can tell them exactly where your spark is the most useful. That becomes your occupation. They tell me I have one of the strongest sparks there is. So what's my occupation?

Well, that's complicated.

Every decade the person with the strongest spark becomes the Magician. Just one. The Magician controls all the sparks. The Magician single-handedly controls the safety of the modern world by controlling all of the Magic left on Earth. A new Magician is set to take over on January 1.

I may be the most coveted occupation in the galaxy.

Or, my worst nightmare could come true. Because for the first time in history, there are two of us who have that strong spark. If she gets the job, I could just be the girl who was almost Magician.

December 27

Tanya

The hallways between classes always border on chaos. Everyone is trying to grab a minute with friends or lovers before dashing off to another class. On top of that, we all came from simulations that may have been dark or dangerous. It's high stress and chaotic, which translates to no fun. This week, with only Seniors on campus, it is a little better. But, honestly, we're usually the loudest and most competitive so it's not a big improvement.

I spot Logan's blonde hair just above the crowd. He's always easy to find because of his height. It doesn't hurt that he was one of the few in recent years to be brought to the Academy from the shores of sunny California, his blonde highlights sparkle under even the harsh fluorescent lights. I push and elbow my way through the crowd, using those sun-kissed tresses as a beacon.

Like a scene from a brainless romcom the crowd parts and there he is. All tanned skin, tight shirt, popping six pack, and board shorts package. He's exactly the kind of guy who is supposed to be the love interest of the leading lady. Exactly the kind of hero for the girl who will be the next Magician, the most powerful woman in the world. He's exactly who I should be with.

He smiles when he sees me, crossing the last few steps between us quicker than I can. In full view of the whole bustling hallway he slips his arms around me and plants a kiss right on my lips. "Hey babe," he says once we pull apart. "How was class?"

"Pretty good," I answer. "Yours?"

He smiles and steps back. I turn and fall in beside him. It's our routine to walk side-by-side to lunch. "Same old shit." He winks at me. "But I saved the day, as always."

I reach down and grab his hand, squeezing. "Of course you did." He squeezes back and we finish our walk just like that. Hand-in-hand walking the crowded hallway like a power couple.

The cafeteria smells pretty good today. This week, the final week before the ceremony that will change my life forever, the only people on campus are those in their final year. This means that we are all fending for ourselves at lunch. Everyone here has a strong enough spark to conjure whatever food they may want. Logan and I drop into a table where his best friends are already seated.

Angela catches my eye, because Angela is hard to miss. Her hair is light brown but loaded with blond highlights that pop. She always pays such careful attention to her appearance, unlike me. You can tell in the perfect curls floating by her shoulders and the makeup, lightly touched onto all the right places. She's a little chubby, I suppose, but in an adorable way. Like a stuffed animal to my bony skeleton.

I see her come into the crowded cafeteria and drop to the table of her friends. Since we're in competition for one job, it's as if we are playing a game with every decision we make and she plays the game well. Her group of friends is a perfect power move. Cheryl is smart and confident, Steve is an excellent Solver and an adorable hunk. Chris may be a loose cannon on the surface, but he is brilliant and strong.

I look around my own gang. Logan and the group that can only be accurately described as his friends, surround me. They're an odd crew that have assembled by proximity, all near the same age and living in the same dorm. George was originally born to an Asian family living in New York, Frank is a skinny little brunette from South America, and Charlie's family lives in a small village in Africa. They're all above average intelligence and top of their occupations. Really my clique is very similar to Angela's except for one glaringly obvious difference. She seems to genuinely like hers.

"What are everyone's plans for New Years?" George asks.

I give him a don't-be-an-idiot glare. "You know damn well there's a ceremony this year," I say. Man, if words could kill this kid would be grabbing his chest and dropping to the ground faster than you can say, "Magician's Assistant".

"Oh yeah." He throws his hands up like a surrender. "I forgot, Tanya. Damn. The ceremony only happens like once in a lifetime."

"All the more reason to remember it." I wave my hand to produce a big salad topped with all the important things; tuna, cucumber, bacon bits, and cheese. I take a deliberately slow bite, glaring at him as I chew. "Besides, it's once every ten years. I'm sure even you plan to still be alive in another decade."

"Well, I won't be at the Academy anymore in ten years, will I?" He laughs, shaking his head like I'm the idiot. "I wasn't here for the last one either."

George was a late sparker. He joined us when he was already ten, the oldest possible age even scanned for sparks. I wasn't friends with his crowd at the time and I'm not sure what the Researcher can offer me now. Honestly, George is weak in terms of spark.

I, on the other hand, was eight when the Magician accepted her position. I remember the details. Her name before, the one I'm never permitted to speak, was Francheska. She had this natural life and grace up there on the stage. I remember watching her and thinking she was the coolest person I had ever seen up close. She is everything I try to copy.

She stood center stage as they drew a circle around her feet in dirt, to root her, and then in salt, to ward off disturbances. She recited the promise "to control the spread of dark energy in the world and prevent the damage it can cause" in a clear voice that echoed off the far wall.

I already knew then that Angela and I were different, new. Angela was only seven so I'm not sure how much she remembers or absorbed. But even then my thoughts strayed to how our ceremony would have to be different. What happens when there's two of us on that stage?

I watched Francheska absorb the light and sparks from the room. I watched her grow taller first and then hunch her shoulders forward like she was wearing a large backpack. Her eyes widened and she cried out in pain, a short bark that shocked me.

When it was over, she was draped in a black robe and smiled a full smile for the audience, who greeted the new Magician with thunderous applause. I cannot explain it, but I noticed right away her energy was suddenly different. She seemed almost deflated. Ever since then, she's been the same commanding, dry, serious Magician. But I will never forget the confident girl who first took the stage.

That ceremony changed her right in front of my eyes.

Fall, Age 10

Emily

Some singing competition is on the television screen. It's not something I'm watching. Maybe I can change the channel. I quickly glance to the other side of the room and see Mom's rapt attention fixed on the image. Her eyes are actually welling up with tears. Clearly, she's buying into the sob story they've written for this character. I wonder how much of it is even true. I sigh. No way I can suggest changing the channel if Mom is watching.

Beside Mom on the couch, Dad is not even pretending to watch. There's an open magazine on his lap. Even that doesn't seem to be getting his full attention. He's just flipping through pages without really looking. He seems to be staring at some point on the floor.

I grab my cell phone and start rifling through apps. A text message comes through, sounding my phone's charm. It's Tricia.

She's bored. "Me too," I type. Then I flip my phone to silent so I won't annoy Mom if it keeps dinging.

Instead, it rings in my hand. "It's Tricia, I should take this," I say. I slide my thumb across the answer bar at the same time that I push myself up off the couch and slip into the hallway for a little semblance of privacy. "Hello."

"Hey, we're going to go to the park for no reason at all. The one between our houses. You're coming, right?" Tricia says all of this in one breath.

"Who's 'we'?" I ask.

"Me and my brother. Ask if you can come. He wants to shoot some hoops or whatever. I'm allowed to go but only if he goes, you know how they are. See if you can come. Micky is an adult, technically. Remind them of that."

That is a technicality. Micky turned eighteen literally yesterday. "I can ask. No promises," I tell her. Then I hang up and walk back into the living room, smiling.

"Ask us what?" Dad says. He wants to make sure I know he heard my side of the conversation. I wonder, for just a second, if he used Magic or if I was that loud.

"Can I go to the park with Tricia and Micky? Micky's going to play basketball. I'll bring my cell phone, I'll stay safe, and I won't be gone for more than ninety minutes." I start high. I'd actually be perfectly fine if they counter-offered forty-five minutes.

"It's a school night," Mom says, checking her watch.

I already know what time it is. It's 6:45. My bedtime is 9:00. I have plenty of time. Honestly, when Tricia first called I didn't even really care. But seeing the looks they're swapping between them, knowing that the "no" is coming, I really want to go. It's not fair. Tricia's Mom probably didn't even put up a fight. She probably just agreed right away. Tricia called almost as fast as I texted her. I bet the "yes" from her Mom was that fast. Instant.

When I'm an adult, I think, I'll let my kid go to the park with her friends.

Maybe I can do something about it. I have these abilities. Dad does too. He calls them Magic. He says the World of Magic gifts people with skills. He says not everyone has them. I've heard him tell his friends that he thinks there are levels of Magic. Some people have more of it than others. I'm not sure if I agree with all that, but I can't argue with the presence of my skills.

I close my eyes and think about Dad. I decide that I'll try and change his mind. Try and connect with him. Maybe I can plant an idea.

Except when I open my eyes, I'm looking at myself. I turn my head to the right, Mom. I look down, that's Dad's lap. There's the magazine he was reading.

I panic and draw a shocked breath.

That pulls me right back to myself.

Now I'm looking at my parents, sitting on the couch. Except Dad looks confused. I wonder if that hurt his stomach like it hurt mine. I wonder if he knows what I just did. If he does, I'm going to be in a lot of trouble. I wait, watching. There's looks passing between him and Mom but they're not that "you'll never believe what your daughter just did" kind of looks.

An idea that could either be incredibly brilliant or terribly bad occurs to me. The possibility of being capable of controlling Dad's movements and speech from inside of him is intoxicating. I decide to try again.

This time, when I open my eyes I'm not as surprised because I'm expecting it to work. I can see myself, Emily, looking frozen in time. At least my eyes are open on my body this time, so I don't look like I'm sleeping standing up. I try out the voice. "Emily, if you promise to be back in one hour you can go. Bring your cell phone."

"Magnus," Mom says beside me. Her voice is full of doubt.

"All right, fine. Forty-five minutes," I say in Dad's voice.

Mom sighs and her shoulders slump. I close my eyes and pop back into myself. My stomach lurches like I've dropped off the highest peak of a fast roller coaster. I resist the urge to groan, instead I force a smile. "Thanks, Dad. You're the best."

I'm really glad I'm already wearing my sneakers, because Dad looks completely confused. I can hear them whispering as I flee for the front door. Before Mom can explain what just happened my hand is on the doorknob. I don't wait to hear if I'm in trouble, I just dash off.

Maybe this Magic thing will be pretty cool.

December 27

Angela

I hate this class.

It's a weird feeling, hate. I usually love everything. I love school and studying. I can imagine a vivid future for myself that includes more time spent here at The Academy studying Magic and I love that. I love my friends. I love my family.

But when that bell rings for eighth period, everything changes. This hallway is stark and empty. There's only one classroom in this hallway, at the very end, and that classroom is only used for my eighth period. So when I say it's empty, I mean it. Plus, there's only two other people who may even need to be down here. Today, my footsteps echo back to me. Based on the echo and the absence of other human beings in this hallway, I'm guessing I'm the last to arrive. I pull open the heavily reinforced door at the end of the hallway.

Yup, they're both here. At the front of the room, perched on a desk, is the Magician. The keeper of all the Magic on the planet. She doesn't look like much. She's actually tiny, less than five feet. She has adorable features and not a wrinkle on her face. Her hair is pulled back in a brown ponytail and she's wearing black robes.

In front of her and slightly to her left the only other person in the room turns to look at me. Tanya's green eyes flash with glee at being first, taking an extra point in our constant competition. She wiggles her fingers in my direction as a greeting and her long black ponytail swishes along her back as she turns her attention back to the Magician.

I take my seat, symbolically beside Tanya's. I drop my book bag to the floor and sweep my dirty blonde tresses into a ponytail of my own. We never leave our hair down for this class because you never know what we might get into.

"Ladies, today I will begin your simulation in the control room," the Magician explains. "Your objective remains the same as always. Find the source of the disturbance and implement a strategy to shut it down. You will have thirty minutes."

This is typical. Tanya and I are being put through the training every Magician's apprentice before us has been put through. We've been through all the drills and practice, with a teacher of the school. Now, since we are in the final week before one of us must take over, the Magician herself is taking us through simulations. But no one is really sure what will happen on January 1. Two people with the spark have never presented before, not like this. Training has never before been for two people at once. Hence my hatred. This class that should be my favorite, preparing me to hold all the Magic in the world, is instead a competition.

"Are we ready?" the Magician asks.

I stand up, pop my knuckles, and nod. I am aware of Tanya beside me, also rising, rolling her head in a circle to loosen her neck. We are ready.

The room dissolves and we are inside the control room. The temperature drops at least fifteen degrees, all the technology in here doesn't like heat. Before us there is an impressive array of screens, spanning about ten feet in either direction. All of them are touch screens and show various parts of the earth. They're satellite images, normally live. Of course, this is a simulation so we may be limited to what the Magician is granting us to look at. The screens respond to voice commands as well as touch, we know that from previous experiences. There is one metal chair in front of the middle screen, reserved for the one Magician. This has the potential to be really awkward, forcing Tanya and I to pretend to be chivalrous and allow the other one the coveted place at the control center. Thankfully, this isn't an issue today. The stress of the simulation forces our decision. We stand, watching the screens, and wait for further instructions.

"Your time starts now." The Magician's voice booms into the room as though coming from a speaker.

"Wait, she didn't give us a focus," I say. She always gives us a focus. We come into this room and she tells us to find the disturbance in Africa, or Australia, or wherever. How can we be expected to scan all one hundred ninety-five countries in the world for disturbances in thirty minutes?

"Magician, can we have an area to focus?" Tanya asks.

I count to five before the booming voice answers. "When I am no longer in power, who will be here to focus you? Find the problem. Twenty-nine minutes remaining."

DECEMBER 27

TANYA

"We have to find one disturbance. We don't know how large or small and we don't know where it is," I summarize. "Let's split up. I'll start in Australia and move my way west. You start in Russia and move your way east. Do large scale scans first, only zoom in if you find an abnormality." I don't wait for Angela to disagree or argue, we don't have time. Instead, I step up to the computer in front of me and give my command. "Show me Earth, zoomed out." The image of Earth, full blue ball of life, comes onto my screen. I pinch my fingers in the center of the ball and push them outward, zooming in. I repeat the motion centered over the continent of Australia.

When Australia takes up most of my screen, I start looking. I know what I'm looking for, I've seen it before. I'm looking for waves of energy, rippling and radiating out from a center point. The center point will be something wrong, a problem. Some negative energy. It looks like ripples in water after a rock is thrown. But this far out they will be small.

I squint my eyes at the screen, using my right hand to move the picture around and explore the entire continent. I don't see anything. I allow myself to long blink, rest my eyes, and then they're open again and I'm heading up to Indonesia with my scroll.

I slowly move the screen up through Vietnam, over to Thailand, back to China. I don't bother going north to Russia, I know that's where Angela started. Instead, I push myself to head west and squint my eyes at India. I pinch and zoom the screen when I think I see something, but it's gone when I get closer. Zoom back out, keep looking.

"Wait, I have something," Angela says. Her voice is questioning, she's not sure. I pull my eyes away from my screen, hoping she's right because I don't want to lose my place if she's not.

"What is it?" I ask.

"Yes, look. It's still there. Brazil. Full screen," she commands the computer.

An image of Brazil fills all the screen space in front of us. I step back to take it all in. The ripples are originating near the eastern border. "Rio de Janeiro, maybe?" I ask.

Angela seems to ignore me, but she pinches and zooms closer to Rio.

The map scoots closer and closer, allowing us to see more features of the land and the ocean that make up Brazil. As we draw closer, it's evident the ripples are centered a little more north than I thought. "That island, what is that?" I ask. Look, I'm good at geography, but not that good.

"I don't know. Turn on labels," Angela commands. White letters fill the screen. I squint. My eyes are so dry from trying to find these ripples. We still need to figure out what is happening and stop it. I wonder how much time is left. Do I even want to know? "Ilha do Governador," Angela reads the label for the island.

"Governador?" I ask. "Please tell me that's not Brazilian for government. Please tell me we didn't just locate a disturbance that affects the Brazilian government." Despite how many of these simulations we run, they always feel real. I try to take a calming breath and remind myself that this isn't a real threat, but the racing of my heart doesn't slow.

"I don't know." Angela pinches and zooms faster.

We have to be careful when we are zooming in and out here. The ripples are deceptive. Sometimes they appear to be centered around one thing when they're actually centered somewhere else. We have to watch them pulse for a beat before we zoom further. Once the Magician even gave us a problem that was on the move. This meant the ripples were traveling. We need to know that. A Solver on the ground, our eyes and ears, will need that important piece of information if they have any hope of finding the disturbance. So we pause each time she zooms, making it a painfully slow process.

Further and further toward the western edge of the little island, Angela zooms. I realize I'm holding my breath and force myself to let it out and breathe normally. There are two little semi circle shaped buildings showing on the screen, the smooth gray of concrete making them stand out against the greenery. "Is that what I think it is?" I ask as the circles start to have some defined shape.

"Airport," she answers. "Call the Solvers. We have a location."

I reach for my cell phone. In this simulation room my calls will sound like they're going through, but they're really not. In reality, no matter who I call, it's the Magician listening and judging my professionalism. I know that, but still my pulse quickens. This is the do-or-die moment. If this were real, we had better be right before we make this call.

"Dispatch," the voice on the other end answers. It doesn't sound like the Magician. It sounds like a man on high alert, as it will when that phone really rings.

"This is the Magician's Assistant. We have identified a disturbance. Send Solvers to the Airport in Rio de Janeiro, Brazil."

There's a pause. I can hear some computer keys clicking. Dispatch will be looking for nearby Solvers to send out to the airport. They'll need more information. I wait. "There's a few airports near Rio. Which one am I looking for?" the man asks.

I lean closer to the screen and squint at the little white letters. I have no hope of pronouncing that word correctly on the first try. I spell it instead. "G-a-l-e-a-o."

More clicking. "Got it. Which terminal?" the man asks.

Angela has been zooming in a little more as I talked. "One," I answer. Confidence rings in my tone. I've learned to fake that. People need me to be confident or they panic.

"I'll text you the phone number of the Solver you'll be working with. Give him two minutes." The calls disconnects with a soft click.

"Two minutes," I tell Angela. She nods.

My phone dings. I tip it to turn on the screen and see it's the text message. "I have his number. What else will we tell him when we call?" We are both looking at the screen. Now that we are close to the circles, they're useless. The disturbance will pinpoint a location, we have to do the rest. Angela has zoomed into the first terminal of the airport, near the Federal Police building according to our helpful labels.

But we still have to figure out what we are looking for.

December 27

Angela

"Time's up," Tanya says. For a second, my heart stops. Then I realize she's talking about the two minutes. It's not over. We didn't fail. We just need to call the Solver.

I bob my chin in her direction. "Do it on speakerphone." I am not letting Tanya get all the credit for this when we solve it. No way. She complies and I hear the phone ring once before a deep voice answers. "Solver fifteen on the ground."

"Are you at the airport?" Tanya asks.

"Yes. Approaching terminal one. Awaiting takeover."

"Is it safe to take over now?" I ask. In our practice with the other teachers, Tanya has a habit of doing the takeovers. There's no way I'm letting that happen today in front of the Magician. I want to do it.

I hear the man draw a shaky breath. "Yes."

I don't wait for further permission. I close my eyes and send out sparks toward the man. I don't have to know him. I don't have to know anything more than what I already know because his voice was just filling the room. The cell phone offers that connection, I just have to take it. So I do and it just … happens. It's easy and peaceful. I feel the breeze suddenly, even though we're indoors, and I know it's worked.

When I open my eyes I have to blink against the bright sun bouncing off the windows of the airplanes in front of me. I would love to just take a second and enjoy Brazil. I have never been to Brazil. But I can't. I don't have that luxury.

"Alright Angela, I have you on screen. Look around. Do a slow circle or something." Tanya's voice comes through the earpiece the Solver must have clipped to his ear before I took over. I do as she asks, knowing that she will be able to watch what is happening through my eyes on the screen in front of her. This is new technology that was brought into the classroom because there are two of us. It won't work beyond simulations.

I do a full circle and don't see anything. I want, desperately, to see the answer myself. I have no idea how much is left of our thirty minutes but it can't be much. I take shaky steps out away from the airport building. I'm aware I am stepping toward the police building, but hopefully I won't have to walk that far. I'm trying to feel it out. I'm going off of my gut instinct. I have no idea what I'm looking for.

"Stop," Tanya suddenly commands. "What's that?"

I squint at the item she must be referring to. It looks like trash. I almost dismiss her and keep walking. But why would a bag of trash be on the runway of an airport in Brazil? "I don't know," I admit.

"Come back. Let him check it out," Tanya says.

"No, we should do it. I'll just have a look." It's a bad idea if what is in that bag is a bomb. But if what is in that bag is some kind of Magic technology, I'm the person who should be checking it out. "How much time do we have left?"

She sighs. The phone picks up the noise louder than if I were next to her, it echoes around the room before filtering through the speaker. "I have no idea."

I walk fast. It's a black bag, small. The kind of bag you'd take to sports practice of some kind. It could be filled with a basketball and a change of clothes. I don't see any marks or logos. When I'm close enough to reach out and touch it, I pause. It looks like some kind of nylon. No mesh. Not like luggage. Just a throw away bag. Could've been free at an event or something, if it had logos.

"What are you waiting for?" Tanya asks. The question jars me back to the present. If I'm doing this, I have to do it. I don't have time to stall.

I step up to the bag. The top zipper wraps around the outside, forming a rectangle. I don't let myself panic, I grab the zipper and slowly tug it up, right, and down until the bag is open. I pull the resulting flap back toward myself.

There's no blinking device inside. I don't think I realize how much I thought it was going to be a bomb until the bag is open and it's not. Instead, nestled in the bag like sleeping twins, are two brick sized containers of white powder. "Drugs," I say out loud.

"Get up, look around, is there someone nearby who may be waiting to buy them?" Tanya sounds on edge. Shouldn't I be the one on edge? Out here in the middle of the danger zone? Of course, in reality, whoever this Solver is should really be nervous. This guy whose body I'm borrowing is the only one in real danger if something goes down.

I stand up and turn in a circle, absolutely nothing is out of the ordinary. It's a hot day and the sun is beating down on me. No people in sight. "Why aren't there any people at this airport?" I ask. "Shouldn't it be busy?"

"I don't know. Maybe the disturbance was a drug deal. We take the drugs, we stop the deal. Give them to the Solver. He can dispose of them. Swap places, get back here."

I do as she says. Slipping my (his) eyes closed, I take a few deep breaths and concentrate on being back in the control room. Again, I feel it happen. I snap into place like those children's toys that only fit in one way, with a satisfying click. The air is stale, cooler. I open my eyes and I'm back there again. Facing the screens and standing beside Tanya's skinny little body. She's holding the cell phone.

"This bag you're standing in front of is evidence. It is the source of the disturbance. The bag must be returned to central and destroyed," she commands.

"Copy that," the Solver answers.

December 27

Tanya

One blink. That's what I get. I close my eyes inside the control room and when I open them again I'm back in the classroom staring at the Magician who is now standing at the front of the room with her arms crossed over the front of her black robes. "Time's up," she says.

I take my seat even though I'm nervous and I don't really feel like sitting. I notice, on my left, Angela does the same thing. Her leg is bouncing like it always does when we are done with a simulation. It's like she's a rubber band that's been wound up and that's her way of releasing. We're both silent, waiting for the score and the analysis to be spat at us. The other teachers sometimes wait until the next day. Sometimes they rate us separately, reminding us we are in constant competition. Since we're back from our short Christmas break today, we have no idea how the

Magician will approach the scoring. I don't want to care about a stupid score in a simulation, but I need to win this job.

"You were able to locate the source of the disturbance and report a location to the Solvers within eleven minutes," she begins. Eleven minutes isn't bad, at least I don't think it's bad. "It's a good time, ladies. But I must remind you that in the real world you will not be told to look for a disturbance. You must learn to be on the lookout for them at all times, even without being told to look."

"Is there a way to feel them?" Angela asks.

The Magician draws her eyebrows together. "Yes, if you learn to recognize the feeling." She smiles at Angela, recognition for a good question. I'm annoyed that Angela seems to be impressing the Magician.

"You were able to locate and order the disposal of a bag of illegal substances within twenty-nine minutes. This is a good time. From finding the source to disposal took you only eighteen minutes. Well done."

My insides are positively flying at the praise. I sit up a little straighter in the chair.

"I do have concerns, however." My shoulders slump again. I wasn't expecting perfect, not really. But just once it would be nice. "Firstly, you needed each other all the way through this simulation. When you are no longer apprentices you will not have anyone else. You cannot rely on someone else to trampoline your ideas from." She takes a step closer, uncrossing her arms and laying one hand on each of our desks. "You must be able to make those decisions that need to be made quickly and entirely on your own. Are you capable of that?"

"Yes," we both answer. I turn my head and look at Angela. She is in full I-hate-you mode. Her eyes are narrowed at me and she has a smug smile on her face. Competition turns her into a hissing cat after his tail's been run over by a rocking chair. I make a silly face at her and turn my attention back to the Magician.

"Secondly, you took an unnecessary risk by having the Magician control the body during the opening of the bag." Here, I notice, she turns her attention to Angela. "If that had been some kind of explosive instead of an illegal substance you could seriously endanger your spark as well as kill the body of that Solver or put out his spark. It was risky."

"It felt safe, somehow, in my gut." I'm shocked Angela has the gumption to say that. I lean in my chair a little, trying to put a little space between us in case the Magician's temper explodes.

Instead, the Magician sighs. "While I understand and value trusting your spark and the feelings it gives you, I cannot condone the risk you took. Solvers have some spark as well. Trust the team you are given, even if they are not as strong as you." Angela nods. I'm aware she's dominating this report. I need to find time to speak up.

"Thirdly, and perhaps most importantly, you failed to complete the task."

Wait, what?

"You chose to dispose of the bag, but you made two large errors. One, you didn't ask for the contents of the bag to be analyzed before disposal. Meaning, if this were a real situation, we don't even know what we're dealing with. Two, you took the bag without doing anything about the man who left the bag there." She shakes her head. "Basically, you destroyed the bag but know absolutely nothing about how it got there. This means you will likely have to face this situation again."

"We didn't see anyone around. We were afraid of the time crunch. In the interest of learning from our mistakes can you tell us where the man was to be found?" I ask.

"I'll show you." She waves her hand above her head and behind her the scene pops up. It looks as though she's materialized a screen with the video of our simulation directly behind her. Of course, she's the Magician, she actually may have done just that. On the ground, crouched by the black bag, is the Solver. Of course we know that's really Angela controlling the Solver. He straightens up, turning his body around in a slow circle. The Magician holds up one finger and the video pauses.

"There," she says. "Do you see it now?"

I certainly don't. I look at Angela. She's frowning.

The Magicians sighs. She flicks her finger to the left and the image zooms in on something to the right of the screen. We can still see the Solver's leg but we're looking at something in the bushes along the outer edge of the runway. "What is that?" I ask.

"That," she narrows her eyes at me, "is the man who left the bag on the runway." She turns toward the image for the first time and uses her hand to push the image to the right. Now we are looking on the left hand side of the Solver. "And this is the man who was there to buy them."

I can't believe we missed two people. Sure they were way outside of the clearing and crouching in the trees, but we don't know who they are and that is a huge problem. The job of the Magician is to harness and use all the sparks of Magic that exist on Earth to prevent and stop crime. If this had been a real situation, instead of a simulation, we would've failed. Epically.

Summer, Age 11

Emily

The ceiling in my room has that texturing with bumps all over it that you can really only see in the light. I'm laying on my back staring up at it wondering if those bumps actually serve a purpose or if they're, like, accidents of some roller someone invented and didn't bother to perfect.

But I'm also snapping my fingers and making things happen all over my room. Snap-bedside lamp goes on. Snap-bedside lamp goes off. Snap-closet door opens. Snap-closet door closes. Snap-book flies off the shelf and lands on my bed. Snap-Another book on top of that one.

I don't have to snap, but I like to. It's immediate. It associates the action of using Magic, which no one understands and we're not allowed to talk about, with something most people can do. It also reminds me of that scene from the Mary Poppins movie they're always playing on the old movie channels where she makes them clean up the room by snapping.

I'm trying to keep myself awake because Dad has a meeting going on downstairs. He says it's just some guys from work but I have a feeling it's something cooler. Why else would he invite guys from work over after my bedtime?

I check the clock on my bedside table. It's 10:17. I've heard the front door open and close a few times, but it's been at least fifteen minutes since the last one. Time to see what's going on with this meeting.

I sit up in bed and close my eyes. I focus on my Dad. The first time I popped into Dad's body it was basically an accident. I didn't know I was capable of that. Since then I've tried it a few times. It seems to only work on Dad, not Mom. When I close my eyes and try to reach out for her I can't connect. I can call up a memory, but that's not the same. It doesn't click the same in my head. But with Dad, no problem.

I only stay for a quick second. By now he's used to me trying this out and he tends to get pretty angry. I just stay long enough to look through his eyes and see who else is there. I'm hoping he hasn't bothered to tell any of his work friends that his daughter can take over his body. That seems like a strange thing to have a little chat about, doesn't it?

Back in my room in my own body I'm smiling. Because I recognize one of Dad's friends. This time, when I close my eyes, I imagine that guy. His name is Fred, I think. I've only met him a few times. I'm hoping that's enough.

I open my eyes in my own living room. I look down at the body. Definitely Fred. I settle back onto the couch and try to look normal. There are four other people here, besides me and Dad. They're sitting all around the living room, one is even sitting on the floor. The guy next to me is talking. "What do you do to fight the drain though? How do you re-energize?" he asks.

"Sleep," someone answers. "That's the only cure I've found."

"How much Magic can you do before you feel drained?" someone else asks.

I feel a coldness all over my body. I try not to look shocked or react at all. They're talking about Magic? I know Dad can do Magic, he's told me. I know he's aware that I can. I know Mom can't. But outside of our house, we're not supposed to talk about it.

You can get sent to the Principals' office for talking about Magic at school. You can get a lot worse for talking about it outside of school. People want to study you, use you, or accuse you of dangerous things. This is what I've heard. So why are these grownups sitting around and talking about Magic like it's the most normal thing in the world?

"I'm good for between five and ten good spells," Dad answers. "Maybe three really big ones."

"That's pretty good," the guy on my right answers. "One big one makes me feel like I need a full night's sleep. I can't even teleport myself across the house after healing an injury."

Teleportation. Healing. This is the stuff I need to be learning. I lean forward a little, eager to hear more. Then I freeze. I realize that probably makes me, as Fred, look like I have something to add to the conversation. I try to make it look like I was just adjusting, getting more comfortable.

"Does anyone else have a way to recharge instead of sleeping?" the guy pushes. "There has to be a way we can get more out of a day. How useful am I if healing one person means I need a nap? Imagine how much more good I could do if I could heal hundreds or thousands."

"Can we borrow from each other?" Dad asks. "Could I gift you energy? Can we draw it from an outside source?"

"Like a battery?" the guy on the floor says. "That seems ridiculous, doesn't it?"

"I don't know," Dad admits. "To some people, I suppose, everything we're talking about would seem ridiculous."

Is he giving me a strange look? Does he suspect something is up? My heartbeat speeds up. Worried I'm going to get caught, I close my eyes and bring myself back to my bedroom where beads of sweat are breaking out across my brow.

So now I know two things.

One, there are other people who can do Magic.

Two, apparently you have a limit to how much Magic you can do before you feel drained.

I turn and check the clock on my bedside table. I've been sitting in this room doing Magic for well over ninety minutes now, pretty much constantly. According to the guy I heard at the meeting, I should be tired.

If Magic is like a glass of water, slowly pouring out if you use it and refilling when you sleep, why is it that my cup never seems to run out?

What would it take to limit my Magic?

December 28

Angela

My first period class is full of Solvers. Some of my favorite people and best friends are in this class. After your spark is discovered you come to the Academy. At first you are grouped by age, just like a "traditional" school. It doesn't take long before the teachers have analyzed your talents and spark to figure out your occupation. After that your classes are all grouped by occupation. Kids in your group will still be around your age, but it's not an exact science. It's more important that they are the same occupation as you are and the same level in that occupation. This group is what you'd call advanced Solvers. Except me, of course. I'm not allowed to become truly advanced in anything. I'm learning the surface of everything and remembering shockingly little of it. I have no idea what I'll be expected to do for an occupation if I'm not the next Magician. I don't even know if I'll keep my spark. No one does, we're in uncharted territory here.

I drop into a comfy red armchair surrounding a small round table. This class always takes place in a little room that I imagine was once a library. There are five little setups, each identical. Five tiny little glass topped tables each surrounded by four large armchairs that look like they should be holding some rich newspaper man from way back in the old days. This particular grouping currently holds some of my best friends in the world.

Steve, at eighteen, is the oldest in our group. He's sitting directly to the left of the chair I dropped into. He pats my knee when I sit, winking at me. Chris sits on Steve's left. Chris and Steve are similar in appearance, both with their longish wavy brown surfer hair and thin faces. But Steve has the gorgeous terracotta skin of his family in Fiji. Finishing off our little circle, on my right, sits Cheryl. Currently, her nose is buried in a book. Cheryl is the youngest Solver in the class, at only sixteen. Of course, talent and spark are the only considerations for aging up to a Senior in the program so she's with us despite her age. She's shy and I'm not altogether sure why we hit it off as quickly as we did.

"You ready for this class today?" Steve asks.

I groan. "After my disaster of an eighth period yesterday, yes."

"Disaster? Do tell." Chris waggles his eyebrows at me. "Is it salaciously bad? Did someone die in your game?" Chris is notoriously flippant about our simulations.

"I let Tanya make the phone call--"

"That's your first mistake," Steve notes. He holds up one finger on his left hand.

I scoff. "But I took the takeover. The problem is, I kept control of the Solver to investigate a mystery bag we found."

"Second mistake." Steve adds a finger.

I sigh dramatically. "We found an illegal substance inside the bag.'

"Ooohhhh," Chris howls. "Interesting. Was it explosive? Did someone die a gruesome video-game inspired death? Were there pieces everywhere?"

Steve wrinkles his nose. "That's gross, even for you."

"It was drugs, I think," I say. "We checked for people, didn't see any, and ordered the disposal of the bag."

Cheryl lowers her book, looking at us over the top of the spine. "You had the substance checked first, right?"

I drop my head into my hands and let out a groan that should scare birds out of the trees outside. The room goes silent and I risk picking my head up to see the judgmental looks of my friends. "See, this is why I need you guys when I'm doing these stupid simulations. No, I didn't think of that."

'Uh-oh," Steve says as he puts up a third finger.

"Oh, it gets worse," I say. "The Magician shows up for our scores and points out that we missed not one but two people hiding in the foliage. The buyer and the seller were both nearby and we missed it."

"Damn," Chris says. He draws out the word, making it two syllables.

Steve sucks in air through his teeth. "That's another mistake." This time, instead of adding a finger, he just extends his middle one in a crude gesture echoing exactly how I feel about it.

He drops his finger and turns his attention to the hallway door just as it snaps shut. Sean Roland, Solver extraordinaire and all around hottie, is standing in front of the now closed door wearing a grey vest over a white shirt with the sleeves rolled almost to his elbows. "Let's not waste any time. Shall we begin? You know your mission."

"Man, I love how Rolly always cuts to the chase. Why waste time, let's get our solve on." Steve stands up and cracks his knuckles.

"Yes, let's see how we can mess up the plan today." Chris winks at me.

My eyes are open when the simulation starts so I get to see the blip when it happens, which is always shocking. It's like someone changing the channel when you were actively watching the show without warning you. I blink fast to get my brain to catch up with the change.

I am on a train platform. There are people all around us. I take a second to appreciate the Magic that must have gone into this simulation. In reality, I'm standing in a classroom surrounded by about nine other people. But each of us is inside this simulation thinking we are alone. Basically the Magician has set it up so that each of us will run this simultaneously. My ending may be different than Steve's, for example, but it's starting exactly the same. I don't even know how to do that and we have less than a week left before the power shift.

Focus, Ang.

People are generally moving toward the train, that tells me whatever I'm doing here involves a train that is about to leave the station. I reach my right hand up to my ear and find a securely attached communication piece. Perfect. I push on it and the voice of the Magician fills my ear. "Are you on location?"

"I am at the train station, near an outbound train. What track should I be looking at?"

There's a pause. I imagine the Magician, if this were real, would be zooming around their screens trying to find me that answer. My stomach knots tightly. Solvers are right in the middle of the action at all times, even when they aren't aware of it. They're literally putting their bodies in danger for us. It's scary. "Fifteen,' she answers. "I'm going to need you to board the train before I take control."

I turn around, checking for a number on the wall of the station. There, on a pillar, is the italicized 15. I jog, following the flow of people through the doors of the metallic tube before they slide shut behind me. I grab hold of a bar, smiling to the normal people filling the train.

Most people have no idea about the Academy. They have no idea what we go through to ensure that they are safe. They don't know that we prevent crimes. The United Nations leaders take full responsibility for the safer world and we let them. The leaders of the UN are aware of the Magician and her work but they're the only ones who are.

I click the ear piece again and whisper, "aboard."

As the Solver, my part is done for right now. I close my eyes. Then I open them, at least I think I do. I'm still in complete darkness. I think I also blink rapidly although it's hard to tell when I can't even feel my eyelashes and the little muscles beside my eyes. Nothing changes in my perception. I try to move my arms and realize I actually can't feel them either. I'm in limbo, not in control of my body. If something happens to the Magician while I'm in this state, I may not return. Or I could be jolted back to my body just in time to experience all the pain of whatever mistake the Magician put me through.

Solvers are bodies. They are Magic users who are average in terms of spark and above-average in terms of physical strength. They are stationed all over the world, ready to jump into action and get to wherever they need to be. They are trained to be agile and strong. They get into the situation. When the Magician has the spark identified the Solver will also get out of the situation. It's a dangerous and thankless job.

This time when I open my eyes the train comes into focus. It shocks me enough that I lose my footing, tipping dangerously back. My breath comes in ragged gasps. That is worse than disappearing, for sure. "The man in green directly before you needs to be arrested and brought in for questioning. Tread carefully," the voice in my ear says.

I don't hesitate because to question the Magician is a mistake. I step forward, pulling a set of old fashioned metal handcuffs off of my hips as I walk. The man in green, who looks like someone's television Dad, narrows his eyes at me. "Sir, I need to ask you to come with me at the next stop," I say.

"What seems to be the problem, officer?" he asks.

I don't even have to look down to know what's going on. The Magician changed my appearance. It's what I would've done. One simple spell changes my costume and adjusts the memories of the people on the train car. The average people on this train are now seeing a police officer in full uniform, and their memories of my boarding the train include that same costume. "No problem." I hold up my hands, the handcuffs dangling from my right thumb. "We don't need to make a problem, let's just agree to take a walk." I'm trying to keep this from becoming some kind of crazy scene.

The man stands. I tense my legs, just in case. I'm prepared for anything. He could run, although on a train there's really nowhere to go. He could turn around and offer me his wrists, although I've made it pretty clear he doesn't need to. He could also just shrug and make this easy. Please make this easy, I think.

He holds up his right hand. "Fine, I'll come with you," he says.

But I'm not stupid. I see the left hand reaching behind his back. Damn.

I act quickly, stepping forward and grabbing his left arm before it can close around whatever he has behind his back. I slap the handcuffs down onto his wrist and lock it. Then I spin him around, wrenching his arm behind him.

There it is. The black handle of some kind of revolver, tucked into the waistband of his jeans.

I wonder how many Solvers missed it. I wonder how many ways this could've gone wrong.

As I snap the other cuff around his right wrist the train comes to a stop. I walk him toward the exit, taking note of all the passengers on this train. Just as we're leaving I notice a young girl, maybe five, playing in the aisle.

This could've gone so wrong.

December 28

Tanya

"It's completely her fault," I whine. "She was right there in the action. How was I supposed to see those people? I had to view it all through a screen."

'You're probably right." Logan smiles at me and squeezes my hand. But his eyes are pinched and he said 'probably' which means he thinks I'm completely wrong.

I give him my I-mean-business face. "Alright, give it to me. I can handle it."

"It's just you're supposed to be getting ready to do this job alone. If she wasn't there you would've made the same mistake." He shrugs. "Didn't the Magician tell you she wants you learning to work alone? I just think, maybe, you need to figure out how you could've found those two guys without Angela."

He's right, but I don't want to focus on that right now. "Could you have zoomed around a little more carefully?" he asks. "Are the images there live? I honestly don't know."

I look up into his face. Those gorgeous blue eyes are wide-open and the smile that crinkles his tan cheeks is enough to melt my embarrassment and anger. "Yes. It's possibly a little bit my fault. I'll do better next time." I lean up just a little, enough to close the few inches between our heights, and kiss him on those delicious lips.

The bell rings. First period, another day begins. I pull back and wince. "I should go."

"You should." He doesn't let go of my hips. "One more for the road?"

I laugh a little and give him a quick peck. "See you in study hall." Then I'm off, jogging down the hallway. Another day, another important lesson. My first period class is for Cleaners. Everyone at this school has some of the spark inside of them. That basically means we were all born with a tiny bit of Magic inside of us. The Academy is focused on teaching us how to harness that Magic for the greater good. Of course, when I'm the Magician I'll really be controlling it all.

For this set of classes, the final week for everyone here, we have classes in everything important. Most people have double classes in their occupation.

I slip in the door just as the final bell rings, the one that signals late people. I look around at the people in the class, knowing I should recognize more of them than I do. Cleaners are the people who will step into a situation after Solvers and literally clean up the mess left behind. They show up whether a mission is classified as a solve or as a fail.

Marissa Council and her amazing collection of pantsuits run this class. She's a Cleaner by trade and, rumor has it, someone who would've been the Magician if she had come of age at a time when a new Magician was needed. She is strong, loaded with spark, and capable. She is also currently holding a palmer, my favorite bit of Magical technology. Palmers literally attach to your palm and use your spark to throw whatever substance you command them to from your hand.

"Today the Magician has scheduled us to begin a simulation of a fire that was not prevented, a failed mission. The twelve of you will don a palmer and do your best to get the situation under control. You are expected to work as a team of Cleaners. The grade earned for this simulation is a group grade. Are there any questions?" She glances down at her watch. Running a simulation can be exhausting, using up the Magic inside the teachers. Many of our teachers are full time employees of The Academy after they teach classes, meaning they need their strength later. So many of our class simulations are scheduled ahead of time. They cannot start, or end, early.

I know the speech Marissa Council has just delivered was partially for me. It's a gentle reminder that I am expected to act like a Cleaner here today, even though everyone knows I'm the Magician's Assistant.

No one has any questions.

"You've worked with palmers before, so we are all familiar with their use. Please take your palmer and attach it now. Leave all backpacks and belongings behind. Stand when you are ready."

I do as I'm told, conjuring a palmer as I stand. I push the device onto my left palm. I'm right-handed. The first time I used a palmer I made the mistake of attaching it to my right hand. I was thinking it would be easier to control with my dominant hand, which it is. But that meant my dominant hand was not available for anything else, like opening doors or operating my cell phone. Stupid mistake.

I stand up and wrap my hair into a bun, fixing it in place with a pen. I crack my knuckles and pop my neck. The room fades away with a small pop and it's go time.

The building on the street in front of us is burning. Fire is pouring from the windows on the top floor and people are running out of the front door. The street is full of people screaming and dashing in all directions. It's hot, it's chaotic, and it smells like smoke.

When a mission fails in a way that causes something like this the Academy will use Cleaners on a scene first. If we are unable to fix this and put the fire out, traditional firefighters will show up and handle it. The difference is if they have to do it, it could reflect poorly on us. If we can do it, we clean up our own mess. Plus, they often take three to fifteen minutes to arrive on a scene where we can teleport in and start the clean up right away.

Tamiya immediately takes charge. She came to the Academy when I was six and she was seven. She's tall, dark-skinned, strong, and a little scary. Right now, I'm grateful for her leadership skills. "You two," she gestures to two people on her right, "we need someone on crowd duty. Go. You three," she points at three people clumped together on her left, "head for the floor immediately below the fire. Make sure everyone is out of the building. Work your way down. Everyone else is with me. We're heading to the top. We need the fire put out before it spreads." She doesn't wait to see if everyone agrees with her, she just turns and heads to the building. I don't hesitate to follow.

It's hot in the building. Really hot. It squeezes my lungs and takes my breath away. I use the palmer, concentrating for a beat on sending out clean air like a breeze, to push something easier to breath into my face. It works and I notice a few others copy the idea.

When we reach the top floor I turn my left hand out away from my face and instantly switch it to water. I have a stronger spark than most people, it's why I'm going to be the Magician, so my water stream is intense. I actually have to plant my feet into the ground or I'll end up sliding backwards with the momentum.

I point my hand at the flames and work my way back and forth. The steam rises. It's a welcome sight. Even if I don't feel like the heat and flames are dying down, the steam tells me I'm making some progress.

We don't get to celebrate the fire being out for long before the simulation fades. End goals, that's what that means. There was an end goal of the fire being extinguished. The simulation is set to end when that last ember dies. Just for a second I wonder what other end goals must have been set up. Would it have ended if we had failed and the building had been consumed?

Back in the classroom, Marissa Council smiles at us. "Tamiya, I like how you stepped up and took a leadership role. Well done." She nods in her direction. "Beyond that, the mission was a success." She glances down at the tablet in her hand, reading the report from the simulation or perhaps watching parts of it again. "It looks like we saved all the human lives. The original fire brought one to the hospital and the man who fell on the stairs broke his leg, but he will survive." She looks to a group of boys who give her a thumbs-up. Of course, being part of the group that focused on the fire I have no idea what she's talking about. That is the worst part of being a Cleaner, they're expected to work in large teams. Sure, it's necessary, but how do you know everything that went on? I suppose that will be my job as the Magician. I'll get to oversee the whole thing.

"Alright," she checks her watch, "we have only about a minute until the bell. I'll watch the tape again tonight and we can debrief tomorrow. Have a good rest of your day." She clicks off the tablet and gently sets it on a table just in time for the bell.

Winter, Age 16

Emily

I didn't want to tag along with Dad tonight. He's holding some illicit meeting with people who are supposed to be important in some way. They've invented some piece of technology that is capable of scanning a human being and showing they have the ability to do Magic. The device looks like the old metal detectors in airports. I haven't stepped foot inside of it yet but Dad has. He scanned himself and showed me the image. He claimed the smoky things rolling around inside were the spark, which is what they call the thing that enables us to do Magic. He says mine will be larger than his. That's why I'm here even though I'd rather be practically anywhere else.

I stand beside my Dad as silently as I can and observe the people as they file into the room. As each person arrives, I watch them place themselves into what is quickly becoming a circle. I find it interesting they all choose to fall into this formation like it was rehearsed.

Finally, after four people all wearing expensive clothing have filed into the room, Dad clears his throat. "Let me make the introductions here before we get started," he booms. He holds up his arm as if to stop everyone else from talking. I resist the urge to roll my eyes at his theatrics. No one was talking. Then he lays his right hand over his heart like he's about to recite the Pledge of Allegiance. "I am Magnus and whether you believe it or not I have Magical abilities."

A few people around the room visibly roll their eyes. Whether that's because they think Magic is bogus or because they also think my Dad needs to dial back the drama, I'm not entirely sure. He moves his right hand out and claps it on my shoulder. "This is my daughter, Emily. She is also gifted with Magic."

He continues his introductions around the circle, pointing at most of the people since he can't actually reach them. "Claire Whitman, engineering and design. Steve Wakeman, homeland security. Marcia Rodgers, legislative aide to the speaker of the house." He changes to his left hand to complete the circle, dropping it onto the shoulder of the only other person in the room I actually recognized. "And Shawn Garcia, Vice President of the United States."

"Thank you, Magnus." Shawn moves just enough to force Dad's hand to fall from his shoulder. "Quite a powerful group you've assembled here. Now, can you please explain why the hell we're meeting in the basement of an old building in the middle of the night?"

"Of course, of course." Dad steps to the center of the circle so he is directly underneath the single light bulb throwing its circle into an otherwise dark room. It makes him glow as if he has a halo. "Most of you are skeptical about Magic." As if proving his point the man identified as Steve Wakeman shakes his head. "If you cannot see it, you do not believe it." Dad snaps his fingers and is suddenly holding an apple. "Heck, even if you do see if you often think it's a trick." He shakes the fruit. "You're wondering how I made this appear right now, for example."

I'm not. I know he brought the apple with him from our house. He set it up on the table in the darkness. The little table right beside the scanner. It's hiding over there just like the guy who built the scanner is hiding. All Dad did when he snapped his fingers is teleport that little apple from the table to his hand. That would be a simple thing for someone with a spark to do. Even if they weren't powerful.

"What if I told you," Dad continues, "I found a way to prove to you that Magic exists inside some of us?" Dad stops his slow spin when he is facing me. "What if I told you we invented a device that will allow you to see the Magic inside of Emily just like an x-ray allows you to see her bones?"

"I'd tell you to stop babbling and show us," the vice president commands.

Dad tips his chin off toward the darkness where I know the engineer hides. "Mark, is it ready?"

"It's ready when you are." The parlor trick is effective. The faces of the assembled power team show shock and a little fear as Mark steps into the light. He's holding an ordinary black tablet. He offers a smile, perhaps to show they have no reason to fear them. "This device is connected to the scanner. The scanner itself is the engineering marvel, but this device is what you'll want to be focused on." He hands the tablet to Dad. "I'm just going to step over here and into the scanner myself." He turns back toward the direction he emerged from. "I have no Magical ability so this will give you an idea of …" He stops talking just as he crosses into the darkness outside the circle cast by the bare bulb. He clears his throat. "Magnus, a little help here."

"Oh, yes. My apologies." The smile on Dad's face is cocky and sure. Again, I have to resist the urge to roll my eyes. Surely these people can tell that this was rehearsed. "Emily, can you fix the lighting in here?" Dad asks, following the script he wrote.

Of course I can. I wave my hand like I'm swatting a fly, simultaneously willing electrical energy to flow into long dead light fixtures. I feel the buzz of the energy leave my fingers and suddenly the room is awash with light from corner to corner. Once my eyes recover from the shock of light this allows me to see that Mark is now halfway to the freestanding metal device known as the scanner.

"As I was saying," Mark continues, "I will step into the scanner myself so you can see what an ordinary non-Magical scan looks like. Are you ready?"

Dad hits the button on the tablet in his hand, bringing the device to life. He turns the screen around, resting the back of the tablet on his own chest. This allows all of us to see that there's a blue banner across the top with white lettering that reads "Prototype Scanner". The solid white form of a generic human body, not unlike the kind that would indicate a generic men's washroom, fills the otherwise black background in the center of the screen. "We're ready," Dad says.

I can clearly see that the group is interested, despite their earlier disbelief. They lean in toward Dad. I don't. After all, I've seen all this before. Mark steps into the scanner and a small circle appears, spinning. The adults watch it spin for about three seconds. Then the image of the generic human is back. This time, instead of being white the little person is the color of ripe blueberries.

Mark steps out of the scanner. "Alright, that blue you're seeing is what any normal person will appear as," he calls from across the room. He must have scanned himself before because I think he's too far away to see the screen clearly from where he is.

"He means, of course, those of you without Magical abilities," Dad says.

"Yes, right. Now we'll ask Emily to stand in the scanner and see the difference." Mark holds his hand out to me, fingers curled up as if cupping water. He moves his fingers in a "come here" gesture.

I slowly cross the room. My heartbeat races. I know Dad has done this. I know Mark has done this. I know it's perfectly safe. Despite all that, I feel nerves bundle up in my throat. "It doesn't hurt, right?" I whisper as I drop my hand into his.

"Not at all." He smiles at me. "You don't feel a thing."

I stand in the scanner, staring at my feet. The spinning circle reappears on the tablet. The group collectively steps closer to Dad, who smiles at their interest.

I hear the group take a collective intake of breath. I step out of the scanner and move along the outskirts of the room until I can see the screen, curious how it differs from Dad's scan. When Dad stood in the scanner the image of the generic person was replaced with a black background swirling with white, like smoke.

This image of me is similar, but Dad was right. There is an obvious difference. My scan is filled with so much white smoke it's choking the black completely out. If Dad was a single cigarette smoldering in the darkness, I'm a car with three smokers and the windows rolled up.

"Amazing," Shawn, the Vice President, whispers on an exhale.

"What are we looking at?" the skeptical Steve asks. "What exactly is that?"

"That," Mark answers, "is what it looks like when a Magic spark is caught on a scanner."

Shawn takes a step back and rakes his fingers up through his hair. "This will change everything, Magnus. You are aware of that?"

"I'm aware of that," Dad answers.

Shawn turns to Steve. "We'll be able to see the Magic on a scanner. We can tell if someone is lying about it. We can find individuals who have it, even if they are trying to hide it. We can bring it all out in the open."

Steve rubs the back of his neck. He nods as if agreeing with some argument that was happening in his head and then turns to Dad's engineer pal. "We're going to need more of those scanners."

Mark smiles. "Of course."

"A lot more," Steve adds. He's already flipping his cell phone up to his head as he stalks purposefully out of the basement.

Dad smiles down at the swirling image of my Magic. Truly, this does change everything. He clicks the tablet screen off and addresses the room. "We'll be in touch," he says.

DECEMBER 28

ANGELA

When I pop out of my simulation Chris and Cheryl are already back as well. Sitting in the chairs, Cheryl is engrossed in her book again and Chris winks at me. "How did you do?" he asks.

"Solved, no issues. You?" I wince in anticipation. Chris makes it his mission in life to mess up the simulations as much as humanly possible.

"It was wonderful, exactly the way I like them. I'll tell you all about it at lunch." A flurry of movement comes from the front of the room as Rolly drops his feet to the floor and rapidly begins making his way toward our group.

Steve startles me by popping into the chair beside me. "Whoa, that didn't go like I planned." He shakes his head. "But it worked out."

The bell rings and three of us stand up. Chris, from his seated position, yawns. "That was so much fun, I think I'll do it again." I shake my head at the lame joke. Chris is a Solver. This week he will have two Solver classes. It just so happens that they're back-to-back.

"Mr. Marshall," Rolly says as he drops into the chair beside Chris, "let's have a conversation."

I shake my head, knowing we'll hear about that later, and rush out into the hallway just in time to catch the kissy-face show between Logan and Tanya. I understand wanting to spend a little time with someone else. I understand the physical attraction thing. But can we play the kissing game in some other, not-so-public, standing-in-my-way place?

I shove past them, possibly throwing a little elbow on the way, and duck into my second period class. For this week, that's a Cleaner class. Logan slips in and takes the seat next to me. "Morning," he mumbles.

I just nod. I'm not entirely sure he's talking to me. I shuffle some papers around in my backpack for a few minutes. Then I take out my phone and click around on some apps, wasting time. Finally, the bell rings and Gary Edmund walks into the room. He's this distinguished older guy and Cleaner extraordinaire. He has hair that's practically silver, a long nose that looks dapper somehow, and never has any facial hair. He always dresses like he's going to an important job interview in suits with fancy jackets. His shoes even shine.

He shuts the door. "Today you are entering a simulation following a successful mission. Do what we do best, Cleaners."

That's all he says before the room fades with the satisfying pop of a simulation. On a truly successful mission, Cleaners will report to duty in pairs. I turn my head to see who is beside me and almost groan. Logan. Wonderful, this shouldn't be awkward at all.

"What's the plan, boss lady?" he asks.

We are on a street corner somewhere. There are probably about ten people nearby, it's dusk. In front of us a man wearing all black catches my attention. He has dark hair that shines under the setting sun and dark eyes. He's also wearing a necklace that looks like it's made of coal tight around his neck. He catches my eye and winks as he slips the necklace under the collar of his shirt. He takes a few steps toward us and then, suddenly, he pops out of existence. "Whoa, did you see that?" I gesture toward the area where the man had previously been standing.

"Yeah. I would assume he's a Container," Logan answers.

Containers are rare. There's only one or two of them even known in the world. No one really knows exactly what or how they do their job. We just know that on a successful mission they would report to the scene and assist the Solver in containing the disturbance. Afterall, the human who was apprehended was merely acting on the disturbance surrounding them. The Solver will bring that human in for justice but the disturbance must be contained. I shrug. That is not the focus of my simulation today.

"There's a broken window on that shop there," Logan says. He points to the store in front of us. I can see three people inside the shop pushing glass around or staring at the window. "I can take care of the glass if you take care of the mindwipe," he offers.

"Done." We take the few steps to the store together but I leave him on the sidewalk when I head in. "Excuse me," I call out. The three women all look in my direction. The oldest, who is holding a broom, looks like she's been crying. I conjure a mindwipe, which looks a lot like a big pink eraser. "Ladies, I'm sorry for whatever the disturbance may have done here today. Rest assured we are in the process of fixing this right up for you. You will remember nothing about today. Thank you." I'm sure to them, if they were to remember it, it would look like I'm literally trying to erase thin air. I swipe the mindwipe between us. Their expressions go blank and they freeze in place. "We have ten minutes, starting now," I yell. Mindwipes take time. We start them, finish our job, and get the heck out.

I begin using spells to move furniture around to the places I think it belongs. Chairs are righted, tables are straightened. It doesn't take me long. I turn to see that Logan has managed to Magically repair the window and has moved on to trying to erase some kind of mark from the sidewalk.

I step outside. "Trouble?"

"Yeah, I can't seem to get this to disappear. Maybe because I don't know what it is." He points down. The small circle is black with lines coming off of it. It looks like something exploded right on this spot.

"Maybe we don't clean it. Maybe we make it look like art?" I reach up and pull a paintbrush out of thin air. "Who's a better artist?"

He sighs. "Gimme that." He grabs the paintbrush, kneels down, and works. I watch our witnesses. They're starting to move. It's short, jerky movements at first. They look like they're twitching. But the tallest one is blinking now, rapidly.

"Logan, I think we're out of time." If they wake up they'll remember us here.

"One second. Almost done."

Her blinking is slowing down, looking deliberate. "I'm not sure we have--"

"Done!" He stands up and the brush winks out of existence. I glance down at the sidewalk quickly. It's amazing. He's managed to make it look like a planet is in the center of the circle. The black looks like shooting stars. It's remarkable for only a minute of work. But we have to go.

I grab his hand, close my eyes, and pop us both out of the simulation. Cleaners are teleportation travelers. We often have to imagine teleporting to end our simulations.

We pop back into the classroom and I'm suddenly aware we're still holding hands. I can feel his clammy palm in mine. I drop his hand quickly and use mine to push my hair back against my head. "Good job," I tell him. This is so awkward.

Mr. Edmund approaches us, tablet in hand. "Not bad at all," he says. "Successful mindwipe." He looks up from the tablet, smiling. "You cut it close on time but that paint job was a decent idea. Nicely done." He turns to leave as another partner pair pops into the room.

"Thanks for the idea," Logan says. He turns and smiles at me and I'm shocked at the fluttering it causes in my stomach.

"Yeah, no problem. Good job on the painting. It was really gorgeous." I turn and drop back into my seat. I don't know what else to say to him. I grab my cell phone and check the time. Four minutes left of this class. Four minutes of awkward silence. I open up some apps and start clicking around. Honestly, I have no idea what I'm doing. I just know that I'm trying to avoid looking in Logan's direction.

December 28

Tanya

Logan really likes his Cleaner class. I get it. We often get to play with cool technology there. But it annoys me that he likes it so much for two reasons. One, Angela is in that class with him. I know she's not the reason he enjoys it, but it can cause a jealousy issue if I think about it too hard. Two, it usually means we wrap up chatting in the hallway early which causes me to be early to the most boring class on my schedule, Research.

I walk myself to the table with Frank and George. The heavy wooden chair scrapes along the ground loudly. I squeeze my eyes shut. "Oh, sorry about that," I say. This classroom isn't one where you'll run a lot of simulations. This one is about studying history. We have big wooden tables each with three big wooden chairs on a side. In the center of the table is a stack of books. Usually someone will come along to give us the research assignment, something we need to search for, and then duck out of the room. They'll watch us, I'm sure, through the two-way glass at the front. They don't think we know it's two-way glass but rumors spread. At the end of the time period they'll come in and check to see how many groups found the information.

"How's your morning going?" I ask the boys. Both of them nod, George caps it with a yawn.

"Same as yesterday," Frank answers.

I don't have time to respond before a girl with short brown hair drops into the chair across the table from me. Cheryl. Angela's best friend. The smile I give her is forced so it probably looks odd or lopsided. "Good morning," Frank offers. I notice a little blush creeps into his cheeks. Interesting.

I offer her my hand across the thick wooden table. She eyes my hand like it's a snake. For a second I actually think she's going to leave me hanging. Finally, she slips her little hand into mine. It just sits there, limp. I force our joined hands up and down once. It's a sad excuse for a handshake. When I pull my hand back I'm shocked at how cold it feels. I wipe it on my jeans. "You're Cheryl, right? What's your occupation?"

"Solver."

For some reason that shocks me. Most of the Solvers I have met since I got here are quick and strong. Her mousy little body and limp handshake are at odds with this image. I try not to sound rude. "Cool, cool. I'm the Magician's Assistant." I smile, hoping it's a friendly one and not something condescending.

Her green eyes come up to land on my face and I'm shocked to see a kind of power radiating there. "You're only one of them," she challenges.

"True," I squint at her trying to figure out if we'll be able to work together. I'm trying to decide if I should switch tables when the leader of the course walks in through a side door near the two-way mirror. "Ladies and gentlemen, let's get right to it. Today's situation is this, a man was arrested by a Solver outside of a sporting event he was attempting to enter. When the man was spotted by the Magician he was wearing a backpack and acting suspiciously. He ran from the Solver, losing the backpack somehow in the process. We have a small window of time in which to decide if we have anything to hold him for."

She runs her fingers through her long black hair. "We need to know if there is any legal precedence we can hold him on. You have forty minutes until the class is over." Without asking if we have questions she turns and leaves the room through the same door. Typical.

I turn back to my group, purposely avoiding looking at Cheryl. "Does anyone have any ideas?"

"Legally we can only hold him for two days without charging him with something, isn't that right?" Frank asks.

"Do you suppose they're already looking for the backpack?" I ask. I know that's what I would do. The backpack may contain the proof they would need to charge him with some kind of wrongdoing. That's the assumption the Magician must have been working off of. The Academy has a very clear set of rules for punishments, based loosely on the United States laws. The UN council gives us a very short leash, most of them looking for any reason to hate what we do and shut us down. At least, that's what we've heard.

"It doesn't matter," George says. He's already reaching for a book in the center of the table. "We need to find something to hold him for. She didn't say anything about us finding reason to charge him. That means they're already looking for that. Our assignment is to find some reason to keep him in a jail cell until they have what they need to charge him." He flips to the index at the back of the book.

"What are you looking for? We can help," Frank offers. He waits about thirty seconds before rolling his blue eyes. "George, what are you looking for?" he repeats.

"There is some kind of precedence for sporting events being allowed to refuse service to anyone. There's also some things about your appearance that you are required to follow. I know they can hold people for violating those, but I can't remember the details. Maybe there's something we can use in those rules."

Frank nods. "Alright got it." He waves his hand. "But we'll need a book about the right sport in the right country." He turns to look at the two-way mirror, really waving now.

The door opens and the leader of the course returns. Her high heels click as she walks across the floor to stand beside our table. "Yes?" she asks.

"Hi Alyson," George greets. His cheeks redden. "How are you today?"

"I'm fine, thank you. Is there something you needed?"

Franks speaks up. "What country and what kind of sporting event?"

"England and they call it football. Is that all?"

"That's it, thanks."

She nods once and clicks her heels back toward the door. This time when Frank waves his hand it's in a single circle with only one finger extended. "I'm gonna need a book that tells me the stadium rules in England for a football match." Three books fly off the shelves and toward Frank. He reaches out and grabs two, I grab the third before it can smack him in the face.

It gets quiet at the table as each of us thumbs through the books we've chosen. It doesn't take me long to abandon the one I caught, which describes the rules on the field instead of the rules for the spectators. I push it off of my palm into the air. "Return to shelf," I mumble. The book sails off and I grab for the one Frank has ignored. This one looks a little more promising.

"Darn," George shouts. The room goes eerily quiet for a moment before snickering erupts from the only other table. "This isn't going to work." He slams the book shut. "They have the right to refuse to allow you entrance but they cannot have you arrested unless it's for a violation of a law. I thought maybe we were onto something. I'm officially out of ideas."

"It doesn't matter," Cheryl says quietly. She looks around the table, catching everyone's eye. "It doesn't matter," she repeats, her voice a little louder. Her hand flies up, waving around to try and get someone's attention. "If the disturbance was contained then it doesn't matter what the person might have done while under the influence of a negative spark." The door beside the mirror opens and I hear the tell-tale click of high heels again. Cheryl locks eyes with someone over my shoulder and keeps explaining. "A negative spark would be the problem, not the person it was attached to. Especially if a disturbance was prevented. Do you happen to know if a Container arrived on scene?"

"Yes, and you're the first person presented with this problem to reach that conclusion. Congratulations, team. You may use the remainder of the period for study hall."

Winter, Age 17

Emily

It's late at night when I finally decide to leave Tricia's. Dad trusts me. He knows I can handle myself. But that trust only extends so far. It doesn't usually extend to eleven o'clock at night in the middle of winter when you have no car and have to walk home by yourself.

I stomp my feet on the pavement, cursing my Dad and his stupid rules. The world is starting to learn about Magic, thanks to us. We're allowed to talk about it. We're allowed to use it. But, and he's annoyingly firm on this, we are not supposed to use it for personal gain. That would include, apparently, teleporting oneself home from a friends' house on a school night. So, I'm walking like a normal non-Magical person.

I stand on the corner by the park wondering which way I should go. I can cut through the park, shaving ten minutes off my arrival time. Or I can go around, where it's well lit and arguably safer.

In the end I decide to go through the park.

I stick to the concrete path, steering clear of the trees and corners of darkness. There's a lingering darkness at the edges of the soft yellow lights from the occasional street lamp. They're spaced just far enough out to make me consider jogging between them to keep myself in light.

My phone dings. It's a text from Dad. "I'm not kidding, young lady. Get home now."

Another ding. "Where are you?"

I hit the helpful "Send location" button that pops up along the bottom of the screen. Then I turn my eyes back to the real world. There's a man jogging toward me wearing all black. I don't want to be a jerk and purposely step away from him. It's not that there's anything inherently dangerous about a guy jogging in the park. It's just … there could be. You know? So I settle for keeping an eye on him while simultaneously threading my fingers through my keys in my pocket in the event that I need a quick weapon.

As he gets closer I realize he's not actually wearing black. He looks black. I don't mean that in a racial sense. I mean he actually has like a black pulsing aura around his body. Too late, he's past me. I haven't really gotten a good look at him. More to the point, I haven't actually gotten a good look at his aura.

I turn and watch him jog away.

I make the stupid decision on impulse. I'm no longer thinking about Dad and curfew, about getting in trouble or getting home safely. I'm thinking about that aura. Before I can even consider how bad this could go, I'm following a random jogger through the park.

He continues for a while down the path. I'm staying at a decent distance behind him, jogging at his pace to keep up. But the darkness around him is what I'm really interested in. It's pulsing around him in waves. It's darker around his head than anywhere else. Plus, something about it just feels Magical to me.

I try to connect with him, take over his body. Dad and I have been experimenting a lot in the last few years. We've learned it's possible to take over someone with Magic only if their spark is not as strong as yours. We've learned that if you try to take over someone who is stronger than you, it's like running headfirst into a brick wall. If you try to take over someone who has no Magic, it's like they don't exist. There's nothing to connect to.

That's what happens when I try to reach out for this guy. Nothing. It's like trying to connect to a bluetooth device that has a dead battery. No signal going out. Nothing to connect to.

Except that doesn't make sense in this case because I can feel that Magic pulsating around him.

We're catching up to a girl now. She's jogging the same direction we are. She's wearing headphones and looks like she's existing in her own little world. For reasons I don't have to explain to any other females out there in the world, I'm instantly nervous for her. Sure, I'm following this guy but at least I'm paying attention to him.

My fears compound exponentially when he slides his hand into his pocket. What are you doing, dude? I feel like my heart will actually stop beating when the nearest street light glints off whatever he pulls out of his pocket. It's silver and long and it catches the light in a really scary way.

I stop moving, panic coursing through me. I have to do something. That could be a knife.

I act on instinct, grabbing the only thing I've brought with me. My cell phone.

Before I can berate myself for having such a useless tool, I open up an app and hit the live video button. "Hello my lovelies." I'm literally yelling. "What's up this evening? I'm coming to you live from my local park where people more fit than I am are actually out jogging. Can you believe that?" I flip to my other camera. "Hey fit jogger people, say hi to my ten thousand followers."

Okay, so I don't actually have ten thousand followers. I have about four thousand and most of those only came after Dad started releasing the video of the scanner and tagged me in it. But that doesn't matter. Right now, social media is the best tool I have against whatever this guy was about to do.

The guy turns and looks at me, briefly. Then he's off again, faster and in a different direction. I'm completely relieved when I see him tuck the object back into his pocket. "I'll catch you all next time," I say in a more normal tone.

Then I end the video and do something I should've done from the beginning, consequences be damned. I teleport myself home.

December 28

Angela

Lunch time is the best time of the day. I always say I'm going to throw some snacks in a bag for my classes or bring a water bottle, but I never do. This is the one time of the day when I get to stuff my face. I also have the same lunch period as the people already sitting at our usual table digging into their piles of food. I drop into the chair they've left for me and take a huge bite of the burrito I Magically bring to the table. Heaven in a tortilla. "How was everyone's morning?" I ask after I swallow and before I take another bite.

"I sat with Tanya and some of her friends for Research today. They majorly overthought a research case. I got the solve," Cheryl says before shoveling a bite of mashed potatoes in her mouth.

I resist the urge to smile at the news that my competition is bad at something.

"I must regale you with the tale of my video game this morning," Chris says. "There we were, opening on a scene of a single Solver on a train platform. I was given directions by my Magician simulation to board the train in order to give control of my body to someone else and sit myself in a timeout until I was once again needed." He pauses long enough to take a swig from his can of soda. "I had two choices at this point, board the train as instructed or take off running and see if I can find the edges of the game."

I should probably stop him from telling this story. I should probably tell him the simulations are learning experiences the Academy wants us to pay attention to. But I don't. Instead, I lean forward slightly.

"I'm on the edge of my seat here, what did you do?" Steve asks. He is only slightly kidding. We all love hearing about Chris trying out things we would never dare to try.

"I boarded the train like a good little Solver. I lost control of my body for a bit and when I came to I was staring at some poor slob who I was told to arrest."

"Was it an older guy in a green suit?" I ask. I always wonder if we truly have identical simulations.

"That's him. Of course, I don't know why I'm arresting him. Do I do as I am told and slap those handcuffs on his wrists?"

"That doesn't sound like you," Steve says.

Chris lays his hand on Steve's arm. "That's the nicest thing you've ever said to me." He removes his hand, using it to gesture as he talks. "Instead I approach the man and ask him if he wants to tell me why he's on the train today. He says he's going to work. I ask him where he works. He says a bank. Now I'm really curious, why am I arresting a banker?" He takes a big bite of his hamburger and chews slowly. He does this a lot, I think he likes seeing how much we lean into him waiting for more.

"Now the old guy is getting a little fidgety, I'm thinking he may be hiding something. So I ask him if he'd like to stand. I tell him I have a bad leg and I'd really like his seat."

"Did he stand up?" Cheryl asks.

"He did not. He refused. He said he also had a bad leg and he would prefer to keep his seat. He suggested I ask someone else. Told me to have a nice day."

"Did you walk away?" I ask.

"Of course not, I had been told to arrest this man. I leaned down toward him and told him that I was under orders to arrest him. I asked if he had any idea what I may have been told to arrest him for. He said he had no clue. I told him to take a guess. He said it may have been for parking tickets."

"Parking tickets? That's a lame excuse," I say.

"That's what I told him. I said I somehow doubted that was the reason. I put my hand on his arm and asked him to come with me and we would clear this all up."

"I'm thinking he probably didn't like that," Steve says. I'm wondering if Steve saw the gun I saw.

"He did not, my friend. It turns out our little green suited man had a gun. I believe I was told, by the instructor shaking his finger in my face, that a total of ten humans were injured when I turned the train incident into a two-player shootout game. That is a quote."

I shake my head. "Don't you ever think it could be worth your time to actually learn something from the simulations?"

Chris shrugs. "Don't you think it would be worth the Academy's time to teach us all how to use our sparks instead of training most of us to be pawns for the Magician?" It's his favorite question. I never have an answer.

"Maybe someday I can change it," I offer.

"I await that day with bated breath." He smiles at me. "Until then I draw enjoyment from reminding them these little video games are useless."

We slip into silence while we all dive into our meals. Steve lets a respectful amount of time for the seemingly serious tone Chris ended on to lapse before he clears his throat and changes the topic. "I hurt myself in Phys Ed this morning."

Because most of our occupations require us to be fit and healthy, physical education is still considered an important class at the Academy. You have it every year regardless of occupation. For Steve, who is a Solver, cardio will not make up more than fifty percent of his physical education time to ensure he can move quickly and not overwork his cardiovascular system. I hope his injury isn't serious. "How did you do that?" I ask.

"In typical, anyone-can-do-it, non-Magical, fell off the bleachers fashion." He gestures toward his right leg. "It was embarrassing and stupid."

"Did you Magic the pain away?" Cheryl asks.

"I tried. I don't think I'm strong enough. It faded, but it's not gone." He looks at me slyly out of the corner of his eye.

I chuckle. "Allow me," I say. I shove the last of my burrito in my mouth and reach for his calf. Touching it lightly I can feel that there is a bump under the surface, maybe a bruise or maybe something broken. It doesn't matter. The point is, he tried to dull the pain without treating the injury. Amateur. I close my eyes and focus my spark on the leg, imagining the inside. I visualize something that looks like shooting stars moving out of my fingers and into his leg. I hear his sharp intake of breath and feel the warmth leave my fingers. I pop my eyes open just as I swallow that bite of burrito. Then I grab my cell phone and tip it up to turn the screen on to check the time. "We have eight minutes," I say.

"I better run. Sixth period is all the way across campus," Cheryl shoulders her bag and picks up her tray. "I'll see you guys after school."

"Hey, it feels better," Steve offers. He moves the leg around a little, feeling it out. "Thanks, Ang. You're the best."

"I know." I stand up and wave my hand, disappearing my tray. "I gotta run. Text me later." I offer Chris a side hug, trying not to be bothered by the fact that he still looks annoyed. He smiles but it doesn't reach his eyes.

December 28

Tanya

Logan and I stand up from the lunch table practically in sync. It looks rehearsed, which is a ridiculous thing to think we may have rehearsed. It is, however, intentional. People notice. I see their eyes take us in. Some roll them, some glaze over looking dreamy.

"I want to check in on my family before phys ed," Logan says. "I'll be right back." Same as every day, Logan ducks out of the cafeteria toward the corridor that holds the hallways to the restrooms. This close to the start of sixth period the hallways should be empty to afford him some privacy.

I step to the doorway and prop my right foot up on the wall. There's no reason to check on my Dad. He'll be at work. If I call him he will have to step away from a patient, which he won't appreciate. He knows where I am and what I'm doing. At least, he thinks he does. In reality, he doesn't know about Magic and he doesn't know this place exists. But he knows I'm at a boarding school finishing out my last year before "graduation." More importantly, he knows how to find me if he needs me. Dad's the only one left I would call. He's all I have and sometimes I think that's even too much family for him.

My phone has a little red indicator floating over the email icon. I click into the app and see an email from theMagician@Academy.org, an email address that will become mine in less than a week.

Tanya,

I have decided a worthy score for yesterday's simulation is 72%.

I believe you'll find it generous and yet it leaves room for improvement today.

Magician

"Oh my God." I don't even care that I just yelled that out in the cafeteria. I don't get Cs. I am a straight A student. C's are for average students. I am not, nor have I ever been, average. I sure as hell don't want to become average now, one week before the ceremony. I angrily smash the trash button and the whoosh sounds loud in the emptying room.

Regret trickles in. I probably shouldn't delete emails from her, even if I don't agree with them. I click the "undo" button that popped up on the bottom of my screen as if it knew deleting was a major error in judgement. The email returns itself to the inbox.

I click it open again, this time selecting to move it to a folder marked "Grades". My email inbox now proudly stands empty again.

"Ok, I'm ready." Logan is standing directly in front of me, smiling like someone who just returned from vacation. "Are you good?" he asks.

I push off from the wall. "I got a C," I whine. When I start walking, Logan falls in step beside me.

"Yeah? In what?"

"Magician." I grind my teeth. Just thinking about what could happen, or not happen, if I don't win this job is so frustrating.

"That sucks." He takes my hand, squeezing. "I'm sorry. But you should be fine, grade-wise. It's one simulation."

"In the most important class." My voice is too loud for the hallway. I'll have to try and calm down a little.

"It doesn't matter, T. Not really. It's not like they're going to do a grade point average check to decide which one of you gets the job."

"We have no idea what they're going to use," I remind him. "I need to make sure I am going to win no matter what they check."

He sighs. "You will. Besides, wasn't that a simulation you did together? She probably got the same score."

Just outside the gym I spot someone turned toward the wall. He draws my attention because he looks like his nose is stuck to the corner. His hands are shoved in his back pockets as if he's looking for something. He keeps my attention because I recognize him. I just don't know what he's doing here in this corridor right now.

I steal a quick glance at Logan. He still looks focused on our conversation, concern for me written all over his face. He doesn't appear to notice the guy in the corner.

I stop in the hallway. "Shoot, I need to pee. Meet you in the gym?"

Logan checks his phone. "You only have like two minutes."

"So I shouldn't waste one of them arguing with you. Go to class." I lean in and kiss him before turning toward the bathroom. I take two slow steps as Logan's footsteps fade. In case anyone is looking I quickly cast a spell that will make them forget my lame excuse. Then I spin around and angrily stomp toward the gym.

My feet stop directly behind the boy facing the wall. I poke him in the shoulder blade as hard as I can. "What is so important?" I hiss.

He turns, smiling like a satisfied cat. "See you later." He winks, drops a folded piece of paper in my open hand, and saunters off.

I unfold the square of paper, sure there were better ways to get me information.

Quad. Midnight. Bring a snack.

Sighing, I crumble the paper and lob it at the nearest trash can on my way through the doorway just as the bell rings.

Emily

Dad is standing behind the chair he was sitting in when I popped into the kitchen. That's one of the tell-tale signs he's really angry. It's like he's too mad to relax in a chair, he has to stand. The other tell-tale sign, the grinding of his teeth, is also happening.

When I left the park I wasn't really thinking about being sneaky or cautious, I was just trying to get home. I didn't think to come in quietly or teleport myself to the front door. I just popped right into the kitchen to find Dad sitting at the table, a cup of something amber colored in front of him. "Sit," he'd commanded. I'd sat. I'd explained the darkness around that guy in the park. I'd shown Dad the video. That's about when he stood up, leaning his weight down on the back of the chair as he leaned toward me over the table. "If you had left on time none of this ever would've happened. Do you understand how badly this could have gone?"

"Yes," I answer in my meekest voice. I'd rather fast forward through all this yelling and get to the heart of the issue.

"You could've been hurt."

"I know."

"That woman could've been hurt," he continues.

"I know."

He sighs. I risk pulling my eyes from the table. Dad's head is hanging down toward his chest. He shakes his head. "I'm glad you're safe."

Now it's my turn to lean forward. I put my forearms on the table. "Dad, what was that black stuff though? It felt like Magic, but I couldn't reach the guy. He didn't have a spark."

He snaps his head up and narrows his eyes at me. "Emily, this is not a time to discuss Magic and what it could mean for our future. This is a time to discuss you listening to your father. This is a time to discuss--"

"Oh my," I whisper. It's enough to stop him mid-sentence. "I've never noticed it before, not really. Maybe it was the lighting." I stand up from the table and cross to Dad, who is staring at me like I've lost my mind. Maybe I have. There are wisps of blackness around Dad's head right now. It's not as dark as it was on the jogger, it's not pulsing. It's almost as if Dad is generating the smoke.

I reach my hand out and try to touch it. It scatters from me.

"Did you see that?" I ask. At his puzzled look, I explain. "The black smoke stuff that was floating around you? Did you see it?"

"Emily, are you feeling alright?" Dad reaches out like he's going to lay his hand on me. I shift to the right and his hand stays frozen in place where my shoulder was a second before. "What's going on?" he asks.

"I don't know. You got mad just then and there was a sort of wispy smoke coming off of you. I haven't noticed it before, not really. But what if we can do that when we're mad? What if we can put off some kind of bad feeling? What if that's what I felt on the jogger?"

Dad's eyes, although still narrow, looked intrigued now instead of angry. "Are you saying you think I put out bad feelings?"

"Not just you. What if all Magical people do?" This is sounding ridiculous, I'm sure. But something inside me is telling me I'm on the right path. "Actually, you know something, the wisps looked a little like the whirling smoke in the scanner image."

Dad shakes his head. "No, now you're saying I'm giving away my spark when I'm angry. That's ridiculous."

"No, I don't think so." Is that what I mean? "No, that can't be right. If you gave away your spark then I would've felt it when I reached for the guy. Whatever he had surrounding him didn't belong to him. It wasn't anchored inside of him. It was just, like, following him."

"Clinging to him," Dad corrects.

"Yes, exactly. What does that mean?"

"I think that means," Dad says, "we have some experiments ahead of us."

December 28

Angela

The door opens, bearing the Magician. She's wearing blue jeans and a black t-shirt today. Her hair is pulled back again and she's slipping a pair of dark sunglasses up onto her head as she enters. "Ladies, good afternoon," she greets. "Today we are trying something different. Angela, you'll be with me controlling the simulation from the inside. It's important that you understand how to project them and how to control them." She turns her eyes to Tanya. "You'll be inside the simulation alone. Are we ready?"

How do I answer that? Am I ready for what? I have no idea how to run a simulation. Sure, I need to learn it. But why am I learning it alone? Is this punishment for my abysmal take-over of the Solver yesterday? I can't question her lesson plans, she's the Magician. I stand up. "Ready as I'm going to get," I answer.

Beside me Tanya is also standing. I don't want to look at her face. I don't want to see that smug little smile. I don't have long to worry about it because the room disappears. The room I land in looks remarkably like the control room except there are two chairs in front of the large screens. The Magician gestures to one of them. "Have a seat," she offers. I drop into the one on the right and wait for her to take the one on the left. "I went ahead and opened a session, which you will learn how to do at a later time. What you will see on this screen here is the simulation recording of what Tanya is doing and going through." She taps the screen and Tanya appears in the control room. She is already zooming around the image of Earth looking for disturbances.

"What is she looking for?" I ask.

"Honestly, right now there's nothing there. You have to program whatever you want her to find." I hide a small smile thinking about Tanya in there panicking knowing there's really nothing to be searching for yet. "You'll need to give a voice command. We will use the command 'begin simulation' and then follow it with details of what you are thinking. Would you like help brainstorming a good one?"

"I'm not really sure." I look at the board, trying desperately to think about all the simulations I've done. "I just have to think of a scenario that may happen that would be caused by a bad spark, right? Can it be something I've seen in a simulation before?"

"Absolutely. Everything you've seen is based off of something I've encountered or that has been encountered and documented by previous Magicians. The things you will see day-to-day are all variations of things that have come before. What are you thinking about right now?"

"There was a simulation this morning in my Solver class. A guy was arrested on a train. I'm not sure what he was doing there. I wondered what the Magician saw, since I didn't get that angle. I wondered what caused us to have to arrest him. I could fill in that story, I suppose."

"I know which one you are talking about. I program those and send them to the various classes. What reasons can you think of that we may arrest someone on a train?" Her eyebrows arch with the question, making her look highly interested in my answer.

"Well, the way you asked that question makes me think the train was relevant. My first instinct was to say he had committed or would commit a crime when he got someplace, but now I'm wondering if the train may have been the target. Perhaps he was planning to take the riders of the train hostage or--"

"Always go with your first instinct when running a simulation," the Magician interrupts. "We don't want to get bogged down in planning. We don't have that kind of time. Remember, the work we do here at the Academy is important but it is our secondary job. Start that one. Give the computer the details in your mind by speaking them. More importantly, feel it with your spark as you talk about it. Your Magic guides the program."

I close my eyes so I can focus. "Begin simulation. Train platform with passengers boarding. Passenger is an average looking male, middle aged, wearing green. He plans to take the passengers on the train hostage with a revolver he has tucked into the waistband of his pants. He plans to demand a large ransom for the passengers. The act must happen between stops. He will wait for a time when he has more than five minutes between stops. He has been riding the route frequently." I don't know where the words come from. The ideas just flow. I open my eyes and the screen is glowing sort of green around the edges. I watch it pulse.

"I didn't say where it was happening," I say as I realize my mistake.

"That's probably fine. The Magic often picks up on things you were thinking about that you didn't speak. I'm sure we'll have a location. Let us watch. With a live simulation like this, as opposed to the ones I set for class, we can make changes in the moment. We use the phrases 'edit simulation' or 'add to simulation' to do that."

"How do we set end goals?" I ask. I've often wondered about this.

The Magician turns to me and smiles. "We speak them. Try it. What are the end goals for this simulation?"

"Set end goals: passenger is arrested safely," I think about all the ways it could have gone wrong this morning. "Or any passenger is shot, Solver is killed, or ransom is paid." I can't think of any others so I stop talking.

The Magician nods, an impressed look on her face. "That is certainly a good list to start with. In the event that the simulation heads in a direction you did not foresee, we will simply edit to include other end goals. We can also force an ending or set a time limit."

"We have a lot more control when they are live simulations then?" I ask.

She bites the inside of her cheek as she thinks. "Yes, but it is valuable time we are using. The real control room is under the care of someone who doesn't have a spark as large as yours, mine, or Tanya's during this time that I am with you. Always remember that the Magician's time is precious." She turns her eyes back to the screen as Tanya groans and frantically zooms around Earth.

December 28

Tanya

I have checked everywhere. There is absolutely no disturbance in the sparks. I don't see a single area. Sparks are odd. They are live bits of Magic inside people. Positive sparks, like the one inside me, are natural gifts. You are either born with them or you aren't. They don't fade but can be broken, injured, or killed. The Magician has full control of all the positive sparks in the world.

Negative sparks are different. They are created. Anytime someone with a spark puts out negative energy into the world it sort of hangs there, small. But if you put a bunch of them together, you'll have a negative spark. Anyone can be infected by a negative spark. It takes over their soul and makes all the bad things they're thinking about larger and louder. That's what we see as disturbances. Someone who has absorbed negative energy and is now radiating it. They're putting it to use. It will dry up but not before something comes of it. Something bad, dark, or scary.

There. I found it! Negative energy centered somewhere in the eastern United States. Zoom. Wait. Possibly New York. Zoom. Wait. Definitely New York. Zoom. Wait. The circles are centered east of the Hudson, I can see that. "Turn on labels," I command. The white labels pop up, confirming my geography was correct. East River, I read. It looks like I'm looking for a little island on the East River.

I keep searching even as I hit the button to call the Center on my cell phone. "Dispatch," the voice greets.

"This is the Magician's Assistant. I'm going to need Solvers on Roosevelt Island in New York." I keep zooming in as I talk. It was risky calling this soon, without a solid location. But the circles are large, which means this is a strong negative spark. This could be bad. "It looks like we're looking at the Roosevelt Island Subway Station. Get me a Solver on the ground and I can get you more information."

I hear typing. "I have someone one minute out. I'll text you her number."

"Thank you." I hear a soft click and pull my phone away from my ear. I've actually been to this subway station before, I think. It's one entrance and underground. I have a bad feeling on this one. My screen is no longer helpful. I've officially found the location, but this version will not let me go underground. I need to wait for the Solver.

The text message comes in. I can't handle waiting so I just click the number and dial. "Solver eighteen," the voice is breathless. "I'm going as fast as I can. I'm almost there."

"It may be a bad one," I admit. "I'm going to need you underground."

"Got it, give me thirty seconds." I can hear her breathing at a steady fast pace. She's running, I think. I close my eyes and try to hone in on her spark. I don't want to take over, just observe. This takes focus because I'm usually much stronger than they are. Too much of me and they'll be just forced out of the body and into limbo.

I'm seeing through her eyes, watching as she jogs down the escalator. She's rather rudely pushing past people but I don't mind. I let my gut guide me, this is what I'm good at. I can find this. A subway car pulls up and stops, people are getting on. "Get on that train and then I'll take over," I say. Suddenly I'm sure.

She does as she's told and then I let my own spark take over.

December 28

Angela

"She got on the train pretty quickly," I note.

"Show time of simulation," the Magician commands. A small set of green numbers shows at the top right of the screen. Currently they read 10 followed by a decimal point and then numbers ticking up too quickly to count around the 15 area.

"Is that ten minutes and a little more?" I ask. I try not to sound impressed. I thought us finding the previous location in eleven minutes was good. Tanya just beat that time solo.

"Yes. That timer would've begun only after you started a simulation." She pointedly looks at me, making me aware she probably knows what I was thinking. "She will not be penalized for your time creating one for her. Typically a timer, if you turn one on, would only tell you how long it had been from the moment you began zooming in on a potential disturbance since real events don't have an official start point like a simulation does."

"We can start our own timers? Can we do that during a simulation?"

She turns away from me but not before I see the little smile play at the side of her mouth. "Of course. You are in a fully functioning control room when you are in a simulation. You have all the powers of the Magician in there."

Well, crap. That would've been good information for us to figure out.

I turn my attention back to the screen. Tanya has taken over the body of the Solver. On the screen it's not much different, but I know her. She absolutely hates to wait for someone else to do the observing. She likes it best when she is fully in charge at all times.

The Solver, wearing black skinny jeans and a tight red t-shirt, is looking around the subway train skeptically. Her head is turning slowly, watching each passenger on the train. I see him because I put him in the simulation. He looks identical to the man in my simulation this morning. The spark inside me must have sent a pretty clear picture. I'm watching for signs that may tell us he is up to something. He is fidgety, a little, but nothing I would notice if he were not already on my radar.

"When I'm the one inside these, for real, how do I know who I'm looking for? I'm good at finding items that are out of place but people ... " I trail off because I don't know how to explain what it is that I don't know.

The Magician nods her head. "People are tricky." I'm pleased she agrees with me. "I've heard rumors of Magicians in the past who were able to see black smoke surrounding people who were affected. It's unlikely either of you will have that gift. More likely, you have to use your spark like I do. You use it to sort of reach out. You can feel the disturbance if you are tuned into it. It feels like it looks on screen, like ripples at the edge of your awareness. You have to find where the ripples are coming from. Feel it more than see it." She turns to me, scrunching up her eyes in a way that makes them wrinkle a little at the edges. "It's difficult to explain."

I don't know what to say so I turn back to the screen. Tanya, in the Solver's body, has taken a step closer to the man in green. He is seated along a row of seats facing the center of the subway car. I can see profiles of them both from this angle. I see enough to know she is doubting him, for sure. But does she know anything at all? Can we ever know anything for sure?

She turns to the lady sitting beside the man and smiles. "Excuse me, can I possibly trouble you for your seat?" I notice a large bag pops into existence in her left hand, which is behind her. She pulls the bag out so it is visible. "I can't stand to hold this for too long."

The lady gives up her seat. "Absolutely, no problem."

"Thank you so much," Tanya/Solver says. She turns to the man. "Hello there. How are you today?"

"Fine." It's little more than a grunt. He doesn't even look at her. He is distracted. Tanya reaches into the bag now resting between her feet on the floor. She pulls out a small ball, orange and light. I smile, it's exactly what I would've done.

Tanya

A truth bomb. That's what we call them. They're manifested by a powerful spark, like mine. They are good for exactly one honest answer. You have to get the mark to take it at just the right time. It can be tricky. If you ask two questions, for example, you can only guarantee the one they answer first was honest. Sometimes honesty can beget honesty, but you can't be sure.

I play with it a little, passing it back and forth between my hands. I hope he doesn't ask me anything while I'm playing or the one question would be wasted on myself. We are not strong enough to produce more than one during a single day. At least that's what we're told. I've never tried. This is actually the first one I've conjured in a while.

I turn my attention to the man, knowing I have to phrase this just right if I'm going to make use of the ball. "What are you doing on this train today?" I ask. As the word train slips from my mouth I toss the ball again. It looks like I'm aiming for my left hand, as I've done every time. But I overshoot on purpose. It's now tracking directly to him.

He catches it. I sigh with relief.

"They're going to pay for firing me. I'm here to make them suffer." He looks shocked. I try to keep my face carefully arranged so as not to reveal anything. Perhaps he will think he imagined answering that question. He tosses the now dead truth bomb back at me. I drop it into the bag between my feet and stand.

"Excuse me for just a moment." I leave the bag where it sits at my feet, I'm done with it. I head for the door connecting the subway cars and use Magic to gray out the area. This makes me basically invisible to anyone looking. Then I change my appearance. I'll now look like a police officer entering into this car from the other car. I close my eyes and give control back to the Solver.

December 28

Angela

Almost exactly the way I would've solved it. From the truth bomb to the police officer, she's nailing this. Maybe I gave her a simulation that was too easy.

On screen the Solver is hearing Tanya's voice in her ear. "The man in green on your right needs to be arrested. He should be considered armed and dangerous. The next stop should be soon. He will need to leave with you. Take him without harming anyone."

Good details. Better details than the Magician who was in my ear at the simulation this morning. Now Tanya will need to watch with us. We are at the mercy of the Solver. Of course, Tanya can have more of a front row seat because she can watch through the Solver's eyes. I suppose she could take over again if she didn't like how it was going, but it's not recommended. So we watch.

"Excuse me, sir. What is your name?" I squint at the screen. That is an interesting technique.

"Thomas," he answers. I can hear his confusion. He wants to know why she's asking. At least he's answering, I suppose.

"Thomas, I'd like to ask you to please come with me at the next stop. We have some important information for you at the station." I like her style. She makes it sound like he's not under arrest or suspicion. Whoever this virtual Solver is, she's smart.

"Is everything alright?" he asks.

"I'd rather not discuss it here, Thomas. Would you please come along with me?"

He stands. "I suppose so." He hesitates. I remember how this went in my simulation so I'm already on the lookout for it. The Solver doesn't see it coming.

"His hand. She's not watching his hand," I yell. Sure enough, his left hand snakes behind him and seizes on the handle of the revolver I know is there. He has it pulled and on the Solver within seconds.

"Actually, I think you'll be coming with me," he says.

DECEMBER 28

TANYA

"**O**h, shit." It's not brilliant, but it leaks out anyway. I have to get this under control. I focus on keeping my spark tuned down where it is right now. I shouldn't take control again, not after yesterday when Angela was chastised for not trusting our Solver. This Solver is highly trained. She can do this. I slip myself fully back to the control room, because I'm not sure I'm strong enough to be in two places at once. It's torture to not be able to at least see what's going on.

"I need the subway map for New York City Roosevelt Island stop," I command the map. It pops up, filling the left hand side of the massive screen. I squint at the little letters and numbers. If the train was going west it's headed to Lexington Avenue. If it's going east then the destination is 21st street. I could use time to tell me, but I need to hurry. I check the screen of my phone. It's 2:38 now. Times are not on this screen. "I need subway times for the F train in New York City." Another screen pops up, this one center. Now I have the map on my far left, the timetable in the center, and the satellite image of the entrance to the Roosevelt Station on my right. Crap, it's a three minute ride to Lexington and less than that to 21st street. Wherever this subway car is headed, it's already there.

I punch the number on my cell phone at the same time that I allow my spark to slip back out and check in on the Solver. I can still communicate on the cell phone, but I can see what she is seeing. I'll get my answer.

"Dispatch," the voice answers. The subway car is not stopped, but it is slowing down. Pulling into a station.

"I'm going to need a second Solver as fast as you can. We are in the Lexington Ave subway station on a subway coming from Roosevelt Island. We have a situation. A passenger with a gun trained on the Solver."

"It looks like that's a busy station, can you give me anything more?"

"It's the F line, I know that." Begrudgingly, I pop myself out of the Solver and back to the control room. I use the left hand screen to click a few times and follow some links. I say a small prayer that this information on Wikiwhatever is valid. "It looks like you're looking for the Rapid Transit Station. Ground level."

I slip back into the Solver while there is clicking on the other end. "Hey, look he's shoving her off the car. There's a lot of people around here, he's causing a lot of chaos. We are going to need a second Solver NOW. Get me whoever you have. Immediately."

"I can have three Solvers there in under thirty seconds. Do you want them all?" the voice asks.

"Yes. I want them all. Tell them to run."

December 28

Angela

"It wasn't going to happen at that spot. He was going to ride around to another location. That was too short of a ride." I'm thinking out loud.

"You're thinking like a Magician now. But that information is not relevant to what is happening right at this moment. Think about the simulation. Do you need to modify anything?" the Magician asks.

I set an end goal of passengers being shot. Since they're no longer on the subway, technically these people are not passengers. "Maybe I should amend it to end if anyone is shot. I said passengers the first time," I say.

"You could do that, yes." She doesn't want to give me answers. I resist the urge to groan. I've never done this before.

Would I want the simulation to end if the gun was fired? If a person was shot?

"Add an end goal of any innocent hit with a bullet," I say. At that point, it's basically already over anyway. If that happens, we lose.

DECEMBER 28

TANYA

He has his hand clamped tightly on her upper right arm. They're walking together, I know she's letting him walk her. She wants him to move away from the crowds. She has her arms up. I wish I knew a way to get her a message, to tell her that there are three more Solvers coming.

Before I even need to tell her anything, they've arrived on the scene. Two are dressed as police officers, but I have a feeling that third guy in plain clothes is ours too. He's out of breath as though he's been running. I'm at their mercy, I hope they have a plan.

"Sir, put the gun down," the taller one dressed as an officer commands. His voice booms out over the concourse. Anyone who was nearby takes off running, even the guy I thought was our third Solver disappears into the shadows on the left. "She's a cop, man. You don't want to shoot a cop."

"I'm not getting out of here alive, I know how you all operate. I'm not getting out of here and neither is she," the guy, Thomas, says. His voice is shaky.

"You don't want that. What if I can promise to take you in myself, alive? Will you lower the gun and come with me?"

I hear something on our left but she doesn't look. I wish I had a way to look myself. But without taking control of her again, which is obviously a bad idea, I don't. I'm at her mercy just as she is at his.

"Do you think I'm stupid?" Thomas asks. His voice is loud in the ear of the Solver I'm occupying. "All of you are the same. You kill a guy as soon as you can. If I give you one iota of a clear shot you're going to take it." He's wiggling and moving a lot. She turns her head a little bit and I can see the gun waving wildly around. He's talking with his hands. That means he doesn't have a clear shot.

As soon as I think it, there's a slam and a sharp pain and then I'm back in the control room blinking wildly at the screen. "What happened?" I yell. "What's going on?"

"Suspect down," the voice on my speakerphone is the Dispatch from the Solver center. I thought she hung up on me. "Suspect apprehended."

This time the entire control room disappears with a pop and I'm back in the classroom. The Magician is standing in front of me with a smile on her face. Angela is wearing an even bigger grin.

I stand up and get right in Angela's smug little face. "What the hell happened in there? Why did I get shoved out before it was over? Was that your idea of a joke?" I'm angry. I should be controlling myself, especially in front of the Magician but I can't help it.

Angela grins, just enough to piss me off more. "That wasn't me. The third Solver you called slipped into the shadows when the guy wasn't looking." She holds up her hands and slaps them together right in front of my face. "He slammed right into the guy. I'm guessing that shock is what forced you out."

The fight goes out of me. I notice the Magician is still smirking beside us, watching this play out. She crosses her arms over her chest. "Oh, so that's how they arrested him. They did good," I say.

Angela brushes my arm with her fingertips. "You did good." I pull my eyes away from the Magician and back toward my competition. "Calling in backup was smart. We could see that station entrance, it's like a weird little door right on the street. If he had gotten above ground there were so many people around. It could have gone really wrong, Tanya. Really wrong."

"Was that … did you … are you complimenting me?" I stutter.

She widens her eyes and turns away. "Sorry, it won't happen again."

The Magician clears her throat. "Are you quite finished, ladies?" We both look in her direction. I nod. "Good. Angela is the official starter of that simulation so your grade will be based on the feedback she just gave you, although I will officially process that into a score." She turns to Angela. "Your score will be a direct reflection of the end goals you set up and the way you commanded the simulation. Any questions?"

We both shake our heads.

"Wonderful, then I will return to the real control room. You two ladies have a restful evening, I'll see you tomorrow."

Spring, Age 18

Emily

"Why don't you explain what you've learned for me while Mark takes care of programming this access I'm giving you," the tall lady in the gorgeous pantsuit says. She's here from the United States Government. Sitting in our living room with Dad and I while Mark, Dad's engineering friend, taps away at the computer inputting some codes or something she delivered to give him access to the World's satellites.

"Our experiments have discovered that Magic users, like myself, can put out dark energy when they are feeling a dark or negative emotion," Dad explains.

"Like what?" she asks.

"Anger, frustration, depression, anxiety, or pure hatred all seem to work," I answer. "Basically if we get irritated at a traffic jam, for example, we emit darkness."

She crosses her left leg over her right and begins tapping her foot. "That sounds dangerous."

"By itself it's not," Dad says. "But we've also discovered that the dark energy will be drawn together, forming larger pools. Those larger pools are then drawn to a non-Magical source of this same darkness."

Her foot stops. "You can see this?"

Without stopping in his clicking, Mark answers. "With the technology we've Magically enhanced, yes. We can see when this pool of darkness collects around the host."

"What does that pool do?" She addresses Mark. When she realizes she doesn't have his attention, she turns to my father and repeats the question. "What happens next?"

"Basically the darkness gives the host more energy for his or her negative thoughts. It forces the action. We've seen evidence of criminal activity being considered or even attempted while in the presence of this darkness."

Her hand flies to her mouth. "Are you telling me that Magic users all around the world are basically putting darkness out into the world and creating criminals?"

"No," I answer. "We're telling you that dark Magic is collecting around hosts and enhancing what they were already thinking or feeling." I lean forward. "We're also telling you that we can see it the second it collects. Before the host does anything."

I let the silence ring until she's had a second to process. "I'm telling you that it may be possible to separate the darkness from the host before a crime is committed."

Her hand drops back to her lap and her leg resumes its bouncing. "Show me," she commands.

"That's the idea," Mark says. "Just give me one more second."

We watch him work as he clicks through screens on the computer faster than I can even process them. Finally, he opens one that holds a satellite image of what appears to be our state in all its glory. "All set," he says. "Gather 'round."

The three of us cross the family room and take up stations behind Mark, who is seated in front of my family's computer in the corner. "Magnus and Emily here have called in a few favors," he explains. "We've sent a few Magic users down to a local park along with a single non Magical representative." He turns to our guest, smiling. "All five of the volunteers were told to wallow in their angriest thoughts. They can read an article or something that will make them angry. Does this make sense so far?"

She nods. "If what you've told me holds up, that means the Magic users will all be putting off dark Magic right now."

"Exactly," Mark agrees. "Then we'll call our non Magic person and have them walk through that same location. If our previous experiments hold up, that dark Magic will latch onto the host. Then, if everything I've done to adjust the satellites works, we should see it show up here."

"I hear a lot of the word 'if' in that plan," she notes.

"Yes, well." Mark rubs the back of his neck. "Make the call," he says.

Dad swipes his phone open and hits Mom's face on his favorite's screen. "You're all set," he says. Then he clicks it closed again.

On the computer screen, Mark zooms in just a little. The park is center screen but it isn't all we can see. I'm watching, counting in my head. I have no idea how long this will take, not really. I get to 24 before the concentric pulsing circles show up. "There," I shout, pointing.

The woman squints at the screen. "That's it? How can you be sure?"

"I'll be right back," I say. Dad nods. I close my eyes and reach out for Dad's friend in the park. I feel the click that tells me I've connected. I open my eyes and I'm in the park, exactly as planned.

My mother is directly across the grass from me and she's completely surrounded by a black cloud. In all our experimenting, we've really only found one way to successfully send the darkness back out of the host. In Erik's body, I break into a run. I don't stop until I've slammed into my mother, sending her sprawling onto the grass.

The black smoke dances away into the night and my mother winces. "We have to figure out a better way to do that," she says.

I close Erick's eyes and pop myself back into the living room. We're all still facing the screen. "Wait, where did those circle things go?" the woman asks.

"Emily was occupying the body of a Magic user," Dad explains. "She went to separate the host from the darkness. The circles disappearing from our radar means that the disturbance has been set free."

She turns and looks at me. "Is this the case?"

"Yes, ma'am."

"And you could do this again if you had to?"

I look at Dad. He nods, telling me to be honest. I smile. "Yes, ma'am."

"Excellent." She claps her hands and turns her attention to Mark. "You will have the equipment you requested and the set up you need available in two weeks. It's a pleasure doing business with you." She offers her hand first to Mark and then to Dad. Both shake her hand heartily. "We're going to need to speak again before I go before the United Nations."

"Of course, Madam President," Dad says. "I look forward to it."

December 28

Angela

I drop my bag onto the floor just inside my dorm room door, which I leave open to the hallway. Then I flop onto my bed, and stare at the ceiling. I use Magic to conjure up a can of Coke and then call my Mom. The image, since its Magic, will show up wherever I'm looking.

She answers, thinking the call is Facetime. "Hey baby, how was school?"

"Good." It's not what I want to say. I don't want to give her one word answers. I want to tell her that I finally learned how to start a simulation. How it's easier than I thought because the computer controls everything. I want to tell her about the simulation this morning in Solver class. I want to tell her everything. Instead, she gets one word. This is my life. In a week, if I'm chosen as the next Magician, this will be my permanent life.

"That's great. We really miss you. Are you coming home for New Years?"

In the past I've always been allowed to. In fact, if it were any other year, I'd be home right now like the underclassmen. I sigh. "Not this year, remember? There's an important assembly on New Year's Day. It's only for graduates."

"When is graduation? Did they give you that date yet? I'd like to get it on my calendar."

"Mom, I don't know. I'm sure they'll tell us eventually. You don't have to come though." You can't come, it's fake.

"Of course we'll come, don't be silly." She waves her hand at someone I can't see. "Oh, your Daddy is here. Ed, come talk to your daughter."

Dad's face pops up over Mom's shoulder. He's a good head taller than her so I can imagine him bending down behind her, probably wrapping his arms around her thin little waist in a hug. "Hello, pumpkin. How's school?"

I smile at him. My Dad is the kind of guy you can imagine was cute back in his day before he gained a few pounds from Mom's cooking and his hair started turning gray. He's a happy guy and always seems to wear a smile no matter what life throws at him. "It's good."

"And the boyfriend, what's-his-name? How's he?"

I laugh. "There's no boyfriend, Dad."

Mom smacks him on the arm. "Oh stop teasing her."

"One of these days, she's going to slip up and say his name. Then I'll know for sure." He kisses my Mom on the cheek and steps out of the shot. "What smells so good?" he asks.

"What are you making for dinner?" I Magic the smell to come through the image. My dorm room fills with the odors of roasting chicken and spices. My stomach groans.

"Chicken, roast potato, and corn on the cob," Mom answers.

I Magic myself a plate of the exact same dish. "Sounds good. Hey, listen, I should go. I have homework to do. I'll talk to you all tomorrow, okay?"

"Sounds good, sweetheart. Love you," Mom says.

"Love you, kiddo," Dad yells from somewhere behind her. "Be good. No kissing people without their permission." Dad gives weird advice like that all the time. It makes me laugh.

"I promise. Bye guys." I end the call and bring the plate of homemade food to my lap as I sit up. Best part of my day, by far. I love these guys. Sometimes I wish I was not Magic. I'd be sitting down to dinner with my parents and sister, complaining about normal homework. Actually, I probably wouldn't have homework at all this week because of the holidays. I'd be hanging out with friends.

I sigh dramatically. The things we do to keep the world safe from dark sparks.

December 28

Tanya

Since we all live at the Academy, it's set up more like a college. The classes all take place inside one giant building, which is on the north side of the campus. On the east and west side there are two identical dorm buildings, one for males and one for females. On the south side is the administration building which also houses the real control room and the dispatchers. In the center of the whole thing is what we call the quad. A small grassy area perfect for studying or enjoying the outdoors.

The quad is really dark at midnight, it turns out. I can see the darker areas that must be trees, but nothing defined. One such tree seems to have a darker shape underneath it. I walk directly toward the figure.

"Make it quick," I say in lieu of a greeting. I don't have a roommate like a lot of people at the Academy, probably because I've been here so long, but my self-appointed dorm mom could wake up at any point. I'm pretty sure I'd have to have the world's shittiest luck for her to be awake and able to see me in the darkness, but still … I'm a worrier, what can I say?

He sighs. The area around him lightens up a little, enabling me to see him in the darkness. I'm sure he's using Magic. Hopefully it only extends to us. "Did you bring a snack?" he asks. "I'm starving."

I Magic an apple and launch it at his stomach as hard as I can. He's sprawled across the grass, hands looped behind his head. He moves quickly, owing to the fact that he's almost finished with Solver training and has a great reaction time. He catches the apple and frowns. "Healthy stuff? I should've been more specific."

"Magic your own snack next time. Now what did you need? We can't be seen together. I can't be linked to you."

He takes a bite out of the fruit, the crunch sounding ultra loud in the silence that is midnight. "They're suspicious," he says.

I don't have to ask who he's talking about. He is not easily scared, which should make me nervous. But I sigh, not willing to show him how much this conversation bugs me. "Look, part of the problem here is they're self-important narcissistic jerks. How is suspicious behavior different from all the rest of their typical actions?"

"It just is." He lets go of the apple with one hand and grabs my calf, the only part of me he can reach. "Trust me. They're watching more closely. Something changed." His eyes cloud. He's scared.

"It's fine," I say. My voice shakes a little. I clear my throat and try again, forcing myself to sound like I'm not worried. I need to stay strong in the face of his fear. Despite the fact that we absolutely cannot be seen together, I need him for my plan to work. "They're probably just on edge. Everyone is. We're less than a week away from finding out exactly what happens at a ceremony when there are two Magician's Assistants. This has never happened before in the history of Magic."

"In the history of the Academy," he corrects.

"True." Technically we could both be right. We don't know what was going on in Magic before the Academy, they've made sure of that. I've tried to find out. I've tried reading books in the library, but the only library I have access to is this one. There are books with literal pages cut out. How am I supposed to learn about what I'm getting into when my only source of information is heavily redacted documents?

"We're running out of time," he points out. This is why I hate meeting with him. Every time we meet he makes me feel like I'm under a bigger time crunch.

"I know. We're close."

"But it only works if--"

"I know," I interrupt. "I know the plan. It's my plan." I take a calming breath. "Look, just keep gathering information for me. You never know what I'm going to need once I'm the Magician. We're going to need to work fast after the ceremony."

"Okay." He smiles at me. He really is cute. The smile takes up his whole face. "Do you ever wonder what will happen to Angela when you win?" he asks. "She won't see this coming. She doesn't know anything about life outside of The Academy."

I shrug. "No one does." It's all I can bring myself to say on the topic. "I'm gonna go get some sleep. Thanks for helping me."

He smiles. "No problem, I believe in you." He winks. "Goodnight, Magician lady."

I chuckle as I turn to head back into the darkness toward my dorm. "Goodnight."

Fall, Age 18

Emily

The screens in front of me are impressive. There's really no other word for it. Each screen is about the size of the old whiteboards in the elementary school I went to before Dad started homeschooling me. They are mounted side-by-side across the wall and there are three of them. The result is that the entire wall lights up at my voice command or touch.

In front of it is a grey table, only wide enough for maybe a plate of food and a mug full of coffee. There are devices that power the large screens, hard drives and things, but they're all stored on the other side of the wall in a small temperature controlled room designed specifically for that purpose.

I crack my knuckles and stand directly in front of the center screen. "Show me the world map," I command. This is my first run on this massive computer system without an audience.

It's been here, fully functional, for a month. I've used it. But I've always used the new system with Dad, Mark, and some random combination of important people from around the world watching me work. This is my first solo mission. I am less nervous without the audience.

On the center screen the globe appears. I pinch and zoom the screen until it's filled with the image of North America. I've learned a lot of new things since starting the planning for this new project. One of those is world geography. I'm forcing myself to label a map of the world every day, first thing in the morning. If I can't do it with 90% accuracy, I try again after a cup of something caffeinated.

I slowly move the map around on my screen, looking for the circles that signal dark disturbances. My Magic is infused through a lot of this equipment. It should make me tired, running all of this, but I've learned that I can draw more strength from other Magic users around me. Specifically, it seems that I can draw from positive energy and thoughts that they put out without draining them at all. We've recently hired a few Magic users to make my process here more streamlined. Some of them are stationed right here in this building, down the hall manning a phone and waiting for me to call them for assistance. I don't even have to be able to see them to draw from their energy.

On screen I'm now centered over Sierra Leone. My screen is filled with brown, green, and red. But something inside me is telling me to stop and zoom in close. I close my eyes and work my fingers on instinct alone, hoping the Magic inside me will guide my hand. The World of Magic is not satisfied when things are out of balance. When our darkness is used to guide the hands of non Magic humans in cruelty, Magic wants us to fight back. I stop moving my fingers and open my eyes, feeling like I've found something.

Just above the center of my screen is a collection of something that looks like it may be the tops of buildings. Surrounding them on all sides is trees, grass, and dirt. More importantly, there are large concentric circles pulsing around the entire image. Big ones.

Times like this are the reason we have the network of Magic users at my command. It's not like I can get myself safely to Africa without someone's interference. I slowly zoom out, looking for more information on exactly where we are. Really this seems like a remote location. I'm east of a Wildlife Sanctuary and south of a place the map is identifying as Makarabai.

I tap a button on the computer and hear a ringing echoing through the room. "Good Morning, Em," the voice greets. He sounds like he's smiling. "What do you need?"

This is one of the new hires we've stationed down in the room. He'll have his own single screen computer where he can access all kinds of information. Including registered Magic users who have agreed to help us with our project all over the world. These people would be paid by the project on an as needed basis, like contractors.

"Do we have anyone in Africa?" I give him the nearest latitude and longitude coordinates to the center of the circles.

"Well, that's the middle of nowhere isn't it?" he asks.

"Sort of looks like it. There's a small town of some kind near there, but it's not where the disturbance is showing up," I tell him. "I'm hoping to get someone down there to show me a live image."

I can hear him clicking on his keyboard. "I have three guys in Africa but the closest one is probably half an hour away from there if I could get him on the phone right now. You want me to get him there and you can keep looking? Is the disturbance moving?"

I watch the circles for a full count of thirty. "They aren't moving right now, but they're pretty large." I close my eyes and take a deep breath, feeling my Magic spark for signs of fatigue. I'm good, feeling healthy and strong. I open my eyes again. "Connect me to whoever is closest, I have an idea."

"You got it, boss."

The sound of ringing fills the room again before I can ask a guy who's likely at least ten years older than me not to call me boss. "Hello," a voice says in clipped English.

"Hi, it's Emily. Are you available for a contract job today?" I ask.

"Yes."

"Great." I close my eyes again and reach out for him with my spark. I can feel him, but I don't take over. When I open my eyes I'm looking through his. He's in a building sitting at a table with a plate of food in front of him. He appears to be alone. I'm not trying to be intrusive. I mostly wanted to see if I was able to access him from this far away. Turns out, I am. "Do you mind if I take over and teleport your body to another location?" I ask. My voice sort of echoes in my own head because I'm in his on the phone.

"You can do that?" he asks.

"I'm going to try."

"Ok."

That's all the permission I need. I push all the way into his body. It is hot and muggy in the room he's sitting in. It's also quiet. A quick check around reveals that I was right about him being alone, which is good. Sierra Leone is still working on their acceptance of Magic use in public.

I think the latitude and longitude in my head, close my eyes, and command my spark to take me to the location.

The change I feel is mostly in my ears. The noise is different here. Not louder, just different. I can hear movement that may be trees blowing in the breeze or it may be people. I open my eyes and my breath catches in my throat. In front of me there are four huge elephants.

I watch them, smiling at the chance to see this in real life, for a full thirty-seconds before a scary thought occurs to me. Poachers. The disturbance could've attached to a poacher, making them more willing to try something dangerous like hunting an elephant in broad daylight this close to a Wildlife Sanctuary.

I push myself back out of this helpful man's body and into my computer room. He should still be on the line. "Sir," I say.

"Yes." He sounds like I felt. Hesitant and in awe of the beauty before him.

"I think we may be looking for a poacher. Someone with a gun. My satellite image here is about ten minutes old. I'll help you look for things here if you'd like or I can come back and take over."

"You search there," he says.

The spot I brought him to is under a tree, in the shade. It's also just outside of where the circle appears to be fully centered. That means he may be just outside of the eye site for whatever we're looking for. With any luck, it's far enough away to keep him safe.

December 29

Angela

Cheryl is on the phone when I make my way through the crowd and into the hallway outside our Solver class. She bobs her head at me in a sort of "hello, I see you, but I'm on the phone" way, complete with a toss of her hand in the direction of the phone stuck between her ear and her shoulder.

As I draw up next to her she makes a show of rolling her eyes. "All right," she says into the phone. Her voice has an annoyed edge to it. "I get it." She rolls her eyes again. "Yup." She holds up her hand and mimes the universal sign for "this person talks too much" pushing her thumb against her other fingers repeatedly. "Yes … yes … okay."

I chuckle a little, shaking my head at her signals. Suddenly she spies something over my shoulder and her eyes go wide. I spin around, searching the hallway. There's nothing going on back there that would make that expression.

"Hey, I gotta go. I'll call you later." Cheryl clicks the call off. She leans toward me, setting her arm on my shoulder and pointing at something. I follow her finger. She's pointing at a tall, thin man wearing slick black pants, a button up black shirt rolled to the elbows, and a dark grey vest. His hair is so black it's almost blue under the fluorescent lights. He's wearing dark sunglasses indoors. He's also talking to Rolly. The pair of them in their immaculate expensive looking outfits are a sight to behold, for sure. But I have no idea why she's so excited. "Who is that?" I ask. I spin around to face her again.

Her eyes are still wide and her cheeks are rosy. "That is Mark Thompkins."

I steal another look. You can see the muscles rippling under his shirt. "Who?" I ask.

She sighs, annoyed with my naïveté. "Mark Thompkins." She must see the confusion is still all over my face because she rolls her eyes. "The Container."

I look again. If you had to think of a person who matches the description of that mythical job that people only hear about, the kind of person who is supposed to be quietly doing his job without anyone noticing, you'd imagine this guy. "Well, we have to walk right by him to go to class. Are you going to be able to handle yourself without fangirling hard?" I ask.

"Yeah, of course." Her mannerisms are completely at odds with her appearance right now. She's practically vibrating with excitement. "Can you imagine being the only Container for Magic in the entire world? Like it's his entire job to contain and destroy dark sparks and he's the only one in the world who does it."

This time it's me that does the eye roll. Yeah, I can imagine. The Magician is the only being in the entire world that controls positive sparks. I guess that means this guy, Mark Thompkins, is the exact opposite. One controls positive, one controls negative. I wonder where he trains to learn how to do that, since there isn't anyone here who attends Container classes.

"Good morning, ladies," Rolly greets us at the door. "Cheryl, can I borrow you for just a second?"

Oh good lord. I give her my best smile, hoping to send a little encouragement, and walk into class. I drop into our usual section with Chris and Steve, whose attention is clearly on whatever is happening in the hallway.

Cheryl continues to look star-struck. She stands nearby while Rolly and this Mark guy have a conversation we can't hear. She doesn't seem to be bothered by the fact that she was, apparently, brought out there for absolutely nothing.

The bell rings to start class and Rolly makes no attempt to enter the room, talk to Cheryl, or finish his conversation. Time ticks by. Finally, Andrew Martin, the teacher for our morning Dispatch courses, brings a student I recognize up to the group gathered in the doorway. He looks nervous. At this, Rolly nods and enters the classroom, closing the door.

"What the hell?" Steve whispers.

"Who was that kid?" I whisper back.

"His name is Frank. He's a Solver too. He's in my advanced seventh period course," Steve answers. He catches my eye and then looks down. "He's friends with Tanya."

Any other conversation we may have been preparing goes out the window when Rolly clears his throat and starts class. "Sorry about that delay. We had a little Academy business to attend to. Today is the day of your essay test."

"Our final essay test," Chris says. He wiggles his eyebrows.

"When the paper appears before you please do your best to answer the question completely. We are looking for thorough answers that address all the possible steps you could take in the simulation described. You may use a spell check spell, but all other Magic has been disabled. Good luck."

A paper appears before me with a single prompt at the top. I have to read it twice before it actually makes sense, since my mind is really on what could be happening in the hallway and where the heck Cheryl has been taken.

I write an entire essay, use a spell check spell, and read a chapter in a book I brought with me.

Cheryl never makes it to class.

December 29

Tanya

We're all uncharacteristically silent at lunch. Logan, Charlie, and George seem to look as worried as I feel. Frank was pulled out of his first period Dispatch class, which he shares with Charlie. Charlie caught us in the hallway between classes to report that Frank hadn't been seen since.

At the time I told everyone not to worry. But then Frank was basically escorted into our Research class and sat alone at a table with Cheryl and some handsome guy with dark hair the entire time. They didn't appear to be working on the research project, which my group completed only because George can't stand to leave one uncompleted. When I tried to use a spell to listen in on their conversation all I got was static, like someone untuned an old fashioned radio.

There have been no further sightings of Frank, Cheryl, or the mysterious tall guy. Hence the fact that none of us are eating right now. Logan is pushing food around his plate with his fork, but that's the closest any of us are getting. This could mean Frank's spark has been taken. It could mean he's being sent home. Just as quickly as we are identified, we can be contained and dismissed.

"Why so glum, chums?" Frank saunters up like he hasn't a care in the world and drops a plate with a sandwich and an apple onto the table with a loud smack.

I jump. "Where the hell have you been?" I shout.

He laughs. "I got a new schedule."

"What? Why? It's your final year. You need two advanced Solver classes. What could you possibly need a schedule change for?" Logan asks. He looks easily as shocked as I was to see Frank pop up on his left.

"Well," Frank takes a huge bite out of his sandwich, which appears to be grilled cheese. Thankfully, he swallows the mouthful before continuing. "It appears that the Academy has detected a new powerful student," he points to himself, "to become the next Container."

"Whoa," Charlie's eyes grow wide. "When was the last time we got a new Container?"

Containers aren't popular. What they do isn't well known. The only people who know what they really do to contain dark sparks are, I suppose, other Containers. An odd feeling starts in my stomach, like I might be sick. I think I realize the answer a split second before Frank says it out loud. It only makes sense.

"Coming up on ten years ago, now. Apparently they're usually appointed in secret at the same exact time as the next Magician."

This is a development I wasn't expecting and suddenly I feel so stupid for not seeing it. The Container has to be as powerful as the Magician, or nearly. It only makes sense. One to control all the Magic in the world and one to Contain any that gets out. I cover my face with my hands. No big deal, right? This isn't huge. Frank is a friend. Frank and I can talk about what needs to happen. We can get on the same page. It's not like ... wait. I drop my hands to the table with a satisfying slap. Everyone turns toward me. "Cheryl?" I question. "You were sitting at the table during Research with Cheryl."

"Yeah, well apparently that's an issue they didn't foresee. It's why my schedule change didn't happen sooner." He runs his hand through his hair. "There are two of us who are presenting. Mark figures it's related to you and Angela both being Magician's Assistants." He shrugs. "He assumes only one of us will take over, but he said if there are two of us it can only help."

I blink too quickly. "Two of you? What would that look like?"

"It's a big job. Every successful solve has to have a Container. He gets around to them all quickly enough, but we could divide the world somehow if we had to." He takes another bite of grilled cheese.

This could be a problem. I think, for my plan to work, I have to be the strongest Magic in the world. I have to be above reproach and punishment. I don't know if a Container is considered an equal, but it's really starting to sound like that.

Logan lays a hand on my arm. "Hey, don't worry." I shake my head and look at him. He's intently focused on me, his eyes narrowed with concern. "That doesn't mean that you'll both be allowed to stay Magicians. Just because this Mark guy thinks that's how it can work with Frank doesn't mean that's what will happen to you two."

I hadn't even considered that.

"Besides," Logan continues, "how bad can that be? Half the job, all the glory, and no risk of losing? Sounds pretty good to me." He finally takes a bite of the food he's been pushing around. I still don't bother to conjure anything to eat. I have no appetite right now.

Apparently, there's a lot I didn't consider.

FALL, AGE 19

EMILY

I'm nervously pacing the floor behind the stage. I can hear the audience shuffling into their seats, chatting and laughing with each other. The sheer number of people that must be present to make that much noise has my heart fluttering at maximum speed inside of my ribcage. The operation has grown too large for me to handle with my small group of helpers. So we've expanded. But expanding raised questions. Who would train the newcomers? With that question came the idea that has taken on a life of its own. The idea that has led the United Nations to finally sanctify the use of Magic, fully and completely.

Beyond that curtain sit hundreds of Magic users. For the first time in our history they are all there, waiting. I can feel the satisfaction in my spark. The World of Magic is so happy with what we have done. I close my eyes and allow the surge of happiness to ratchet my heartbeat down a notch.

I open them when someone calls my name. "Are you ready?" he asks.

"If they're ready for me," I answer. The house lights blink a few times. I watch them below the curtain. This is the signal for the gathered crowd to take their seats. I listen as the noise quiets to an almost complete silence. Then I step out onto the stage.

I'm wearing a long black robe. It seems archaic, in my opinion, to have the person in the role I'm agreeing to undertake today wear a robe like an old wizard in a children's cartoon. But it was Dad's idea and one that my advisors loved. Plus, if I'm being honest, it required very little work on my part. So I caved.

I stop myself at the center of the stage on the small X someone has helpfully made for me out of a roll of regular masking tape. I roll my shoulders back and face the audience. "Good afternoon," I greet them. "Welcome to the home of the future. Welcome to The Academy of Magic."

There are genuine cheers all around the room. Not the small kind like you'd expect from a polite audience. These are the cheers of a group that has been told to hold their gifts in secret for too long. The cheers of my people. My smile widens and emotions surge in my chest.

"Here we will train your children in the use of their Magical spark. We will prepare for the mission we have accepted. We will control the dark energy put out into the world and prevent it from being used to commit crimes."

I hold out my arms. "With your permission, I accept the role of Magician. I will do my part to keep the World of Magic satisfied by maintaining balance. In that role it may be necessary to call on the spark inside each of you. But it will make us stronger as a community. I will use this gift to teach you what you are capable of and you will use it to train each other and share your gifts. No longer will we operate in darkness and shadows of secret. Tonight, we step into the light." This time the cheer explodes from every corner of the audience. I let it ride its natural course before lowering my hands. "I will take that as your permission," I say. This brings the silence again.

It also brings out a helper with a small canister of dirt. She walks around my body, drawing a circle by slowly upending the canister. "We root this woman to the Earth," she says in a loud, clear voice that echoes back to me off the far wall.

Another person enters the stage with a matching canister just as she finishes her circle. Their paths cross and they offer each other shy smiles. This man slowly pours a layer of salt out on top of the dirt. "We ward off disturbances," he explains.

I wait until he also exits the stage, letting the silence radiate. It feels as if the entire auditorium is holding its breath. No, I correct, the World of Magic is the one waiting. "I ask you to bear witness today as I take control of the Magic sparks around me. Magician, the title I am being granted by you and by the World of Magic, is one that commands respect. It is also one that reminds me that I am no longer a mere individual. For the rest of my days I will stand for all who have shared their spark with me. When you give me full control today, you will be entrusting me with your safety and security."

This time the applause is reserved, polite. The people are suddenly nervous and they should be. I have realized that it is only right to ask them to do this. When I take over a body, I am invading it. I do it without pause because that is the right thing to do in that situation. But the people who have been taken over explained to me that they are existing in a sort of sensory deprivation. They know what has happened to them, to some extent. I can take power from all of these people in attendance, whether they want me to or not. To me, it is so important to do it with their permission and with promises that I will not abuse what they are giving me.

"I promise to use the power you are sharing with me to control the spread of dark energy in the world and prevent the damages it can cause."

Like a switch has been flipped the power in the room flows to me all at once. My breathing grows ragged and I have to shut my eyes against the onset of skills and life experience that threaten to bury me.

I was always a powerful Magic user. I open my eyes again and smile for the crowd as Dad steps forward. "Ladies and gentlemen, the Magician of The Academy for Magic," he bellows.

The room explodes and people everywhere rise to their feet. I can tell they're all glad they don't feel any different. I haven't taken from them. They still retain their skills until the moment when I need them. But I have a new perspective. I can see inside of their sparks in a way I couldn't before. I can reach any of them, right now, without knowing a single thing about them or having any connection to them at all.

Yes, I always knew I was powerful. Now, I can tell I am the most powerful Magic user that walks the Earth. I must use it wisely.

December 29

Angela

"I'm honestly excited for you," I gush. We are walking as a group from lunch to study hall: Cheryl, Steve, Chris, and I. Cheryl spent our lunch period explaining her new opportunity. She seems excited, which gives me hope even if I don't fully understand how this is all being sprung on her less than a week before the ceremony.

Chris, on the other hand, seems like the news sent him into a strange funk. He's distracted and not making any jokes, which is odd for him. I eyeball him when I think Cheryl isn't looking at me. He's watching the ground as he walks in that way people do when their mind is somewhere else. Steve punches him on the arm. "Check us out, we now have two famous friends."

"Not famous," Cheryl adds. I notice she does smile though. "None of you even knew who Mark was before I told you. That doesn't equal famous."

That's true. Even I, who should know everyone, didn't know who he was. It's something that will make me realize I don't really understand what I'm getting into if I think about it too long. I decide not to think about it.

The study hall room is pretty empty today. Our study hall looks like a library. Tables and independent study corrals are randomly placed among stacks and shelves of books. There's no teacher here. Sometimes people who have graduated will use this space. Teachers who are planning lessons will also pop in here occasionally. Basically the idea is that anyone can be watching at any time, which is worse than the threat of a teacher.

The four of us choose a section near a large window. Cheryl drops into an armchair, casually flipping her legs over the side. I sit nearby at a hightop table in one of four rolling high chairs. I love high top tables, which is something my friends are privy to. They always make sure to sit in a section that offers one for me. Steve and Chris drop to the floor between us facing each other.

Cheryl pulls a book out of her backpack and starts reading. Steve pulls a chart of Solver tools and a set of flashcards out of his bag and situates them between him and Chris. I Magic a stack of Magician reports I'm supposed to be analyzing onto the table in front of me and grab a highlighter.

"Are you seriously reading that garbage?" The venom in Chris' voice draws my attention. His eyes are fixed on the cover of Cheryl's book.

She peers around the edge of the book to take in the cover as if seeing it for the first time. It's all black with smoky grey lines running up and down around the words The Dark Truth About Containers. She shrugs. "I have to know the rumors."

"What's it about?" I ask. "Besides the obvious."

She lowers the book a little. "I don't know yet." She pinches pages with her left hand, drawing attention to the fact that she's only about a tenth of the way into the thick book. "Right now it's about the history of Containers." She glares at Chris. "Which, in light of new developments, we can all agree I should know."

"C'mon, we need to study," Steve says. He holds up a flashcard. "What tool is this and what is one side effect?"

Chris doesn't let himself be redirected. He shifts his body toward Cheryl. "I'm just saying, that's a book you would've looked down on me for reading. That seems very anti-Academy."

Cheryl's sigh echoes off the window. "It's not anti anything. Mark went to the Academy, he's a teacher of record here. I am a student at the same place as you. I'm not saying this book will be valuable, but how can I accept a job without knowing the negative things people say?" She keeps her voice calm. I know she's angry because she's clutching the book so tightly that her knuckles are white. I'm impressed she can keep it out of her voice.

"Let her read it," I say. "I'm curious myself. Maybe we should all read it."

Chris throws his hands up. "Fine. Whatever. You know if Containers are so important, why does the Academy keep what they do such a big secret? Anyone ever think of that?" He turns his head back to Steve. "And that terribly named tool is a rod. Side effects include looking like a jackass while using and feeling light headed after about two minutes."

Steve checks the card, shrugs, and lays it down. "How about this one?" he asks of the new card now showing. I turn back to my notes, trying to pretend like Chris didn't just raise a really good question.

DECEMBER 29

TANYA

My seventh period is as far away from the quiet, lonely hallway of Magician class as you can get. It's below ground level, dark, and bustling. No matter when I come down here there are always so many people. Really it's more people than there should be here on this final week of the year.

I slip my way past a cluster of adults wearing bluetooth headsets clipped over one ear. The soft blue lights flash at regular intervals. These Dispatch officers are connected to the network right now. For some reason, the thought gives me chills. It reminds me that everything we are practicing for with our simulations is based on something real. Something with real lives on the line.

I push open the door and enter the crowded room. There are tables and desks covering every available surface and they all point toward a huge screen showing a map of the world. This map is very similar to the one that the Magician can use but it has one major difference. On this one there are blue dots representing every available Solver across the entire planet. It's an impressive display, a blue reminder that Solvers are everywhere. Living their lives, knowing that at any time the Magician can take over their bodies, forcing their minds into a terrible limbo they can't escape from.

The room is full to capacity with both students and real Dispatch agents. Although we will be given simulated phone calls on our headsets once we connect them, this final week of Dispatch experience is the same as the real one. The room will remain full, the screen will be available to us on a laptop or on the large screen, and we can always ask for assistance if we need it.

I slip the bluetooth device into my right ear and power up the laptop at an abandoned table toward the back of the room. I notice when Angela's friend, Chris, sits next to me and powers up an identical laptop. "Here we go again," he says. I smile, but since I don't turn to look at him I realize he may not see it.

The phone in my ear rings. Real Dispatch agents are queued up in the order they log into the computer. The calls automatically rotate down to the next available agent, even if they're standing in the hallway. I assume it is the same for students. I click the earpiece. "Dispatch," I say.

"This is the Magician." Two things occur to me in that split second. I'm not sure what makes them pop in my head, but there they are none-the-less. One, this really sounds like the actual

Magician. Two, why do we need to identify ourselves? Who else would call this number? I shake my head to focus myself. "I need a Solver at Grand Avenue and 107th Avenue in Arizona," she continues.

I click on the map on my screen and type the crossroads into the box at the top. When I hit enter the screen jumps to the location. A big difference between this map and the one in the Magician's room is that this one is instantaneous when given a location. You don't need to wait for it to load. Apparently that has something to do with this image being a few minutes old. There are eight blue dots within a five mile radius. "I have a Solver," I begin. "Where along that intersection am I sending him?"

I click on the closest blue dot. This will alert the Solver to finish up whatever he or she is doing and prepare themselves to be dispatched. I can give him more information as I go, he is connected to my map screen as soon as he opens his app.

"There is a grocery store on the southeast corner. I'm seeing the disturbance centered there, possibly in the parking lot."

I click the store she's talking about, which now marks it as my destination. Along the bottom of my screen white numbers appear. "He will be on site in just under two minutes."

She sighs. "Be specific."

I freeze. Something about the way she said that makes my blood run cold. Little hairs stand up on my arms. I look around the room. Why would she say that? Why would this simulation have been precoded to respond condescendingly to a time input that was not specific? "Um," I check the numbers again. "One minute, twelve-seconds now."

"Thank you." The click tells me the call was disconnected. On my screen a button pops up. Text information? I click the small green checkmark. Just like that the Solver and the Magician will each receive a text message with each other's information, meaning it's one less thing I have to do. Actually, I suppose that also keeps their personal information in as few hands as possible.

I pause my program and sit back. I still feel uneasy. Something about that didn't feel right. I turn my head to look at Chris, wanting to talk to someone about what I'm thinking. He's on a call. I can see him running through the same steps I was.

"All right, Magician lady, it looks like there's a lot of businesses around there. Or perhaps you need homes. Where should I send this poor Solver who is pulled out of his regular life to be sent to limbo for you?" he asks. I shake my head at his obvious flippant attitude. This guy needs a t-shirt that says, "I hate authority".

I recognize the look that passes over his face. His eyes connect with mine and widen. He blinks twice. "Right, I'm sorry. You're right. I can have someone there in thirty-eight seconds." He disconnects and hits the green checkmark. Then he clicks pause, removes his earpiece, and looks at me. "What the hell was that?" he whispers.

"Did yours seem real too?" I ask.

He nods. "That wasn't a simulation. I have spent all of my years up here screwing up simulations. In the beginning they weren't coded for that, so they kind of looped back to something familiar. Now they are coding more for it so sometimes I can incite a pretty crazy reaction. But that was … " his voice drops lower. He leans closer. " … the real Magician."

"What did she say?"

"She called me by my name. She said, 'Chris, that is enough of that nonsense. Give me the location.'"

My hand flies to my mouth automatically. "How did she even know it was you?" There are other questions that come on the heels of that one; how was she on the phone with both of us at the same time? Was this a simulation? Why would she waste her valuable time connecting to our calls and sending us simulations herself? No, this one had to be real. But if it's real, why is she using underage Academy students for real Dispatch situations? Have they all been real and we just didn't realize it? Did we just send real Solvers out into the field?

I can't voice all those questions. I feel like everything has just shifted underneath me and I'm not sure I trust myself to speak at all.

The computer beeps, angry that I have been paused for too long. I'm approaching my limit. Chris points at my screen. "What now?" he asks.

I shrug. "Do we really have a choice?" I answer my own question by clicking onto the laptop with shaky hands. I'm relieved when it doesn't ring right away. I click back out to the main map, watching the blue dots pulse as if they were breath being drawn by Solvers around the world. I wonder, for a second, if someone would notice if that breath stopped. When a Solver is extinguished or killed in the line of duty, does anyone notice the dot leaving the screen?

A call comes in. I steel myself as much as I can and click the button. "Dispatch,"

"This is the Magician." Except it's not. I feel my shoulders unbunch. "I need all Solvers in the vicinity of the White House immediately." There are a few phrases we are trained to react differently to. This is one of them. My shoulders relax even further. This is a test, plain and simple. Normally a true attack on a leader of the World would require forward planning. Our system would identify the disturbance in earlier stages. We haven't had a true attack to be concerned about in a really long time, at least not during the reign of this current Magician.

My pointer hovers over the purple button at the top left of my screen, the one for this emergency situation only. Here's where I will know for sure. If I am inside of a real call this will project my map onto the large screen at the front. My call will take priority and immediately put the calls of all other Dispatch agents on hold. All eyes will be drawn to my problem, the Magician will go on speakerphone, the senior Dispatch agent will handle talking to the Magician, and we will watch this one play out all the way to its conclusion. If it's a simulation I only take over the screens of the other students in the simulation.

I click the mouse.

I'm relieved when the purple hued map takes over only the students around the room, ignoring the main screen. Beside me, Chris sucks in a breath.

His screen remains live.

158

SPRING, AGE 20

EMILY

I spend roughly sixteen hours a day pacing in this little control room on the campus of The Academy. Most of it is spent searching for disturbances, calling Dispatch, and taking over Solvers positioned around the world. Some of it is spent recording simulations and sending them off to teachers to use in training situations. They are supposed to help them walk through situations I've really faced, help them understand what could be facing them when they are fully trained.

It's important work that we are doing here, I know that. So why do I always feel so drained? Why do I always have that nagging feeling that we could be doing more in the face of this danger?

I tap the screen to my left. "Show me Solver class," I command. This is something new I've infused into our technology. As it turns out having this many Magic users in one location has made me powerful in a way no one ever anticipated. I haven't found a limit to my ability yet. More importantly, it strengthens each person connected to me by spark. They're no longer tired after completing a few simple spells. Most of them can last a full day before they truly need a rest. Me, I still have yet to find my limit.

My screen shows an image of the Solver classroom in the training building. Ten students are standing as still as skyscrapers in the classroom. The teacher, a Solver who has been with me since the beginning, is sitting with his feet propped up and a tablet perched on his legs. From here he can watch the simulations of all the students at once. I click on one child. "Show me her simulation," I command.

There's a little tingling from my spark, like electricity almost, and then my screen shows me the interior of a convenience store. I remember this one. This is a robbery she has a chance to prevent. In reality, this one will always stick with me because I didn't find it. Now I see it, the guy outside who seems like he's filling his car with gas. I feel the pulsing in my stomach that tells me he is possessed with that dark spark even while I watch the simulation. But the first time I wasn't drawn to him. The first time I was drawn to the man at the back of the store buying bags of chips. I feel the same draw from him, I thought he was the only threat. I brought a Solver into the store, sent him along to bump into the guy. The disturbance was effectively separated, sent loose back out into the world.

The bigger problem came when our friend outside entered the store carrying a gun. He demanded the money from the register. He demanded everyone get down on the floor.

My original Solver decided to be a hero. He ran at the guy, intent on knocking that darkness out of him. He was shot before he got there. I stood here in this room, desperately bringing other Solvers closer to the location. Ultimately, I lost control of that one. The local police department had to come in. I had to answer a lot of questions with local authorities. It raised questions about what we are really doing up here.

Questions I couldn't answer.

What happens when we release that dark Magic back into the world?

Was it possible that the darkness left the first man and immediately went out to strengthen the darkness of the shooter?

Isn't what we are doing really about recycling darkness?

Is there a way to contain it?

The shooter was arrested and charged with the murder of my Solver. I visited him in prison to ensure that the darkness was no longer surrounding him. I convinced myself he was an ordinary citizen by trying to take over his body, hitting that wall that told me he had no spark. The government considered it a win that he was arrested. They believed me when I told them he was no longer under the influence of a dark spark. He is sitting in a jail cell even as this simulation runs, awaiting his murder trial. But visiting him brought me more questions.

Once he was free of that darkness, shouldn't he be let go?

Would this man have committed a crime if it wasn't for the dark influence?

Is he an innocent man or a guilty one?

If he is innocent, if the fault lies with the dark Magic that took hold of him, are there other innocent men in jails awaiting sentences they don't deserve?

I swipe away the image of the simulation from the screen and focus myself back on the map of the World, slowly searching for disturbances. I cannot answer all of these questions, not yet. The best I can do is keep doing my part to keep the World of Magic satisfied. To keep the balance between good and bad sparks in the world.

One disturbance at a time.

December 29

Angela

"So glad you could join us," the Magician greets just as the door clicks closed behind me. She's smirking at me with narrowed eyes, an expression that perfectly matches her statement. Tanya is standing beside her, arms crossed over the symbol for some band I've never heard of. Their hair is already pulled into ponytails.

I look at my watch. "I'm not late," I say.

"You certainly weren't early," the Magician adds.

Oh good lord, I wasn't aware early was the expectation. I resist the urge to shout that, instead I focus my attention on dropping my backpack onto a nearby chair. I pull my hair back and smile at them. "Ready." That's the moment when the bell rings to start class. See, I wasn't late.

It's also the moment when the classroom dissolves. I'm standing, alone, in the control room. "Must be Tanya's turn to run the simulation," I say out loud. I'm not expecting anyone to answer me, but I know they're listening. I realize Chris must be getting under my skin because I'm feeling argumentative today. I close my eyes and take a deep breath, commanding myself to focus.

I sit in the chair and pop my knuckles. Then I lean back and let myself look relaxed. There's really two reasons for this. One, it will make Tanya crazy because she'll think I'm not taking her seriously. Two, and probably a better reason, I know there's nothing for me to find until she starts something. It took me a minute or two to get a simulation started. I have a bit. No point in searching now, there's literally nothing to find.

I can feel the silence in the room like it's breathing. I start to get nervous. How am I supposed to know when to start looking?

The clock.

I remember what the Magician said. Normally, when we are in a real situation, it will just show the time that has passed since I commanded the clock to start running. But in a simulation, it should show the time of the simulation. So what happens if I bring up a clock now? Will it restart when the simulation has begun?

"Show simulation clock time," I command.

In the top corner of the screen a timer begins at 00:00:00 in bright green. I watch it tick up for a little while, nervously wiggling around in the chair. I know they're watching and that's the worst part. I have no idea if my little clock trick is going to work.

I decide I'll give it exactly one minute longer. When that clock ticks over to 00:02:00 I will start searching, no matter what.

Tanya

"Start simulation," I say. It's such an easy command. It's ridiculous, really. We have been able to command this thing to start with the most inane phrase in the history of the world and yet none of us have tried that. Of course, none of us have been alone with the real equipment before. At least, I don't think we have. "Criminal is riding along the street," I pause, trying to think of more details. My Dispatch call is still rolling around in my head, so I decide to borrow from it. "He's in Arizona and he's in a car. The car is full of explosives. The plan is to abandon the car in a public place."

It's really not fair to Angela that I am building something on the move. But I need to buy some time alone with the Magician. I have some things I'd like to ask her. "The car will be on the move, but this has been a long time planning so it will be a large disturbance." I hope that sentence works as an explanation for the Magician as well as for the simulation.

"You will need to include end goals." Her voice comes from behind me but wraps around the room and echoes off the computer screens in front of me.

"Set end goals," I take a guess at the simple command. Something on the lower right of the screen clicks on with a green glow. I guess I had it right. "Bomb explodes, bomb is deactivated." Really, do I need any other goals? "I think that's all of them."

"You can always addend them if you need to. Our simulations can be edited at any time." She steps up until we are shoulder-to-shoulder. She points at the screen. "The screen on the left will be a full video of the simulation you have started. Normally, you won't have access to everything. You're aware of that, yes?" I nod because it seems like she actually plans to pause her little speech until I do. "But because we have started this one ourselves you get access to the entire video. On the right hand screen you will be able to see everything Angela sees. Again, this is not something we normally have access to. Finally, in the middle you'll have access to the camera inside the control room that Angela is using."

I notice with irritation that Angela's little strategy was effective. The clock she started earlier ticks back over to 00:00:00. I roll my eyes. Again, so simple. What we were doing wrong all this time is assuming that the commands would be something complex, difficult. We needed to think like children, apparently.

My left screen fills with the image of a clean cut man driving an old green car down an otherwise deserted road. It's dusk, darkness just starting to swallow up the edges of the scene. The sun's rays are only visible on the horizon, and only barely. All around the road there is dirt in both directions. I see a few houses, but they're far off. Wherever he is, it's not heavily populated.

I check in on Angela and see that she's started her search in the Americas. Meaning it won't be long before she finds what she is looking for. I can only hope that she is delayed a little by the moving circle.

I'm going to need to act quickly to take advantage of the fact that the leader of all Magic in the World is a captive audience behind me. I clear my throat. "Magician, how would a student know whether they are inside a simulation or a real experience?" I ask, thinking about the screen in Dispatch that obviously was connected to the real server.

"Why would a student ever be inside a real situation?" she asks.

Fine, play coy. "I'm just wondering if it will feel different. The first time we are out in the real world, working on the real server, are there differences? Is there a way we can tell?"

On screen Angela has started her little zoom on the state of Arizona. I'm watching, I'm aware, but my focus isn't really there with her. I'm holding my breath, awaiting the answer from the Magician. I'm also aware that absolutely nothing she can say will change my mind at this point.

"The feeling is different, but the equipment is exactly the same. We are preparing you for working with the technology in the best ways that we can. Before the Academy, Magic was wasted. It existed, but it was not harnessed to the best of our ability. The Academy brings it all together to keep everyone safe. We teach you the tools you need to be able to control the future of the World."

I'm afraid to move. This is the most anyone at the Academy has ever talked about the past. I've tried to get teachers to talk to me about why we do what we do, they simply give you the required answer. This is the closest I've ever been to getting someone to talk about the past, to tell me the truth I've only read in books. I have to tread carefully here or she may shut down. "If the students at the Academy are supposed to control the future of the World, isn't it possible they could be helpful on a real case?" I'm willing myself to play dumb here. We both know that was her on the phone with me in Dispatch. I assume she knew it was me. I even tried to give her a hint right now by setting my simulation in Arizona, the same state as the call she gave me. Doesn't she know my voice as well as I know hers? Besides, didn't she need to make a choice to include students in that call?

"None that I can think of. We have trained adults to handle those situations."

On screen, Angela breathes a sigh of relief and hoots. She's found the disturbance.

December 29

Angela

Finally! I was starting to get nervous. When I first started searching I was running on the high of having come up with the timer idea, which was a stroke of genius. I was starting to be afraid that I had missed something. I was worried that I was going to waste valuable time and have to circle back to where I started.

Then I noticed the circles centered on Arizona. That figures. If I had thought about it long enough, I bet I could've realized she'd start there. Tanya is as close as someone can get to being obsessed with the desert.

I watch the circle, which is actually rather large, as I zoom. I'm moving in toward the center of the state. Maybe a little south of center. "Turn on labels," I command. Along with the little words a small yellow star pops up. I'm west of the capital of

Arizona, by a little. I keep zooming, watching as I get closer to the center of the circle.

Green national forests populate my screen. Interesting, I guess I didn't figure a desert southwest state for national parks. I'm west of the large one, for sure. Zoom. East of the green area labeled as "White Tank Mountain Regional Park". All of this map appears to be labeled in a grid pattern, which seems oddly satisfying from an aerial view. But this area the circles are centered over is approaching something that isn't. For some reason, that gives me a bad feeling in the pit of my stomach.

My hand freezes over the screen. Did the circle just shift? I swear I was getting close to closing in on a location and then suddenly it was off center. I hold my breath and watch. The screen flashes and I make a noise that most closely resembles a scream of rage. "It's moving," I moan.

I zoom out a little and watch the circle carefully. From this far out I can judge the direction the circle is moving if I'm careful. I force myself to slow down, watch. "It's moving north." I'm not sure who I'm saying that for, I just know that it makes me feel better to say it out loud.

I scan the area north of the circle and grab my phone, hitting the button to make the call. "Dispatch," the voice answers.

"This is the Magician's Assistant. I think I have a major disturbance headed for the Luke Air Force Base in Arizona. How fast can you get me eyes on the ground?"

"I have eyes on the ground at the Air Force Base, ma'am. If you need someone, they're always available. But if you need someone in the air it will take me about …" her clicking is loud in my ear, "two minutes."

"Yeah, let's do that." I hang up. A text message comes through, giving me the phone number of a Solver located inside the base. I can start there if I want. Otherwise, I wait out the two minutes and a Solver will be in a plane or a helicopter to give me eyes in the sky.

I decide to wait.

I really hope that doesn't cost me the solve.

December 29

Tanya

"It seems she has identified your location," the Magician says.

"Seems that way." For a second I was actually proud of myself for throwing Angela for a loop. She seemed confused at first, the moving car really messed her up. But now she seems to have it figured out. Whatever, it's just a training simulation anyway. I can't imagine anyone getting completely lost and not solving them. We always know there's something to be doing.

"When you're looking at a real map, aren't there times when there are multiple disturbances at once? How do you know what to focus on?" I ask. I'm not sure it would matter, ultimately, to hear her admit something incriminating. But it would give me a modicum more respect for her. I can't see her face, but I can imagine that she's standing behind me with her lips pierced, angry and annoyed with me for asking. I don't expect her to give me an honest answer.

"You focus on where you are needed the most," she answers.

I was right. That's not an answer. That's an answer that invites more questions. That's a riddle. I roll my eyes. "How would I know what that is?" I ask.

"The larger the negative spark, the larger the circles you see and feel. It's not difficult."

But that's not an answer, either. Because, in reality, you'd see one at a time. How would you know whether the one you are seeing is the largest one that is happening unless you keep looking? It seems to me like two things are possible; either you solve them in the order you see them, or you have insider information I'm not privy to yet. I'm not sure I'm happy with either possibility.

On my left the driver has entered into an area that appears to be more populated. There are houses on the right-hand side of the road now. Lights are on in a lot of the houses. If this wasn't a simulation that I had created I think I'd be worried about all the people living in those houses. They could all be in danger.

On Angela's screen I watch her look down at her phone to check a message and then dial a number. My guess is she's connecting with a Solver in the air.

December 29

Angela

"Solver 3382," the voice answers. There's a lot of noise in the background.

"This is the Magician's Assistant. Are you my eyes in the sky?" This is not normal protocol, but then it's not normal to involve some kind of government base in your simulations. Tanya went for broke on her first try. This is likely an Air Force official who also happens to have a spark. It's important to have them on our team, but stressful for them.

"Yes, ma'am. I'll be able to give you eyes on the scene but I'll need you to promise not to take full control. That is, unless you know how to operate an airplane."

"I certainly do not." I tell him. Just the thought of taking too much control makes my hands sweat. I push my consciousness out to him, finding his spark and closing my eyes so I can focus on what he's seeing. It's overwhelming. We're not in a helicopter, as I was hoping. We're in something really, really fast. It's hard to see anything. I say as much into the phone.

"I'm not going to be able to go much slower, but I can go higher."

"How is that going to --" I stop because I understand now. He went higher and I got a wider lens. Which means I can actually see the grid I was seeing on my computer, but live. There's one major difference. From the direction I was watching there's a cloud of dust kicking up. "What is that?" I ask, pulling myself further out so he can focus.

"I am not sure." His voice is hard now, edged with the nerves of the situation.

"That is our primary concern. What can you tell me about that location?" I am not familiar with the area. He is.

"Lock down the south gate," he says into his headset. That information is not for me, I'm guessing. He must be connected to the Solver on the ground. "We have a vehicle approaching the area along Cotton Road from the west. I have reason to believe he's headed for the base. My estimates will put him along the south gate in about three minutes. Be aware." That message was for both of us.

Do we call this a solve?

I wait for the scene to dissolve, for the classroom to reappear.

It doesn't. I sigh. That means Tanya has bigger plans besides finding the car and alerting the appropriate authorities. She wants this to be hard.

December 29

Tanya

"Do simulations always go so differently than you planned?" I ask. This one is certainly not taking a route I had imagined. I was imagining a small building or something. I never said anything about an Air Force Base with massive security and gates. There's no way this guy is getting inside that base. These people are bound to have plans in place for keeping people like him out.

"Simulations fill in the blanks based on the information they are given," the Magician answers. "If you aren't going to be specific, they'll often just do what needs to be done for a simulation. You cannot argue with the results. You are, in fact, looking at everything you said with some details filled in."

"But a military base? I didn't think of that."

"You are assuming that Angela has found the correct solution." Her voice ticks up at the end, like she's asking me a question.

"I suppose I was." I hate how my natural reaction is to do what she asks. My brain automatically wants to please her. I have to remind myself that what's really going on here isn't so simple. "In the real world, are you ever wrong?"

"Wrong, how?" she asks.

She's playing dumb. I'm sure of it. They've been wrong before. I tread carefully. "In the wrong location, arrest the wrong person, something like that." I'm not turning around and looking at her. I'm not sure if she'll be able to read my face or not. I'm not sure I want her to try.

"I suppose mistakes have happened, yes. But is the mistake of taking in an innocent person for questioning really a big mistake, in the long run?"

I can't help myself. I whip around, my ponytail turning into a weapon as it flies toward the screen. "It can be. When someone comes in for questioning because we called them in it's really like guilty unless you can prove otherwise. Isn't that the point of that Research class half the time? You have an entire Academy working on how to hold that innocent person you brought in because you were wrong. You don't have an extra screen over here showing you the real criminal. You don't have Science to back up any of this."

Her eyes flash dangerously and she takes a slow step toward me. I may have gone a bit too far. "Young lady, you are advised to take a breath and calm down. You've put your partner in a high stress situation that you are overreacting to. You certainly can't mean what you are saying to me right now. Am I correct?"

No. I mean all of it. But I can't say that. This woman is the most powerful wielder of Magic in the world. It would be nothing to her to cast a spell that erases my existence. Less than nothing. I try for a smile. "Of course not. You're right, I'm stressed." I turn back to the screen, pretending like I care about what it shows.

But my hands are still shaking.

December 29

Angela

I pull back into the control room and dial the number for the original Solver, on the ground. "Solver eighty-six," he answers.

"This is the Magician's Assistant. I hear you're going into lock down at the south gate. If you don't mind, I'd just like to watch what happens. I know you'll have plenty of backup there." I stop myself, swallowing my urge to further ramble. I don't know how to explain to this guy that I understand he doesn't really need me but my simulation hasn't run its course. Of course, technically, this guy is part of the simulation. He can't have real feelings. He's a computer program. That thought makes me feel a little like Chris. I shake it off.

"No problem," he says.

I push myself through just enough to see through his eyes. He's standing on a large guard shack looking out over a line of people who are holding weapons behind a large, closed gate. If you need an image to instantly conjure up the idea that you are safe and they have this under control, that's a good one.

I watch as a long green car pulls into the area. A man turns the car off and exits, his hands in the air. He's having a conversation with one of the armed gentlemen, who is pointing back out in the direction the man came from.

Is it possible I was wrong? Is this guy not the source of the disturbance?

I watch them surround the car. The small man driving steps away from the vehicle without incident. It takes maybe five minutes before he's handcuffed and seated on the curb.

Why am I still here?

The simulation should end with his arrest, shouldn't it?

I back out of the Solver and turn my attention to the map. I absolutely hate the idea of looking at the map again but if I was wrong about this guy then I've already wasted too much time.

The map doesn't appear to have any other disturbance circles. I can feel myself getting frustrated. If I can't figure this out, Tanya wins. I put myself back out to the Solver. I can't shake the feeling that the answer is right here at the Air Force Base.

They're checking the trunk of the car. What in the world is going on? What did Tanya do?

I have just enough time to wonder that before there's a huge explosion. A fireball of orange fills my vision.

When it fades to the classroom, my heart is pounding and I can't seem to calm it. "What the hell was that?" I yell, stepping toward Tanya.

The Magician steps between us. "That was a fail. Can you tell me what you did wrong?"

I blink rapidly. It takes me a few seconds to process what is happening. There is no way to handle this transition smoothly. A bomb just exploded in my face and now I am here. I can't focus.

"There was a bomb in the trunk," Tanya explains. Her voice is soft, apologetic. "The simulation was not set to end unless the bomb exploded or was disabled."

"You …" I don't even know what to say. I am so angry. I'm angry at her for creating a ridiculously hard simulation. I'm angry she didn't edit her end goals. I'm angry at myself too, because I should've been able to do it even if it was hard. I shake my head. "You can edit end goals in a simulation."

"Yes, she can," the Magician frowns. "But in the real world you can't wait for someone to end it for you." She shrugs. "Really, she's preparing you. Now use it as a learning experience. What could you have done differently?"

"I don't know. The military base made everything harder. I couldn't really control anything. They seemed to have it under …" I stop myself because they obviously didn't have the control I thought they did. The big explosion proves that. No one jumps in to save me from what is quickly becoming a lame explanation. "I thought they could handle it," I conclude.

"Girls, let me explain something to you." The Magician steps back and leans one buttcheek on the desk behind her. "Everyone in the entire world with a spark has been trained here in our ways." She grimaces, narrows her eyes. "But many of them are further trained. If you are told two paths to follow and both are slightly different, how do you choose which to take?"

I try to think literally. I imagine a wall before me, brick and seemingly endless except for two doors of equal size. Both are open to reveal two identical hallways seemingly leading the same way. The Magician is pointing to the door on the left, marked Path A. Tanya is pointing to the door on the right, Path B. What would I do?

"I guess that depends which training you respect or value more," I answer. Because I can't imagine ever taking the route Tanya suggests.

"True," the Magician answers. "But if one is a respected Magical institute and the other is a respected branch of the military, what then?"

This time I imagine the Magician is still pointing to Path A but an endless line of military men and women in starched uniforms lined up and pointing to Path B. Do I take the path she tells me or the path of the majority? Both are trained in providing me safety. Both are valued, respected. This decision is much harder.

"You take the one you've immersed yourself in," Tanya says.

She's right, because I know I would take Path A. I would trust the Magician to protect me from harm and anything the military could dream up as a consequence for not listening to them. Is that because I am living at the Academy now? As Tanya says, I have immersed myself in this life and this training.

"Exactly," the Magician nods. "The men on that base have lived and trained with average humans since graduation. Those methods always come first."

"But the goal is the same," Tanya pushes. "We all want to keep people safe. Why can't we agree on how to do that?"

I think of what would've happened if I had followed Path B. The military men could've flanked me, led me to safety. But if the Magician decided to punish me, what then? Really, what defense can anyone provide against the full power of her Magic?

December 29

Tanya

Why can't we agree on how to do that?

That's what I asked her. Really, the shared pronoun was a nice touch. It implied the problem is with the entire Academy, the military, maybe the world. That's not what I meant. What I meant was why do you have a problem with that?

But I know better than to say that. The little narrowing of her eyes has me wondering if she knew what I meant, what I was implying. Then she smiles. "That is the million dollar question. One that, with any luck, one of you can solve in your decade of service."

Usually in this room she acts like any other teacher. She dresses like them, she walks like them, talks like them. Today, for whatever reason, she decides to do it her way. She waves her right hand in a tight circle and disappears from the room.

I don't think I can explain why that bothers me.

Let me try. I live in a World, the same one as you, but I know Magic is real. It surrounds me all day. I can do it. I use Magic to complete tasks. I use it to make something faster or easier.

But I have never used Magic exclusively to shock.

Fall, Age 20

Emily

I have been summoned to appear before the United Nations. This time it is not because of an epic error, loss of life, or a failed mission. It's simply because there are changes happening in Europe which have resulted in new leaders who have questions for me regarding our agreement.

I stand in the center of the bowl while leaders from all over the world stare down at me with a mixture of contempt, confusion, and interest. "Good afternoon," I say into the microphone in front of me. They've explained to me that translators are in the ears of all assembled who would require one. "You requested my presence this morning."

"We did. There are a few questions we'd like to ask you, if that is all right," a small woman says from directly in front of me.

"Fine," I answer.

She indicates a spiral bound notebook on the podium in front of her. "These questions have been recorded for me but they come from many of the assembled leaders." I nod that I understand and she lets her eyes drop to the paper to read the first one. "Please explain the process of crime detection at your school."

"The Academy of Magic is a training facility for students around the world who are shown to have the spark of Magic inside of them," I say. Someone behind a sign that reads "Lithuania" shakes his head. "But that is not what you mean, I'm sure. You are wondering about the fully trained people who work at The Academy and what we do." I smile. "My software taps into the satellites orbiting our planet. They feed me live images which I infuse with my Magic spark. This allows me to find dark disturbances, or negative Magic, in the world which has collected within a host. I send out a Solver, someone who also has a spark and has been trained by The Academy, to separate this negative Magic from the host. Hopefully, this all happens before a crime can be committed."

"What happens to the disturbance?" she asks, reading off her sheet.

I suppress a sigh. "It is sent back out into the world, unfortunately. We have a Research team attempting to find a way to destroy or contain it." The entire auditorium is so silent I could literally hear it if someone were to drop a pen or cough. It's unnerving.

"Interesting," she says. Then she gives a little start, like she is shocked to find that she said that out loud. Her eyes drop back to her paper, her pointer finger tracing down the page to find her location. "Approximately how many people are employed by The Academy?"

"That is a difficult question to answer. As Magician I have access to the sparks of everyone in the Magical community whether they work for us or not." I let that sink in for a second. "But there are close to 1,000 employees working either on campus or around the world at any given time."

She clears her throat. The noise sounds decidedly uncomfortable. "Do you believe The Academy is truly necessary in crime prevention? What services does The Academy offer that cannot be fulfilled by law enforcement agencies?" she asks. Her eyes find mine and she grimaces as if trying to apologize for the painful question.

I try to freeze my face in my most serious mask in the silence that follows. I hope I look stoic. "We are the only law enforcement agency in the world that can prevent a crime from happening. We still default to using the other agencies, which we have a good relationship with, in the event that we are unable to prevent it. In other words, madam chairperson, we concede that we are not experts in solving crimes that have happened or in dealing with criminals." I smile. "We are, however, the experts in handling a crime before it has the chance to happen."

The smile she flashes me makes me feel like I may have nailed that answer. "How effective is this process?" she asks, without looking down. I wonder for a second if this is an official question or not.

"My average solve time is just under seventeen minutes from locating disturbance to displacing the negative energy." This time is something I am quite proud of. When we first began working on these programs it took me well over thirty minutes in most cases. With the extra personnel and the added strength I draw from those near me, I was even surprised by the increase in speed.

"We have just one more question," she says. Again, her eyes track down her paper. "In your opinion, is The Academy necessary for continued peace and security in the world?"

Around the room there is some shuffling, possibly preparing to end the session they have had here today. I know I was the last item on their agenda. They are likely tired, ready to move on and get back to their countries. I allow myself a few breaths to consider what I will say in the face of this question. I remember what it was like before my father and his crew invented the scanner that proved Magic was real. Before I opened the school that brought it out into the open.

"In my opinion, this is an important step to take in the eradication of crime. We had thousands of years of handling crimes in a reactive sense, and we did a fine job of it. The World of Magic is allowing us to use it in order to deal with crime in a proactive sense." I throw my arms out dramatically as if readying myself to embrace the entire room. "We have always been good at defense, Magic allows us an offense. I certainly wouldn't want to go back to the world as it was before," I say honestly.

When the polite applause begins, I turn my palms up and curtsey. Then I drop my hands to my side. "Thank you for having me today. I hope we will continue our partnership."

I am swept off the worldly stage and into the wings before the applause is finished. I smile at the large man in the suit who guided me from the bright lights. "Have a good day," I tell him right before I teleport myself out of New York City and back to the control room of The Academy.

December 29

Angela

I'm suddenly aware my mouth is hanging open so I snap it shut. "Well, that was different," I offer. "She normally leaves through the door."

Tanya shrugs. "I was just thinking the same thing." She widens her eyes at me and opens her mouth like she's going to say something else. She takes a deep breath and then pauses, holding it. Then she looks down at her pocket and frowns. She pulls out a cell phone in a purple case and turns it so I can see the incoming call screen lit up with a shot of Logan that looks like it belongs on a magazine cover. "Saved by the phone," she says. She walks away, toward her backpack, as she answers.

I slip out the door and walk quickly toward the exit. At the end of the corridor I slow down. I hear voices nearby and I don't want to interrupt. One of them sounds like it belongs to the

Magician. " … give him a real one. We will see how he handles that," she says.

"If he treats it like he's done the rest of them he's really in jeopardy of losing his spark," a different voice answers. This one is familiar but I cannot place it. It's deeper, more masculine. I swipe up on my phone, opening my camera. I flip my finger to turn it to video mode even though it's still directed at the floor. I can't see their faces but I want to try and figure out this other voice later.

"I understand that," the Magician answers in a condescending voice. "One of two things will happen. He will either succeed by doing things correctly, which is a chance for us to positively praise him and hopefully turn him around."

"You think that will happen?" Whoever this is he's feeling equal enough to the Magician to interrupt. Not a student.

"It may. Or, more likely, he will mess this one up as well. If he damages his spark we have no choice but to send him home."

Send him home? We don't go home. We are pulled from our families when we are young. We are brought here. We live here. We are allowed to go back for holidays and breaks, but even then there is no talking to our families about what is happening. We are taught in our first year at the Academy how to perform a mind wipe spell, in case that should become necessary. I know there are a few students here who no longer have families who would recognize them if they even tried to go home. We don't have homes we can just go back to. The Academy is what we have. A cold sweat breaks out on my upper lip and along my back. I am not supposed to be hearing this.

Behind me I hear something else. Footsteps. They're slow but they're coming.

"How am I supposed to get him into something real without him knowing?" the voice asks.

"What time is the class?"

"First period. We start right away." The voice clicks in my head and steals my breath.

"I will handle it," the Magician answers.

I stop the video. When I stand up straight I slip the phone back into my pocket and turn around just in time to face the person approaching me. I'm not at all surprised to find Tanya staring at me. "Why are you still here?" she asks.

"Tying my shoe," I lie. "Gotta go." I have to call him. It's Chris they're talking about. Who else could it be? Chris is the only person I can think of that throws simulations on purpose as a way of showing The Academy that their training is useless. Plus, that voice, that's Rolly. We have Rolly first period.

I adore Chris. He was one of the first people to open up to me from the Solver class. There's only a new candidate for Magician's Assistant roughly every ten years. Rumor has it a little girl in early primer is one now but I've never met her. She'll be trained by whichever one of us is chosen, eventually. My point is in a school where your future occupation matters so much, being unique is the same as being lonely.

But Chris never treated me that way. Chris welcomed me right in. I can't risk the chance that he may walk into a real situation unprepared. He may throw the chance, mess things up on purpose, because he can. From what I just overheard I can be sure no one will stop him before it's too late. He could damage his spark. Someone could die.

I have to warn Chris.

December 29

Tanya

My phone chimes with a text message alert just as I'm tossing it away to try and focus on the case study in front of me that I should be reading. I snatch it up again before it even hits the bedspread, secretly glad for the further distraction.

"Midnight on the quad. Bring snacks."

Sometimes he texts instead of handing me a scribbled message during a stolen moment in the hallway. The message is always the same.

In the beginning it was an unlikely pairing. We caught eyes after an unexpected moment in class. It was a total "did that mean what I think it meant" moment. The meetings started soon after. Always at midnight. But lately, the exchanged looks happen more frequently and lead to more midnight visits. I want to ignore him sometimes, especially when there is too much in my head. But I can't. I won't.

I delete the text and check the clock. 9:15. I have just under three hours.

***

He's in the exact same spot as last time, under the tree on the quad. This time, however, it's a challenge to spot him. His knees are pulled up to his chest, his arms firmly wrapped around them. He no longer looks relaxed.

I hold out the harvest berry granola bar as a peace offering. A bright green package of "I'm sorry you're worried." He hesitates for a second. Long enough to affix a fake smile to his face. "Thanks," he says.

But he doesn't open the snack. Doesn't take a big bite. Just clenches it in his fist. "Have you seen this?" he asks. He waves his free hand and a newspaper headline arranges itself on the air between us. "Explosion in Washington, DC" the headline reads.

I forget it's not real for a beat. It comes back to me when my hand swipes the cold air. I hope he's making up the whole thing. Pretending. I decide that if he is I will forgive him for his sick joke. That's how badly I want this to be fake.

"No. Stop telling tales." I conjure a newspaper, a real one. The only one I can remember the name of, New York Times. It appears quickly and the front page story steals the air from my lungs.

In an apparent attack on the US government that is yet to be claimed by any organized crime syndicate, a bomb exploded in the capitol building at 7 AM EST. Officials report that the loss of life was minimal. There were only two US Senators in the building at the time of the bombing. Senators Michelle Hill (VA) and Randy Hawkins (NH) are both in critical condition at this time.

"Why didn't this get attention here? We were still allowed in the Dispatch center for class today. Something like this should've halted our classes, all-hands-on-deck," I say. This is the kind of disaster the Academy seeks to end.

He shakes his head. "I think this is what we feared." He catches my eyes. Even in the dark I can see the fire burning in them. "They're striking first."

I roll my eyes. "No." It's ridiculous. "Something this public, this garrulous ..."

"It was seven o'clock in the morning. No one starts a government session that early. Only two people were there, only two people were hurt. That takes more than luck. That takes careful planning. Plus," he brings up pictures of the two senators in the air. "Hill and Hawkins openly opposed the Academy bill."

I pinch the bridge of my nose, focusing on the dull pain it causes. The Academy bill would allow the school to continue "business as usual" including "acquiring, training, and controlling" those individuals born with the spark. It extends a previous agreement, set to expire in six months. Without it, the Academy has to shut down and close all operations.

I drop to my knees beside him in the cold grass. "Are you suggesting someone here ordered an attack on two US senators as a way of pushing a piece of legislation forward?"

He narrows his eyes at me. "Why not?"

I throw up my hands. "Because it's extreme. It's against everything she stands for. It's --"

"Like allowing a student who hasn't finished schooling to field real calls?" He shakes his head. "We need to put the plan in motion now. She's out of control. Dangerous."

I reach out and squeeze his hand. I offer him a smile. "Three more days, Chris. Three days and we can start."

He squeezes back and nods. "Fine. Three days. But be on your guard, Tanya. Promise me."

"I promise." I only hope that's enough.

Fall, Age 23

Emily

"Suspect has been separated from the disturbance," the voice in my ear says.

"Thank you for your assistance and diligence," I respond before clicking the button to hang up on the call. My left hand immediately reaches out and starts scrolling through the world looking for any other disturbances. Lately, the number of issues popping up world wide has been extreme. This is evident in the dark circles under my eyes and the coffee mug beside me that has been empty for so long it is cold.

The door to the control room opens. I do not turn around but I do push out my spark a little, feeling for who may be disrupting me. It is a high ranking and powerful teacher, one who I have asked to lead Solver operations. "What is it?" I ask, still without turning. He cannot take my attention away from the world, but he has enough of my respect to not get yelled at for interrupting .

"I'm sorry to bother you. There has been an unusual scan I thought you should see."

"I don't need to see the scans of students. They are to be trained if they have the spark. How old is this child?"

"Fifteen," he answers. His voice is wavering a little. I turn my head slightly so I can see him out of one eye while still keeping my attention focused on the screen. He's holding something. A folder, perhaps.

"Why are you bringing me his scan?"

"Well," he clears his throat. "It's unusual."

I grunt in frustration. "Unusual, how? Be specific."

"It's black," he answers.

I turn very slowly away from my screen. I reach out a hand for the folder, certain this will be a mistake I can clear up quickly. He lets me take it. I flip open the plain manilla cover to reveal a print out from the Academy's scanner. This is the strongest scanner on earth. I have many that I have sent out to schools around the world that will scan for the presence of a Magic spark. But this one is special. This one will help identify who may have what it takes to rival my own strength. I won't live forever, afterall.

The picture inside this folder is white with black smoke. The negative of what it should be. I flip the folder shut. "The equipment is malfunctioning," I say. "I'll come by and look at it after I'm done here."

"That was my first thought as well. I ran a test myself."

I look up at him, narrowing my eyes. "You made a mistake."

He shuffles his feet and rubs a hand through his hair. "That was my second thought. So I called your father."

That stops me. My father knew about this problem before I did? My father has seen this scan? I flip the folder open and look at it again. The image of the generic human body form is white. Normally, our images would be black to allow the contrast of our spark to show. If someone has no Magic it will normally be blue in appearance. I have never seen one stay white.

Beyond that, the amount of the spark that appears inside an image usually correlates to how much of a spark that person has. This child, Tom, according to the name printed along the top of the page, has as much black as I have white. I flip the folder closed again.

"What did my father have to say?"

"I believe his exact word was, 'extraordinary'". He found no fault in the scanner."

I slip the folder under my left arm and turn to the computer screen. "I will meet the child tomorrow. I will handle one class period a day of his training myself. Keep his differences a secret until I determine what is going on with him. That will be all."

There is no response except for the soft clicking of the door as he closes it on his way out. I open the folder again and look at the scan one more time. Tom, without a doubt, is something I have never seen before.

I can only hope that he isn't something dangerous.

203

DECEMBER 30

ANGELA

"You've reached Chris, leave a message." I hang up instead. I'm not leaving him a message. He always has his phone with him. I click the green banner under his name again. "You've reached Chris, leave a --" I hang up again.

"Still no sign of them?" Cheryl asks. I didn't even hear her walk up, I'm so engrossed in the phone in my hand.

"I didn't sleep a wink. I can't get Chris or Steve on the phone. Did they answer you?" She scrunches her nose up and shakes her head side-to-side. Not good. "I'm getting really worried," I tell her. "I feel like I should tell someone. But the highest authority in the school is in on the plan."

"Look," she says. She checks over both shoulders, steps closer to me, and drops her voice to a whisper. "They're Solvers.

Solvers have to be on location for this all to work. You work from the control room. Their Magic is more like a receiver, no output."

"That's true." The bell rings. We're officially late. Cheryl grabs my arm and yanks me across the hallway. "Where are we going?" I whisper. We are definitely not headed into the classroom we were supposed to be entering.

"Bathroom," she answers. Her voice is a hiss. It's a warning. I shouldn't talk right now. Let's just get to the bathroom.

She lets go of me once the bathroom door closes then proceeds to check out all the stalls. Satisfied that they're empty, she turns to me and smiles. "I have an idea." She stands with her back flat against the inside of the bathroom door, holding it shut. "I want you to reach out and try to connect with one of them. Whichever one you're closer with. See through their eyes."

"Cheryl, that's a bad idea." Technically I'm strong enough that I may be able to reach one of them. Maybe. I don't need the cell phone connection that we use during simulations if I'm in front of or actually know the Solver. It's possible but not an exact science. "It might not work, I might not be able to reach them."

Cheryl's grin looks almost wicked in the bathroom's fluorescent lighting. "But you might be able to. Who are you closer to?"

I sigh, knowing she's right and I'm going to have to try. "Right now with all this fear in my gut pointed at him, Chris." That's not always true and she knows it. But it's the truth for today. Without another word I slip my eyes closed and reach out mentally, looking for Chris.

I feel a sort of click, like I've dropped into place. I open my eyes. I'm looking into a classroom. My excitement boils just under the surface. I found him! He's in class. We didn't even check the classroom. Maybe he was just early. Maybe …

Wait a minute. This isn't my first period. I look down and let the connection fade. With a pop I'm back in the bathroom looking at Cheryl. "Not him."

"How did you know?"

"Chris may be gay, but he's never in his life worn a pink skirt to class. I hit the wrong person. This is hopeless."

Cheryl smacks me on the shoulder. For a petite girl she can really hit. I rub it and frown at her. "One failed attempt does not equal hopelessness. Try again."

I glare at her before closing my eyes and thinking of Chris. "Where are you?" I whisper. I open my eyes on another soft click. Now I'm facing a male who I don't recognize. I look down. These clothes could be Chris', but where are we? It doesn't look like a classroom. I push myself deeper, taking control of the body so I can look around. Whoever I just took control of is going to wonder how they got shoved into limbo during their first period. I have to be quick.

We're in a classroom, but I don't recognize the furniture or the people surrounding me. I pop back out. "Cheryl this isn't working," I tell her. "Look, it was a good plan but I just don't have the spark to make this work. I'm not good enough."

She's not looking at me. She's looking at her cell phone. Rude. She hits a button and holds it up. "You've reached Chris, leave a message after the … "

The voice did it. When I open my eyes I'm looking at Steve. Quickly, I push myself deeper and send Chris into limbo. "Where are we?" I ask. My voice is Chris'. Steve shrugs. We're on the street somewhere, literally sitting on the curb of a sidewalk as cars whiz by in front of us. There's an adorable little red awning behind us and a black one labeled with the name of some sushi restaurant across the street. There's a four-way intersection with stop signs to our left and tall buildings rising up nearby.

"I think it might be Chicago, but I'm not really sure," Steve answers.

I want to ask how they got to Chicago, but there's no time for that. Not really. "Steve, listen to me." Chris' voice sounds more urgent. Steve must pick up on it because he turns to me and crinkles his forehead with concern. "It's Angela, I took over for a second. I don't know what's going on or why you two are not at the Academy but I think whatever is about to go down is real. I overheard a conversation. I think they're giving Chris something real. If he fails he may damage his spark. You have to warn him."

"The Magician zapped us here herself, Angie. It's supposed to be a field test. We're supposed to be observing something. She's not going to use us. We're underage." He looks concerned, but not nearly as concerned as I want him to be.

"She was the one I overheard. I think she'll use Chris. I think he's in danger."

Steve takes a deep breath and lets it out with a sigh. "I can't tell him that." He rakes his fingers through his hair. "He would do it on purpose." He shakes his head. "I'll do my best to keep us safe and make it a successful venture, whatever they have us do, but I can't tell Chris." He traps me with a fierce gaze. "You know as well as I do that losing his spark and getting out of here is his ultimate goal. I cannot tell him there's a chance for that."

He looks so sad, suddenly. "You have to go," he says with a sigh. "Whether this is a field test or a real situation the Magician will be watching. She can't hear us, I don't think, but you can bet she sees us. Get out of here before she wonders why we're doing too much talking and not enough observing." He shoves me. "Go."

I don't have a choice. I close Chris' eyes and feel the pop that brings me back to the bathroom. Cheryl is right in my face, staring at me with intense eyes. "What happened? Was it Chris? Did you warn them?"

"Steve was there. The Magician zapped them somewhere, he thinks Chicago. They were sitting on a curb."

Cheryl's intake of breath is jagged, slow, and loud. "Why did she zap them out of the Academy and into a city somewhere?"

"She told them it was a field test or something. They're supposed to be observing." I shuffle my weight from foot-to-foot. "I think they're in trouble." I rub my fists into my eyes. "Steve doesn't want to tell Chris. He thinks Chris will welcome the wreck of his spark."

Cheryl shakes her head. "You have to get back there. You have to watch them."

I know she's right. I know I have to be ready to call in reinforcements of some kind. I know I could never focus in class right now. I may be needed here. I know this is important. But I'm also scared. "What if she notices I'm missing?"

"Who?" She rolls her eyes as she realizes, a silent chastising for not noticing who I meant sooner. "The Magician, right. Maybe we should tell someone else." She reaches up to her shirt collar and frees something underneath it. It's a necklace of some kind. The circles are black, so dark they feel like they're sucking light from everything around us. I stare at them and notice they're not really circles. They're irregular clumps, like coal. They're mesmerizing. Cheryl's hand is clutching them. Her thumb is chasing lazy circles around one. "Maybe we should tell Mark," she says.

"What?" I don't take my eyes off the necklace. I can't. I feel like my gaze is glued to it. Am I even blinking?

Suddenly, they're gone. I can still see them there, like an outline of the sun that lingers after you close your eyes. I shake my head. "Mark. That's a good idea, actually." My brain feels cloudy. "What is that necklace? Where did you get it?"

"Don't worry about it. Not right now. I'll tell you later. We need to get moving. We need to find Mark."

I don't know much about the Container guy, Mark. But I know he's supposed to be powerful. Maybe he's the right person to tell.

December 30

Tanya

My heart is not in this today.

I push open the door of my Research class and let my feet guide me to my normal table. George is already nose deep in a thick, black book. The smell of old paper wafts to my nose and I wrinkle it at him. He doesn't notice.

I slam my backpack onto the floor. It's loud but George barely looks up. Fine by me. I don't feel much like chatting anyway. The news yesterday has barely even had an impact today. I heard the DeAngelo's in the hallways gossiping about it on my way in but it doesn't seem to have reached the students. Last I checked both Senators were still alive. Maybe that's the reason it hasn't caught on. Which, if you think about it, is a really macabre thought.

The bell rings to start class. Frank is alone at his small table. No Cheryl and no dark haired Container man. I wave to him and signal the empty chair beside me. He nods, gathers up his belongings, and heads over.

"Where's your partner in containing today?" I ask.

George looks up from his book. He still has his finger pointing at a specific paragraph, holding his place. He nods in Frank's direction in silent greeting before returning his eyes to the text.

"I don't know. What are you so engrossed in, G?" Frank asks.

"Research," George mumbles.

I roll my eyes. "That was vague." I plan to make another joke but the door opens to allow Ms. DeAngelo to enter. Today she is in a navy blue dress with a white sweater. She looks ready to board a yacht in the Hamptons, not lead a Research class in Magic.

"Our case today deals with a pending arraignment in which a Solver was overheard discussing 'limbo' with another Solver. The line of questioning must not lead to the heart of this information. Case details have been emailed to you. Please review them and find a reason to exclude the Solver from the witness list."

I wait for the door to click shut before I lean into the table. I consider my options and decide these two may actually buy my "stupid" routine. I sigh. "Why would the Solver be on the witness list to begin with? Shouldn't he have been clear of the scene before the police arrived?"

Frank nods while logging into his email on his phone. "Yeah, but if the victim or innocent heard him talk about limbo he may have stuck around. Maybe he knew he messed up."

"How did he know?" I ask.

Frank shrugs. "I have no idea. Let's see if the case file tells me anything."

I sigh, really laying into the routine. "What does it even matter?"

George's head snaps up. "The general public doesn't know about Magic. Can you imagine if a member of the Academy was asked questions under oath?" He shakes his head. "The secret would be out and it would change everything."

This is the party line. The standing opinion fed to the students. I drop my voice even more and lean in. "What's the big deal, really? I mean the government already knows about us. Why do we have to keep it from everyone else?"

Frank looks over his shoulders, checking to see who may be listening. I do the same. There's a few tables full of kids actually researching and, of course, the two-way glass to the teachers. Nothing else.

"Mark says people would expect favors if they knew about Magic. He says the Academy would constantly be bombarded with people asking us to use Magic for frivolous things," Frank whispers. "The way he described it, we would never get anything done. We'd have to have committees and procedures for hearing requests and deciding what to grant."

"That sounds like more jobs. Why would that be bad?" I ask.

George waves his hands between us. "I don't care about any of that. I care that the leader of this school, who knows more than us and is stronger than us, told us to keep the secret of Magic contained. I care that this school has managed to keep the secret for decades without letting it slip out. I care that we have the chance to keep it that way and we will." He slams his hand down on the book. "Now help me figure out how we can keep this guy off the witness list."

I widen my eyes like he's shocked me and backup a little. In truth, I'm not shocked. George is spouting what we've been told. He's getting angry at me because he doesn't fully understand it either. He's at war with himself, I just represent the other side of the line. The devil's advocate, as they say.

"Sorry," I throw my hands up in mock surrender. "I just think hiding who and what we are makes us seem like a dirty little secret. If there's nothing wrong with what we're doing, shouldn't we tell the world?" I open up my email on my cell phone, ostensibly to pull up the file. But I risk a glance at Frank. He's buying it, I can tell. His facial expression is different than it was before our little conversation.

He's conflicted.

The main door to the classroom opens. I turn my head to see what's going on and spy the Container guy approaching our table. Before the door clicks shut I spy something even more interesting in the doorway. Why the hell are Cheryl and Angela outside of class right now?

The guy stops beside our table and lays a big hand on Frank's shoulder just as the other door opens and Ms. DeAngelo clicks her way into the room on her impossibly high heels. "A word, Frank?" he says.

"What's the meaning of this?" D'angelo asks.

"I need to borrow my apprentice for a while," the man explains. His voice is so deep and yet so quiet. It reminds me of a bass playing in an orchestra.

"Of course, Mark. You may take him. Will he be back in time to help his group finish the assigned research?" She's sputtering. This guy has quite an effect. Maybe Containers are more powerful than I thought.

"Probably not, if I'm being honest." Frank rises and both men head toward the door.

I knew there was a lot about the Academy that we were not fully in-the-know about. But I have a feeling Containers just jumped to the top of that list.

Fall, Age 23

Emily

Tom stands behind me, fidgeting. He's learned enough in the last two weeks to know that talking to me right now would probably only result in my barking at him. I'm standing in front of the screens for my computer, searching actively for a source of darkness. But this time the plan is different. This time I don't plan to send a Solver to eradicate the problem. Today we have another plan.

"Found one," I call out. I zoom my screen in on Lithuania. I turn to offer Tom a smile. "Are you ready to go?" I point to the screen to show him where I mean.

"Go? Where would we go?" he asks. His voice sort of cracks on the last word.

"We are going to Lithuania, my friend. We are going to run a few experiments on the darkness gathering there and see how you react to it. How does that sound?" I don't wait to hear what he thinks of the idea. We're going. I reach out and lay my hand on his shoulder and close my eyes to teleport us to the location. My brain is getting better at this kind of thing. Thinking those coordinates, 55°11'39"N and 23°54'38"E, now means something to me. It means enough to get me there, I'm sure. When I open my eyes I'm awarded with a cloudy day and a brick building directly in front of us.

Tom does a slow circle, taking in the tall tree lined road at our back and the houses just off in the distance. The low rumbling of farm equipment can be heard over the wind. There's also a row of something that may be storage lockers or containers off to our left. He looks completely shocked that we are standing here only a blink or two since he was standing in the control room at the Academy.

"Where are we?" he asks, his voice showing off the reverence I'd already read in his mannerisms.

"Lithuania. We are looking for a source of darkness, like the ones you've been learning about."

"We're going to separate the darkness from the host, right?" he asks.

I smile at him. "First we are going to see how you react to the darkness."

His eyes widen. "Why would we do that? Isn't it dangerous? Can't I get hurt?"

I hope not. I don't say this out loud because that doesn't sound like the confident answer you'd want from your Magician.

"I'm right here to keep you safe," I say instead, laying my hand on his shoulder. "It will all be fine."

He nods once like he's agreeing with me and then looks out ahead of us again. "What are we looking for?" he asks. "What should I expect to find?"

I point up ahead of us toward a copse of trees. "Let's head that way, I think that will be closer to the location of the darkness I was seeing on the screen."

We start walking, me in the lead. "This isn't the location you saw?" Tom asks.

"Well, that's complicated. The circles I see on the screen are often large. I didn't want to bring us to the exact center of the location. That seemed like a dangerous concept. I dropped us along the circumference of the circle."

There is a man standing under the tree we are heading toward. Even from here I can see the darkness radiating around him, pulsing. "Do you see that man?" I ask, throwing my hand out over Tom's chest to stop him from walking closer.

He squints into the darkness. "Why is he covered in that black stuff, what is that?" He turns his head quickly, sudden realization lighting up his face. "Is that why you call it darkness? Because it looks like that?"

Well, that answers one question. Evidently, Tom can see the darkness in the same way I can. "Yes. As we get closer I need you to pay attention to how you are feeling. Can you do that?"

"How I'm feeling?" He cocks one eyebrow up at the thought, questioning me without having the gumption to question me out loud.

"Yes. Darkness can manifest as a sort of depression. I need to know if you start to feel anything like that. Keep the lines of communication open."

He nods and we resume walking. I watch the smoke around the man. If you watch it closely enough you can see it swirl and pulse exactly like the smoke on our scans. Exactly like the smoke I know is operating inside Tom, dark and black. I reach out with my mind, trying to find the man. I hit a wall, he is as innocent as I expected him to be. No spark, no Magic.

The smoke appears completely unaffected by the presence of Tom. It's as if they are not phased by each other at all, which makes me happy in many ways. The man pushes himself off the tree and starts to head off away from us. Nervous that I will not be able to stop him if I let him get too far away, I break into a jog and do my best to make it look like an accident when I crash into him.

The darkness swirls up and out even as the man starts to berate me in a language I do not speak. I could take the time to cast a spell to allow me to understand what he is saying, but I decide against it because I am mesmerized by the sight of the darkness. It is not doing what it normally does. It is swirling above us in a tornado pattern.

As I watch it begins to spiral downward, descending directly to Tom.

I rush to his side, scanning him for signs of that darkness. "Are you all right?" I ask.

He nods. "I think so. Did that stuff just come into me?" He taps his hands along his chest, patting like he thinks he can feel whatever is now inside him. "Where did it go?"

"Do you feel different?" I ask. There are no outward signs of anything being different. He doesn't appear to have a dark cloud around him. He doesn't seem like he's reacting at all to the darkness that just infiltrated him.

"I don't think it's inside me. Honestly, Magician." He looks afraid of me. Which is funny. Tom is the first person I'm aware of in the history of the world who has what appears to be a black spark inside him. I've put him through tests and it seems as though he is a strong and powerful Magic user. But this is the first interaction we've had that puts him face to face with the darkness and he has reacted to it differently than I expected. He shouldn't be afraid of me and, evidently, I shouldn't be afraid of him either.

I lay a hand on his shoulder. "Call me Emily," I tell him with a smile. If Tom truly is fine, this is a breakthrough I can't help but be excited by. Have we found a way to take the darkness out of the world? "We need to get back to the Academy," I say.

"Yeah, good idea." He smiles. "Why do I have a feeling this is only the beginning of the experiments we'll be doing?" he asks.

I loop my arms through his bent elbow. "Because you're brilliant," I say.

December 30

Angela

"That's everything I know," I finish. The room stays hauntingly silent. Mark is nodding, lips pierced and eyes narrowed. He hasn't said a word since I launched into the story. Cheryl, having already heard the story, is quiet for different reasons. She's chewing on her fingernail, a nervous tic. Frank looks like he might be sick.

"All right." Mark claps his hands together. The sharp sound echoes through the room. I blink my shock away. "I want to believe in the integrity of the Academy but I can see this worries you. Let's check in on the boys together and see how they're doing. That will put everyone's mind at ease."

He pushes off of the wall of his office where he'd been leaning since we walked in, cracks his knuckles, and rotates his head around. A popping sound emits from his neck. Then he closes his eyes and takes a deep breath. I'm fascinated by the calming gestures he is going through. He waves his hands in circles in front of a blank wall. His lips are moving but I hear no sound, despite straining my ears to try.

He pops his eyes open and turns to look at us. "All set, go ahead and reach out for them." He's talking to me, I'm sure. He's looking right at me.

"What did you do to the wall?" I ask. To me it looks exactly the same as it did before. But Cheryl and Frank are staring at it, tilting their heads left and then right. They see something I don't.

"I opened a portal so we can see what you see."

"What?" I look again at the wall. It looks exactly the same. There's no disturbance, no change in color, certainly no video showing what I'm looking at or thinking. "But it looks the same to me." I think about how the Magician always lets Tanya and I see more details of the simulations than we used to see, before she took over our eighth period. That nagging question returns: what else don't I know?

"We know. In the portal, which shows us your vision, we see that it is a blank wall to you. I'm sorry if that is confusing. Trust me when I say it's less confusing than if I open the portal to you. Then we'd see you looking in a portal of you looking in a portal." He shakes his head. "We're wasting time." He smiles at me. "I'll be happy to show you this later, if you'd like. For now, can we please dispense with the connection?"

I have so many questions. Questions that I'm sure I'll never get answers for from the Magician. Here's an adult with a strong spark who seems to be implying he would answer them. He's offering to answer questions I didn't even realize I had. But Chris is my first priority, he has to be.

I close my eyes and reach for him. I don't feel the connection but I feel a light breeze blowing around me and I know I've done it. When I open my eyes I find I'm still sitting on the same curb in the same spot. Sure enough, when I turn my head, there's Steve. I force Chris the rest of the way to limbo. "Any new developments?" I ask Steve.

He looks confused for a second. Then he narrows his eyes at me. "Are you babysitting us now?" he asks. "We're perfectly fine. In fact, nothing has happened at all. We're just sitting here being boring." He looks away from me again. "Didn't I tell you to get out of here," he asks out of the side of his mouth. "If this is as dangerous as you say it is, you shouldn't be here."

"I know. I have help. Let's just leave it at that. I don't want to explain more right now. I'm going to back out a little, let Chris have control. I'll just observe. Be careful, okay?" I wait for him to nod before I back out.

Chris's breathing picks up. "What the hell is going on?" he asks.

Steve shrugs. "What are you talking about?"

"I was just in limbo, Steve. Whatever you said, whoever was talking to you, it wasn't me." He jumps up from the ground and glares down at Steve. "What did she ask? What was she looking for?"

"Calm down, man." Steve stands up slowly. "It was just Angela. She was worried because we weren't in class today." He lays his hand on Chris' arm. "It's fine. She's gone back to focusing on her own life."

Chris visibly relaxes and lets out a sigh. "Man, what did you think was going on?" Steve asks. "Who did you think it was?"

"I don't know. I just--" he shakes his head. "It doesn't matter. How long are we just supposed to sit here?" he asks. He gestures around him. "Nothing is happening."

Like he summoned it with his words, Steve's phone rings. Both of them go silent and Chris's eyes widen. Steve hits a button on the earbud settled in his left ear. "Solver in training 1853," he answers.

I cannot hear the voice on the other end. I want to, but Chris is my connection right now. I try and wait patiently as Steve's end of the conversation gives me frustratingly little information. Finally he clicks the earbud again, hanging up. "All right, we have to head about twenty yards to the west, we were a little off location. The Solvers should be showing up in about one minute. They want us in a position to observe and remember not to involve ourselves or react in any way. The Solvers are aware that we are on a field test," Steve explains.

"Let's do this," Chris says.

I have a terrible feeling in my gut. I pull myself back to the classroom. I can tell the attention in the room had been on the wall, but they all turn to look at me when I pull myself back in. "Anyone want to tell me what's going on?" I say. "How did the

Magician know that the boys were going to be that close to something that hadn't happened yet? If she knew, why not prevent it before this point? What are they walking into?"

"Angela," Mark stops me from my questioning, which was growing louder in the quiet room. "I'm going to need you to get back in there and observe. You have a connection to Chris that I cannot duplicate. I could call him and connect myself, but that seems like it would raise his hackles more than we need. I just want you to be my eyes. Can you do that?"

I'm taken aback by his comment. How often does he take over people? What makes him so sure he is stronger than Chris? Who is this guy? "I guess I can do that," I say. "But I think I have a lot of questions when I'm done." He just nods, a small smile forming on his lips.

I notice everyone's attention shift immediately back to the wall. I close my eyes and focus on connecting with Chris, fading back into his subconscious.

Chris and Steve have jogged themselves down to the location they were ordered to. Two people, presumably Solvers, run in from the other direction. One of them clicks her ear to answer the call from Dispatch. She points toward a building on the opposite side of the street from Chris and Steve. It's a small storefront with window dressing that identifies it as a nail salon. The two Solvers immediately enter the building.

"Should we move closer?" Steve asks.

"We're supposed to be able to see what they're doing." Chris starts crossing the busy street, just jaywalking right into traffic.

"Chris," Steve yells. I think I hear him sigh before he jogs up behind Chris. Once they're safely on the other side, he smacks Chris on the shoulder. It's hard enough that I feel it even though I'm not completely inside his consciousness. "What the hell were you thinking?" he asks.

Chris laughs. "I was thinking that if she doesn't want us to die she'll make sure we're not hit. If she does want us to die, there are better ways to do it than a car accident."

"You think she's watching us?" Steve asks. I notice there's no questions about who the she they're referring to might be. We all know. The Magician brought them here and she's likely watching this all play out right now.

Chris throws a charming crooked smile over his shoulder. "I know she is," he answers. Then he immediately turns his attention to the glass window that will give him visibility of the Solvers he's supposed to be watching. The girl, the one who took the call, is standing in the middle of a lobby surrounded by nail chairs on either side. She is looking pointedly at the window where Chris and Steve are standing. Chris lifts his hand and waves. "Hello, Magician lady," he says. "We're here for the show."

As we all watch, the Solver approaches a male customer who appears to be waiting for someone else and has a short whispered conversation.

"What do you think they're talking about?" Steve asks.

"Maybe she's asking him who he's waiting for," Chris answers. "That would be the responsible thing to do. Or, on the other hand, she could be telling him to get his ass out of her chair and leave this building immediately." He smirks at Steve. "That's probably how I'd handle it."

Steve rolls his eyes. "I think we can bet she won't take your route."

Chris turns his attention back to the window where the Solver has taken a few steps back away from the man. She looks shocked for a second, her weight shifting back like she's going to tip over. "Goodbye, Magician," Chris mumbles. He's right, I notice. The Magician must have given control back to the Solver. She turns and whispers something to her partner and they approach the man again.

After a whispered conversation, the Solver's hand on her hip like she's ready to pull some non-existent weapon, the man hands her the bag he's holding. That must satisfy her because the two turn and walk out of the nail salon.

"What the hell?" Steve asks the question I was thinking.

I don't have time to hear the answer because there's the sound of a phone ringing. For a second I'm confused, until I realize the sound is coming from my body. I pull myself back to Mark's office just in time to see him answer his own cell phone. "Container," he says.

He nods a few times, swipes his hand in front of the wall, and then hangs up. "The portal is closed. I have to go."

"That was real, wasn't it?" Cheryl asks. "Whatever was in that bag needs to be contained. Am I right?"

He nods. "We'll talk later." He waves his hands again, this time he completely disappears from the room.

"I've been here longer than any of you," I say. "So why do I feel like I have absolutely no idea what the hell we really do here?"

December 30

Tanya

Today when I approach the Dispatch hallway I'm on edge. Chris wasn't at lunch. I mentioned it in a sort of off-hand way to the table and Frank blanched. He looked like he was going to vomit. He mumbled something about field tests, which didn't even make sense. When I pressed him on the issue he shut down altogether. So I don't know what to expect right now.

The hallway is just as crowded today as it usually is. Dispatch workers with their blinking ear pieces line the sides, drinking coffee or talking about sports. I catch a few words about scores here and there. I'm not in tune to much of the information. I don't care, honestly. Aren't there more important things to be talking about? Didn't a couple of US Senators just get injured? Can anyone tell me what the hell a field test is and when we started using those?

In the Dispatch room I spot Chris right away. He's standing off to the right of the room, wringing his hands. He spots me only a fraction of a second after I see him. Our eyes meet and I swear he looks as relieved as I feel. We both walk towards each other, meeting in the middle.

"Where were you this morning?" I ask.

He pulls me by my arm until we're along the wall at the side of the room. "She took me to a fucking field test. She took me and Steve out into the field to observe a Solver on a real case. It was completely stupid. I don't understand why we were there or what the point was. I'm scared, T."

He looks it. His eyes are red rimmed and his face is pale. We are never seen talking to each other during class unless it's casual or looks accidental. He's supposed to be team Angela all the way. I look around to see if anyone notices. So far, nothing. We have to hurry. "That doesn't make any sense. I'll look into it. We can meet tonight and talk about it. At least you're safe."

"Safe? What the hell part of this is safe? I was dragged out onto an assignment on the streets of Chicago before I was ready. Yesterday my computer stayed logged into Dispatch, for real, when you were in a simulation. What part of this is safe?" His voice is too high for the room.

I put a finger up to his lips. "Would you please try and be quiet?" I hiss. "You will certainly raise suspicion if anyone hears you yelling like this."

He shakes his head and pulls my hand away from his mouth. "I don't care." He speaks slowly, each word dropping like its own sentence. "If we don't go now I may lose my spark, or worse. Is it ready?"

I give him a dirty look. A shut-your-face look. I cannot believe he's trying to have this conversation right now, in the middle of the Dispatch room. "We're not talking about this here. I'll see you tonight." I turn and walk away to a computer and log myself in. I try not to notice when Chris sits beside me. I put the earpiece in and connect.

The earpiece rings instantly. "Dispatch," I say. I'm glad to have an excuse to focus on something safe. Something fake.

"I need a Solver at the 1500 and University in Provo, Utah. There's a Home Depot here."

I type the coordinates on my screen. "I'm not finding that location. I see an S. University Ave but I'm not finding 1500. What else can you give me for location?" While I wait I open a second tab and look for Home Depot locations in Provo, Utah. There's only one. "Never mind, I have it." I click the location and blue dots populate my screen. There's not a single Solver near this location. "Hold on, please," I say.

I click on a blue dot at random and click the call button. My earpiece switches to this line. "Solver 753," a voice answers.

"This is Dispatch. I'm going to need to teleport you to a location in Utah. Stand by." I don't wait for a response. If this were real, I would be able to do this myself. But a Dispatcher likely wouldn't have the spark strength. So, instead, I click the little teleport button and then click the parking lot outside the location.

Then I return to the original call and give the Magician the required information. I disconnect from the call and log all the information on the log sheet in front of me.

I steal a glance at Chris. A quick one. One that no one else will notice. I cover it by looking past him and pretending to care about the faces of the other people in the room as well. He still looks pale, nervous.

I tear the bottom corner from the log paper I'm using. Then I connect to the call ringing in my ear while I hand him the small note. I hope no one notices the two little words written on the paper.

It's ready.

***

I'm not expecting Logan to be waiting for me after class. Judging by the sheepdog look I get from Chris as he scurries down the hallway, he wasn't either. I suppose that's the good news. A conversation with Logan is safe, where another one with Chris could raise suspicions. I smile at the boyfriend, thinking how far removed he is from everything I am afraid of right now.

"What's the special occasion?" I ask.

"We need to talk." He doesn't smile. This can't be good.

"What about?" I start walking. There's a long way to travel if I'm supposed to make it to Magician class in time. My heart is already pounding just thinking about being in the same room as her. What Chris told me about the field test means she's into something dangerous. Something even I didn't see coming. I try to hide the nerves from my face.

"It's just that you're completely obsessed with beating Angela lately. It's, like, consuming you." He's behind me a little. I roll my eyes before I turn around and face him.

"She can't win." I don't want to talk about this. I stop myself just shy of throwing the cheap water bottle I grabbed on the way out of Dispatch across the hallway. The plastic crinkles underneath my fingers. It's actually oddly satisfying, the effect radiating through my fingers. I squeeze and release the bottle repeatedly.

Logan reaches out and wraps his fingers around mine, stopping the crinkling. "I'm gonna point out something you absolutely don't want to hear."

I sigh. "Go ahead."

"Whichever one of you is the next Magician will be the right choice for the Academy. Bottom line, you have to respect that. Even if ..." he trails off, his meaning clear.

Even if it's not me.

"Can we talk about us?" he asks, quietly.

I bristle. There is so much he can't possibly understand and I cannot explain it to him in the middle of the hallway. "What about us?"

"You're stuck in your own head all the time. We aren't even really together even when we're together." He stops talking, suddenly looking nervous. He runs the fingers of his free hand through his hair. "I don't know. You seem like maybe you need a friend."

"I do."

"No." He lets go of my hand, moving his to my shoulder. "Just a friend."

His meaning hits me like a bucket of cold water. I pull back and shake my head. "Are you breaking up with me?" I realize my voice is too loud. It's drawing attention from the kids surrounding us, hurrying to get to class. I don't care. "Seriously, is that what this is?"

"It's better for both of us." He takes his hand away and shoves it into the pocket of his faded blue jeans. "This just isn't working. We're not really anything anymore. You'll see it soon. I'm sure." He shrugs. "I have to go."

His next class is closer to this hallway than mine is. He doesn't actually have to go, but I know that's not what he meant. He means he needs to get away from me.

I don't argue. I let him go, watching him walk down the hallway. I don't have time to feel sad about this. Logan was part of the perfect Magician image. Tomorrow, I won't need that. Whatever image I've created will have to be enough because I'm out of time.

But I feel a little twinge of sadness for the lesson I just learned. Apparently when you push someone away enough, they actually leave.

Winter, Age 23

Emily

Tom and I pop back into the control room and he immediately collapses onto the floor. I kneel down beside him and put my hand up to his forehead like I'm taking his temperature. He doesn't look any different, he's not warm, but he is sweating. I take my hand back and wipe it along my robe.

"Three is my limit," he whispers. His eyes are barely open and if I didn't know better my best guess would be that he's drunk.

"Now we know," I say. I smile. "You can absorb two darknesses without an issue but that third one wipes you out."

"I couldn't even teleport back. Good thing I was traveling with you." He chuckles a little and his head lolls to one side. "I just need a rest."

"Yes, you take a rest. You've earned it." I move my legs out from underneath me and pull my knees up under my chin. This has been an interesting few months. Aside from absorbing darkness, which I obviously cannot do, Tom and I are remarkably similar. He doesn't seem to have any other limits to his powers. Like me, he can perform remarkable spells all day long without growing tired or exhausting himself. I cannot absorb the darkness, we've tried. It continues to float around me or dissipate like it does with everyone else. But if Tom is present it collects like a swarm and enters him. Tonight was the first time we have attempted to absorb multiple darknesses to find his limit. The good news is that we found it. The bad news is that it's a rather low number. I glance down at him. His eyes are closed and his breathing is even. I hope all he needs is a little sleep to refresh him completely. This is certainly a promising development. It appears the World of Magic saw fit to send me exactly what I was searching for, a way to contain that darkness instead of just separating it from the hosts.

Contain. Yes, that's exactly what Tom does. He contains that darkness without any consequence to himself. I brush a lock of dark hair across his forehead. "You're a Container," I whisper.

Hesitantly, I reach for his spark. I haven't tried doing this because I'm slightly afraid of what will happen. My father tried reaching for people when I explained to him how it worked. When he attempted to reach out for someone who's spark was stronger than his, he wasn't able to do it. I have always been able to reach anyone I have ever tried to reach, as long as they have the spark. Tom obviously does. But some part of myself is aware that I may no longer be the most powerful Magic user. What if he is stronger than me? We already know he has abilities I don't have. Should he be running this school?

Fear creeps up my spine when I'm unable to reach him. I was afraid of this all along. But really, that's not an answer. Maybe we're simply equal. I'll have to teach him how to reach out for someone. If he can take over my spark, I will step down as Magician immediately.

"Emily," Tom whispers my name.

"What?" I wasn't aware he was even awake.

"You need to relax. Whatever you're thinking is making my spark skip beats. You're worried or something and I can feel it. I'm tired and I need to sleep," he says without opening his eyes.

"I'm sorry. I was trying to take over your body."

"Right this second?"

"I couldn't do it." My voice breaks a little on the admission.

Tom's eyes flutter open. "What does that mean?" he asks, sounding slightly more alert.

I audibly swallow. "It means you may be stronger than me."

There's a long pause in which I can feel my heartbeat racing away in my chest. He's right, I can also feel the tension in his spark like he could probably feel mine a minute ago. "I may be?" He squints at me. "What does that mean? What are the other alternatives?"

"Either you're stronger than me or we are equal." I shrug. "I don't think there's anything else."

He pushes himself up to a sitting position and cracks his knuckles, a nervous habit. "How do we find out?"

I reach out and take his hand. "You'd have to try taking over my spark. But we can do it another time, when you're rested."

"Actually, my strength is already coming back." He flips his hand around so our palms are touching. "Tell me how to do this."

I swallow my fear. "You just have to think of me. You have to imagine my spark as a sort of smoke inside me. You want to connect with the smoke. You want to take over the smoke, hold it in your hands. Control it."

His eyes slip closed. He takes two slow breaths. "Nothing," he whispers. Then his eyes pop open. "Maybe I'm not doing it right."

"Try someone else. Try someone else you know is Magic," I offer.

"Like who? You're the only person I interact with here." He's not wrong. I have kept him a secret because I didn't truly understand what he was. The more I've worked with him the more I've realized that he's shrouded in unknowns and mysteries. I've been keeping it all to myself.

I pull my cell phone out of my pocket and send a text message to a Dispatch officer downstairs. *Come to the control room.* Then I smile at Tom. "I'm sorry about that. Your scan showed you were different right from the beginning. I didn't know what that meant. I still don't fully know what it means but I understand that you have gifts we need." I squeeze his hand. "I didn't mean to keep you a secret. We will fix that."

The door to the control room opens. The Dispatch officer steps into the room, halts, and jerks back a little. Then her eyes fix on mine. "I think we're equals," she says.

I let out a hearty laugh. She jerks again, blinks rapidly, and then focuses on me. "What did you need?" she asks.

"I'm sorry, we were just borrowing your spark for an experiment. Forgive me for wasting your time. Have a nice evening." If she's shocked to be used in such a way, she doesn't say it. She just turns and walks out of the control room. I turn back to Tom. "I assume that was you?"

"It was." He rubs the back of his neck with his free hand. "In the spirit of honesty and equality, I have something I need to run by you."

"I'm listening."

"I think I may have accidentally sent the darkness into this organic substance." He pulls a lump of what appears to be charcoal out of his pocket. "I think that's why I came back around so quickly. Sort of like you were telling me to reach out for your spark, I was sending the darkness into this. I wasn't sure it would work, which is why I didn't tell you. But I think it did."

It looks like an ordinary brick of coal, unrefined. I reach out and touch it. It's warm to the touch. I can feel negative energy pulsing out away from it in waves. I feel drawn to it, mesmerized by it.

Tom's fist closes around the coal. "Let go," he orders. His voice is harsh.

I pull my hand back.

He shakes his head and slides the stone back into his pocket. "Well, that confirms it. It's in there. You looked strange just now. Are you all right?"

I nod.

"I'm going to make a necklace out of these stones. Then we have some experimenting to do." He smiles. "If I can push the negative energy into these each time, I wonder what my limit would be?"

December 30

Angela

The classroom door opens into the control room. I actually step back out into the hallway and try again. Because that doesn't make sense. It should open into a classroom. The Magician can turn it into the control room, but it always starts as the classroom.

When I enter the second time to find the control room still there I do something I've never done before. I sit in a chair in front of the screen. I drop my backpack by my feet and decide to wait for Tanya and the Magician to arrive before I do anything. I pointedly refuse to look at the screen in front of me. The problem is, there's not much else in here to look at. I stare at my fingernails, my outfit, even my phone.

Finally, the door opens. I sit up straight, trying to look like I wasn't completely bored. I turn, fixing a smile to my face. It's Tanya. Just Tanya.

"What the hell?" she says. "Where's the classroom?" She looks down at her cell phone. "How late am I?"

"I don't think you are late. It was like this when I walked in."

She drops into the chair beside me. "It's time for class to start. Should we just start looking for something? Maybe she's not giving us the lead-in this time."

"I guess." I turn my attention to the screen. "Is it brighter than usual?" The colors seem more vivid, which is something I can't explain. It's like someone messed with the visual settings and colors. "Split screen," I command. Immediately the screen shows two identical images of the globe zoomed out far enough to allow us both to enjoy the sparkling blue of the oceans.

"Zoom in on Australia," Tanya says. Figures. She loves Australia. The screens move in sync with each other, zooming in on the continent she requested. "You go west, I'll go east." She's not asking. She's already pinching and zooming around, looking for the disturbance.

I pinch and zoom my way around the western half of Australia. Then I pull the map upward toward Indonesia. I'm careful to check every island, which can be tricky because it's not like there's a checklist here to cross off as you go. I let out a frustrated puff of air when I come up empty and swing up to the Philippines.

"Does this feel different to you?" Tanya asks. She whispers it like the question is only supposed to be for me and not for the Magician, who's surely listening in from somewhere.

"A little." I pull my hands away from the screen. I close my eyes for a second, relaxing them away from the bright lights of the screen. I also stretch and flex my fingers. "Normally she's here when we start. Do you suppose she's making a point?"

"Not really what I meant." She sounds annoyed. I open my eyes. Tanya's teeth are clenched, her green eyes narrowed at her screen.

"What did you mean then?"

"Nothing. Just … nothing."

"Tanya, look, if you need to talk about something --"

"Found something," she interrupts. I lean closer to her and watch over her shoulder as she zooms in slowly like we've been taught. There's definitely a disturbance. The telltale waves are rippling out in concentric circles around her screen. But her zoom isn't making sense. The disturbance appears to be centered on an ocean. No people, no buildings. Her entire screen is filled with shades of blue, slowly rippling with the circles of dark Magic.

"There's nothing here." The annoyance in Tanya's voice perfectly matches with the emotion pumping through my veins.

"Wait, I have an idea." I stand up and shove Tanya's rolling chair to the side with my hip, taking over her half of the screen. I rest my thumbs on the sides of her screen and rotate them clockwise. Then I quickly lower my right thumb which angles the screen up toward the sky.

"You gave me that sim recently on an air force base," I explain. "I thought maybe it was above the ocean." Blue sky is filling the entire screen now. I zoom out a little, making sure. A few clouds dance into the field. But no circles up here. No dark Magic. I drop my hands. "I was hoping that would work."

"If we were looking for an airplane in flight the circles would be moving," Tanya says.

She's right, of course. But this doesn't make sense to me. I was trying to find something that would explain the unexplainable. I blow out air, sending my bangs fluttering up off my forehead. "Fine. Then what is this?"

She sighs. "It's nothing." She swipes her hand across the screen, changing the view. "Keep searching."

"Tanya, no. Maybe we have to figure out -- "

"No. She didn't set this up. Can't you feel it?" She waits for me to answer her. But, honestly, I have no idea what she wants me to say. She throws her arms out. "It's real. This is real. Keep looking."

I can't move.

It's like I'm frozen under a foot of ice. I'm aware of Tanya taking her own advice and resuming her search. "This can't be … we're just kids … why …" I'm stuttering half sentences. It's the best I can do with my brain under ice. I don't even know what questions I should be asking first.

"Ang, relax. Maybe it just seems real. It's just a really good sim." She sighs. "Please help me."

"Why would you even think that?" I decide to ask. "They wouldn't …" But I can't finish that sentence. Because, wouldn't they? Wasn't I worried about Chris being used for real?

"Never mind, just keep looking," Tanya pleads.

I finally decide to join her. I drop into the chair in front of my own screen and force my hands to get back to searching. I don't know what to say. I just know that I'm suddenly afraid real lives may depend on this.

December 30

Tanya

Too close. That was too close. I risk a look up. I don't see any little red or green indicator lights that might mean we're being recorded. I almost smile anyway. I know she's watching. I can feel it.

What is the game here?

Are you watching to see if we're ready? Are you hoping we're not?

"Got something," Angela says.

I don't take my eyes off my own screen. "Zoom in, be sure." If this is real, and I'm pretty sure it is, there could be a lot of dark Magic out there. We just have to find one. One circle that shows we know what we're doing.

"Got it. Computer, show my location on all screens," Angela commands.

My screen fills with the image of a parking lot and a pickup truck that may be more rust than green pain. There's a guy in a blue ball cap sitting in the driver's seat. Wherever we are, it's night time. The circles seem to be centered on the entire truck. I lean closer and squint a little at the screen, focusing my eyes on the front of the truck and the circles. I feel like something is wrong. I use my half of the screen to zoom out just a little.

"What is that?" I ask. I'm not really asking Angela, just thinking out loud. But I hear her leave her chair and join me in looking at my screen. I've moved my screen so that I'm looking at the rear end of the truck and now it's obvious there's something hanging behind the vehicle. "Is that a chain?" I ask.

"I think so." Angela steps away from me, back to her own screen. She doesn't sit down. She pulls her phone out of her pocket, dialing. I assume she's calling this in to Dispatch.

I ignore her half of the conversation, focusing on what I'm seeing. The circles. That's what's not right. It's like there's a second set of circles messing with the outer edges of the ones we're looking at. I zoom out a little further. Now I can see more of the dark parking lot.

The first thing I notice is a second set of circles, which means I was right. They're to the right of the ones we were looking at but they're lighter. Usually that means smaller amounts of dark Magic. But together like this they could mean something big.

I find the heart of those circles, which appears to be a guy in dark clothing standing in the shadows of a building. I have to zoom out even further to see what building we're dealing with. Actually, I'm a little shocked that Angela zoomed so far in. That's bad work. Why would we need to see this particular truck instead of the whole location?

We're at a strip mall. There's a grocery store in the center and a bunch of smaller stores and restaurants on either end. They're all dark, closed for the night. "Why this location? What are they doing?"

Angela, who is obviously listening to me more than I'm listening to her, points at my screen. "Yes, two of them," she says into her phone.

I zoom into the area where she was pointing. It's near the second guy. Maybe she knew about him or maybe she watched me find him.

I sigh. It's a bank ATM. Suddenly the chain on the back of that truck makes a little more sense. These two idiots are going to try and pry an ATM from out of a brick wall of a grocery store using that beat up old pickup truck.

I lean back in my chair just as Angela hangs up. "They have two Solvers nearby. They're sending them both right now."

"We don't have a lot of time before they try something. How far away are the Solvers?"

In the reflection on my screen I see Angela grimace. "Four minutes, minimum." Not good. That's too much time.

"I have a feeling these guys will get out of here with the money before that," I say. There are worse things that could happen, I suppose. "Maybe we should keep looking."

"I'm going to stay on the screen and see this one through. You do what you want." She drops herself back into her chair, turning a little so that she's giving me the literal cold shoulder.

I zoom out, intending to move on to something else. I shake my head. Let her handle the crimes that don't really hurt anyone but corporations. I'll look for something more --

A small dark figure shuts up my mental chatterbox. "Who is that?" I point at him. In between two street lamps, he's basically in the dark. He's casually walking, no circles around him at all. He's just strutting along the street. So why do I care? Because he's heading right for that strip mall. A witness at best. An innocent victim at worse. This changes things.

I turn and look at Angela. "We could get in trouble for what I'm thinking of doing. Now is your chance to leave if you want to keep your nose clean," I say.

"You're thinking of teleporting, aren't you?"

It's frowned upon. Not because we can't. We can. But the Solvers are trained to handle situations that are dangerous. They're familiar to the local police departments in many cases. Some of them even carry weapons. None of that is true about a Magician who teleports to the location. Also, we are seriously risking the secret of Magic if we go there. Because these people don't know the Academy exists. Unlike the Solver, who works for the Academy, these people don't know Magic is real. When we pop into existence right in front of them they may have questions. They may fight back against what seems like a threat.

But, on the other hand, this seems like the only option we really have. With an innocent bystander crossing onto the scene, this could get messy fast. I don't want to take the time to figure out if these guys will try to drive away with this ATM at the exact moment this innocent crosses that street. I don't want to risk him being run over. I don't want to risk him being shot by these two guys because he was a witness. I want this over. Now.

I nod at Angela.

"Do it," she says. She never moves from her chair.

December 30

Angela

The secret of the Academy is kind of a big deal around here. We're under strict rules to not speak about what goes on to anyone. Obviously even my family doesn't know about it. So you can imagine the strict rules the leaders put on using any kind of Magic in front of someone who has no spark. But I'm about to watch as Tanya does just that. If this goes to council, I'll be expelled and so will she.

I wonder what happens to the Academy if both of the Magician's Assistants are expelled? I wonder if not having a precedent for that will save us from being expelled. I know it probably won't. "Wait …" I put my hand out, reaching for Tanya. "Is this really how we want to go down? We'll probably be expelled." I sigh. "Maybe we can teleport one of the Solvers to the location instead. Then we can take over one of them."

"There's a delay in our image," she gestures to the screen. "We could already be too late. We don't have time to explain this to anyone else. We don't have time to argue." She shakes her head. "I can't handle whatever goes wrong here on my conscience. You can leave if you want." She waits, watching me, while my heart hammers away in my chest. Finally, I nod in her direction and drop my hand back to my chest. Some part of me is aware that we're both assuming this is real right now. Really, can we afford not to?

Tanya leans back in her chair and closes her eyes. If she pulls this off, I won't be able to see what she's doing. Then I remember what Mark showed me, the portal to someone's vision. I remember that everything we've learned from the Magician has turned out to be as simple as commanding it. This spark inside of me is strong. I have to learn to use it.

I close my eyes and mentally reach for Tanya's spark. I feel it in a way I can't explain. It feels strong, sarcastic, chaotic. It feels like a wall I can't cross. She's equally as strong as me, at least. But I'm not trying to take her over. "I just want to see what she sees," I whisper, hoping my spark understands. I reach out and touch the computer screen without opening my eyes. "Put it up here," I ask. "Please."

I open my eyes and it's as if I'm standing at the front of the truck, peering right through the windshield. From this angle I can see the driver, who's currently looking behind him. I can also see directly through the vehicle to the guy who is currently wrapping a separate loose chain around the ATM.

It appears the plan is to get the ATM secured and then attach it to the chain on the truck. I assume the driver would then accelerate. That would, in theory, break the machine open. They would then be able to gather up as much cash as they can carry and get out of there quickly. Criminal number two, at the machine, is checking his work by tugging on the chains. It won't be long now.

My angle changes, looking around the parking lot. The innocent is getting close. Any minute now he'll look up and see what is going on. Any minute now they could see him, out for a casual walk at night. The angle returns to the truck, Tanya must have seen what she was looking for. "Hey," she calls out. The voice sounds like it's coming from all around me even though I haven't taken over her spark. The driver looks up, directly at me. "Oh, hello," Tanya says. Something about her voice is different. Something has changed.

Tanya walks around the side of the truck, toward the wall of the building. From this angle we can't see the second guy. What are you doing, Tanya? Then her eyes close and when they open I can tell something is different about the driver. The way he's smiling, the way he's blinking too fast. He must have a little spark because Tanya just took over.

That means I'm stuck right here in her abandoned body and this guy, whoever he is, is in limbo somewhere. I have no choice but to watch as Tanya puts the car in gear and hits the gas. I watch the action, frozen to the scene and wishing I could chase her down. I hold my hand steady over the computer screen, ready to cut my connection the second this gets any more dangerous.

Tanya, in the criminal's body, steers the truck off the scene, careful to avoid the guy walking. Dragging the chain, she drives off down the road. I have to laugh. She's made this an easy solution, really. With no vehicle to use to pull the machine, they have no hope of getting this crime committed. Of course, she's also moving.

I wipe my hand along the screen, closing the portal and returning myself to the room as I hit a button on my phone, calling the Solver who was assigned to my case.

"Solver 49," a voice answers.

"This is the Magician's Assistant. We have a change. The vehicle containing one suspect is traveling north on Main. The remaining suspect is still at the site. Their crime was not successful. I repeat, their crime was not successful."

"Any need for a Cleaner?" he asks.

The basic rule is a Cleaner would be needed if anyone saw anything, suspected anything, or made a mess. I weigh my options here. Really we should admit what we did and order a Cleaner to the truck's location. They'd probably memory wipe the driver.

But, in this case, we'd also be in serious trouble for what we did.

Of course, chances are we're already going to be in trouble anyway. When this sim ends we'll be standing in front of the

Magician being screeched at for even considering using someone with a tiny spark who isn't an Academy employee or student.

"I don't think so," I answer. "It seems like this one solved itself. Sorry I dragged you guys out of bed."

"No problem, have a good night."

I hang up the phone just as Tanya appears beside me and takes a violent, shuddering breath. I lay my hand on her shoulder. "You're back. It's all right," I tell her. "What happened?"

"The driver had a little spark. I don't think he even knew. It felt pretty small. I took him over and drove the heck out of there. I think he shoved me back out," she shakes her head. "But we got pretty far away from the scene, I think. Where is he?" She focuses on the map. There's a small circle that would represent the guy she left at the ATM but the second circle appears to have faded.

"I think we're good," I say.

"He might go straight back there. I don't know." Tanya is staring at the screen, her jaw clenched. "I've never done that before," she whispers. "Usually the people we take over are consciously letting us."

I've been taken over. I know that it's basically like sitting in a sensory deprivation room. I can't imagine ending up there and not knowing what it was. What would it feel like to have someone violently shove your spark back into your own body? How does one even do that? "Was it painful?" I ask. "Being shoved out, I mean."

She winces. "A little." She turns toward me so I can see the sadness in her eyes. "But I can't fault him for that, you know? He had no idea what was going on. I think it scared him." She turns her attention back to the map "I'm hoping it scared him enough that he'll go straight home."

December 30

Tanya

Thank the good lord. I relax my shoulders and let out a dramatic breath. That could've gone really, really wrong. Now we wait and see if the room dissolves back into a classroom and we get in trouble for using a solution that violates the secret of the Academy.

I tap my fingers on the table in front of me.

"What do we do now?" Angela asks.

"What time is it?"

The computer answers me before Angela can flip the phone in her hand up to her face and check. "The time is now 4:13 PM."

"Class is over," I say. I push myself out of the chair and grab my backpack off the floor. "I say we head home and relax."

"Why isn't she here to give us our scores?" Angela asks. "Shouldn't she have something to say about the way we did that?"

"Guess not," I answer. It's the best answer I can give her. Because what I really want to say is she can't give feedback if she wasn't watching. This proves it.

We were live just now and we were alone.

Winter, Age 24

Emily

"Ladies and gentlemen, thank you for coming tonight." I smile at the men and women before me, filling the first two rows of the stadium seating. This is a far cry from the kind of ceremony I received. Tom is standing in the wings, anticipation making him jumpy. He has been with me, working on this campus, for just over one year. He turned sixteen just a few days ago. On his birthday he came up to my control room and we had a very serious discussion about The Academy, our plans, and the future of Magic. We have agreed on a few things, embracing our status as equals.

Tom will be accepted as a Container. He didn't want a full ceremony, like I got, because we're not sure he will have access to all of the spark as I did. The ceremony should be small. He will then spend his years working side-by-side and training with me. I will find disturbances and send out Solvers as I have always done.

But they, in turn, will call Tom. He will teleport himself to the location and contain the dark Magic in the necklace he has fashioned himself of coal.

He will not be responsible for training, much like I am not. We will continue to have scans of new students monitored. In the event that someone with black spark presents themselves, we will hand part of their training to Tom. This is much the same arrangement I have reached with the scanner operators regarding very strong sparks, sparks that would rival my own.

We both have faith that the World of Magic will present us with heirs to our positions when they become necessary. Until that time, we have agreed to let this be the solution we have been searching for.

I stand center stage tonight on the midnight between January 1 and January 2 of a new year. I stand ready to present Tom to a group of about twelve of the most powerful Magic users in the world. These people are top of their fields at the Academy. Each of them is important in some way. They are the group we agreed should be aware of what is happening.

"Tonight we embark on a new experience for the Academy of Magic and one that has been a long time coming," I explain. "As you are aware, we have long been separating darkness from innocents without having any way to do away with it. A year ago a young man was scanned and presented with a dark spark inside of them." Tom steps out of the wings of the stage and into the light at my words. He is standing tall, his dark hair flashing under the lights. He looks stoic, solid, and much more mature than he really should be at only sixteen. "Since then we have learned it is possible for that man to absorb the darkness when it is separated from the innocent. Because of his strength, which rivals my own, and this ability, we decree that from this day forward he shall be known only as the Container."

There is a smattering of polite applause. I let it continue for about thirty-seconds, letting Tom bask in this. Then I raise my hands and a silence falls. "Container," I say. I step back from center stage and wave my arm down toward the floor.

Tom takes my spot. He slowly turns his head left and right, taking in everyone in attendance. I bend down, grabbing the canister of dirt from the spot on the floor. I walk in a circle around Tom, letting the dirt pour out. "I root this man in the Earth." Returning the canister to the spot on the floor, I swap it for the salt. The white drifts down over the dirt. "I ask the salt to be our barrier, keeping evil and darkness from this site during the time of our ceremony." Then I retreat into the shadows to watch as Tom commands the power in the room.

"I ask you to bear witness today as I take control of the darkness in the world," Tom says. His voice is loud and clear and it echoes off the back wall. "Container, the title I am being granted by the World and Magic and by you, is one that commands respect. It is also one that reminds me that I am no longer a mere individual. For the rest of my days I will stand for all who have shared their spark with me." This part of the speech, we decided, would mirror the one I gave. He turns his head slightly toward me and gives a little wink. I roll my eyes at the cocky show of pride in his memorization.

He returns his gaze to the audience and continues. "I promise to use the power you are sharing with me only to contain dark energy. I promise not to take over the spark of anyone unless it is warranted. I promise to always use my spark to contain the spread of dark energy in the world and prevent the damages it can cause."

I wasn't sure what to expect when he said these words. I remember my own ceremony. Those words had acted like a Magic switch, bringing me the control of everyone around me. I feel a tug in my spark when Tom speaks them. Not like he is taking power, but like he has just tied himself to me. When his eyes meet mine, I'm sure he felt it as well.

I walk forward as if in a trance, my eyes never leaving his. "Ladies and gentlemen," I bellow, "the Container for the Academy for Magic."

The room bursts into applause and I'm vaguely aware the people in attendance rise to their feet. I can feel Tom breathing. I can feel his pulse. I can feel that this makes him nervous.

We have connected ourselves in a way I didn't expect and everyone else may as well fade away.

December 30

Angela

I can't stand the idea of being caught. What if the Magician was listening and she just wants to know how long it will take before one of us admits what we did? What if she's waiting for us to confess? I turn myself around and march right back to the classroom. I hesitate at the door, my hand wrapped around the doorknob. The last time I opened this it was a control room that felt distinctly real.

I stand there considering the possibilities. She could have created a really good simulation that felt like we were in the control room. Having us arrive to the simulation already started could either shock us, give us the impression it's real, or just chastise us for being late in the past. That's the most likely situation, I tell myself. This was a really well done simulation.

But there's a little voice in the back of my mind that is not buying that. Oddly, it sounds a lot like Tanya. It's telling me the

Magician also could've turned the doorway into a portal that took us directly into the real control room. It's possible that situation was real.

I shake the thought away and turn the knob, slowly pushing the door in. I close my eyes and send up a silent prayer to whatever God may be listening that the control room is not what I'm walking into. It won't mean anything, because any spell could've been time sensitive. But I don't know what I'll do if I open my eyes and I'm in the control room again.

I open just one eye.

It's just the Magician's classroom.

My shoulders relax and I open both eyes. I look around. The classroom is empty. No Magician, sitting at her desk waiting for me to come in and confess. No Tanya, waiting to stop me from confessing what we did. Just a room with the fluorescent lights that will give you a headache if you spend all day here.

And a cell phone.

I cross to the desk, peering down at the cell phone. This has to be a test, right? Because I'm pretty sure that sleek black case is the same one I've seen on the Magician's phone. I look up at the ceiling while I reach my hand out and flip the phone over. "Oops," I say. I'm not sure why I'm keeping up this routine of pretending I'm being a good little rule follower. I freeze, waiting for the moment when she pops out and accuses me of trying to steal her phone or hack it or --

Hack it.

If I knew how to open her phone I could see if there's a recording of what we did. Maybe there's an email already typed up, ready to shoot off to us, ready to expel us from school. I click the home button. There's a passcode screen.

I stare at it until the screen goes dark again. I have no idea what her passcode could be but I know there are literally thousands of possibilities. I read about something once, but I'm sure it won't work. It was just something stupid, something you can use to unlock a phone. The company probably saw the same news story. Probably pushed out an update that stopped it from being possible. Right?

Still, I find myself holding down the home screen until the little blue line appears under the text "What can I help you with?"

Nervously, I whisper. "Um, what time is it?"

The world clock appears and the phone reads out the local time in a loud booming voice that echoes around the empty classroom. I freeze, waiting again to be caught. Right this second, I can say that I only wondered what time it was. I can say that I only needed to know if class was over, to know if I was allowed to leave. Once I do more than this, I really have no excuse.

I do it anyway.

I click on the clock, bringing up the time management screen. I open the alarm tab at the bottom and click the plus sign to add a new one. I click on the sound option, then click that I want to choose a new one. Her music app opens in the background. Holding my breath, sure that this won't work, I back out of all of it and hit the home button.

Her phone background fills the screen. "It worked?" I whisper. Before I can stop myself, because really I'm in too far now, I click open the email app across the bottom. I was right, I feel the flutter that signifies my heartbeat quickening. There is an email in the drafts folder.

I open it.

But it's not to me or Tanya.

It's a reply to something that she must not have sent. "I'll take care of it." That's all it says. I click back to return to the email inbox. Just as the screen flashes, I think I see something. I open the email again. Sure enough, there's my name. I scroll down so I can see the context. It's the original email she was replying to, copied there in her response.

"You assured us that either Angela or Tanya would not make it to the ceremony. Have you considered what a risk it will be if both girls are given the title to split? How devastating it will be to our progress if they were to, for example, open a second school? Exactly how do you plan to ensure that this doesn't happen? How do you plan on giving the power to only one? How do you plan to guarantee the one you choose will be the one you can mold to your plan for dealing with the black sparks?"

I drop the phone back on the desk and take two slow steps back like it's going to explode. I think of all the things I've been worried about lately. All the reasons why students shouldn't be in real situations. My breathing quickens and my eyes burn with unshed tears. We could lose our spark, we could be expelled, we could die.

If you had to guarantee that one person wasn't going to make it to a ceremony, those are all valid ways to do that. Is it possible the things I've feared when I imagine everything going wrong are actually happening?

The realization comes to me like a bucket of cold water. That situation just now was as real as Steve and Chris' field tests. It was real, it was a test, it had the risk of our spark disappearing.

Then I realize something else. She won't risk turning us in for breaking the rules. She wants something bigger than expulsion.

We're in danger.

December 30

Tanya

This time, the meeting is my idea. I open and close the phone fifteen times before I finally get the chaotic thoughts out of my head. It's irrational to imagine that someone may be looking down at his phone screen, reading the message over his shoulder as it comes through. It's ridiculous to even think my name would be attached to my phone number in his phone, as his is not in mine. But those are the thoughts I have to battle before I send a copy of the message he's sent to me countless times.

Quad. Midnight.

I don't risk walking to the quad when the time comes. Part of me is terrified of being caught. But another, bigger, part of me is just done with her random rules. There's no reason to insist that students not be out of their rooms at night. You cannot convince me that you're worried something will happen to them. With your

Magic map and your control of the spark, there cannot possibly be danger anywhere around us. It's a control issue, pure and simple.

Instead, I steal a quick glance at the hiding spot in my room and then teleport myself to the quad. The complete darkness of the night is shocking when you don't allow yourself time to adjust. I probably should've turned off the lights in my bedroom before leaving, but it's too late for that now.

I see the dark figure that I assume is Chris sitting beneath the tree. His arm flies to his chest. "You scared me," he says. "Why are you using Magic?"

"Why not? Isn't that what we're trained for?" I approach him and drop to my knees on the ground beside his body. "I'm scared, Chris."

"That's a change." His voice sounds softer, wounded. "You're usually the one telling me I'm being irrational. They need us, remember? That's what you keep saying. We're not expendable. We just have to bide our time until you're in charge and then we can put the plan into action."

"What if she knows?" I whisper even though we're outside and seemingly alone. Even though if she's listening somewhere, she can use Magic to hear me anyway. "If she knows what we have, we're a threat."

The outline of his body is coming into focus now as my eyes adjust so I see when he nods. "That's what I'm afraid of too." He lays his hand over mine, the warmth a contrast to the cold coming off the grass.

"We know she's capable of dangerous things--" I start to say.

"But if she wanted me gone, she had her chance when she put me on that bogus field test," Chris points out.

"That's true, that is her style. Manufacture a crime, draw an innocent into it ..." I shake my head, trying to clear the memories that have rushed at me just at those words. I try to change the topic. "What was the point of that?" I ask. "I'm not saying I always understand what she's up to, but this one really baffles me. Why pull you into a real situation? Why have Steve tag along with you?"

"I've been thinking about that," Chris says. "I think it was to scare me."

"Did it work?"

A chuckle shakes the air between us. "You can't scare someone who has been terrified for months." He sighs. "Speaking of the field test, Angela knows more than you wanted her to. I know we need you to be the Magician, but Angela may be able to help. We don't know what will happen to her when you take over, T. Let her in. Talk to her. She hasn't been through the same stuff as us, but she's a good person." He brushes his hand along the sleeves of my jacket, tickling my arm a little. "It's almost over. Tomorrow you'll take that stage, become the Magician, and the old Magician will be powerless to stop you from releasing what you know. It's your plan and it's a good plan. We're almost done."

"We're almost done," I repeat. The words have meaning but they fail to make me feel as good as they used to. I can still feel their warmth, the promise of a future that is more honest, but underneath that is the tremble of fear. The worry that we waited too long and gave her an opening.

We had a plan to take on the most powerful Magic user on the planet and I'm starting to realize how foolish that was.

Summer, Age 28

Emily

I don't startle when Tom teleports back into the control room. I'm expecting him. He gives me a cocky grin as he tucks the charcoal necklace he wears back under the collar of his shirt. "I have a date tonight," he says. "Did I tell you that?" He drops into the empty chair beside me, the one identical to mine.

I turn my attention away from the screen and give him a little chuckle. "You didn't mention that. Who with?"

"A Dispatch officer named Charles." He wiggles his eyebrows. "He's just a bit older than me but not enough to be gross."

"Not like me, you mean." I'm eight years older than Tom. It's one of the many reasons I absolutely refuse to go out to dinner with him, despite him asking me a few times over the years. Actually, this is the most socially acceptable of the reasons. The largest reason is really that I have never really understood the draw to social attraction. I have no desire to date, fall in love, or be with anyone. It's yet another way that Tom and I have proven, over the years, to be complete opposites. I'm basically asexual and Tom considers himself pansexual. He loves all things love and dating and I can't be bothered. Opposites.

"What's that?" Tom asks, pointing at the screen.

I draw my attention back to it, watching the little pulse of something centered over Nevada. "Las Vegas," I answer. "There's usually a lot of activity there but it rarely manifests into anything."

He drops his hand and settles back into his chair. "There have been fewer calls lately," he notes. "Unless you've been taking some without me."

He knows I haven't been doing that. I would never do that. Since Tom became the Container of Magic for the Academy things have been smooth and easy. You can feel the happiness from the sparks inside people. Magic as a whole is pleased with our arrangement. Magic users put out negative energy accidentally, that manifests and gathers around non Magic people. But I can find it and Tom can contain it. Between us, we are cleansing the world and setting Magic right. "I think it's a cycle," I say. "Magic users are allowed to use Magic in their everyday lives. This makes them all happier."

"When they're happier they don't put out darkness," Tom picks up the thread of my thought. "When they don't put out darkness, there's none to collect. I get it."

"Right, but it's more than that." I turn away from the screen again, facing him. "When they don't put out darkness, non Magical people trust them more. When we're trusted more it means we can continue to be allowed to use Magic without making people uncomfortable."

"I was only a teenager when I got my scan, Em. How bad was it before?"

I shrug and turn back to the screen. "No one trusted us. I had to fight for our chance to use Magic the way we do now. When they first saw the scanner Dad created it was a way to catch us lying about it. Honestly, I feared they'd use it to create some kind of concentration camp where they held us all away from the rest of the world."

"That's terrible." I feel the warmth of his hand on my elbow.

"But they didn't." I force my voice to sound upbeat. "They gave us a chance to show that we can do good work that betters the world. We've done that. We will keep doing that."

Tom lets me move the screen around, looking for disturbances. My brain wanders, thinking about what could have been and being thankful that things didn't go that way. I remember the dark days before we found Tom when even I was growing weary of sending darkness out into the world without being able to stop it. Tom is the answer to all of that. I will never forget how much he has changed the process.

"What happens when you and I can't do this anymore?" he asks quietly. "I mean, I'm not quitting on you, but I don't think you'd be as effective with a cane."

I don't have to stop and think about this right now because I've thought about it a lot lately. "We find someone else," I answer. "Someone who will work together with their opposite and keep the World of Magic satisfied. Someone who will always remember that they are not more important than the other people with a spark."

"What makes you so sure someone like that will come along when you need them?" he asks.

This time, I turn my body all the way around. I reach out and brush my fingers along his soft cheek. "Because you did." I drop my hand from his face but keep the eye contact. "The World of Magic sends us exactly what it needs when it is needed. Our job is to listen."

December 31

Angela

I fling open the door to my Solver class and have to suppress a groan. No Chris, no Steve. Of course, no Cheryl either. But that's because she's now in Container class first period. A class I know nothing about.

Shouldn't I know more about it?

After midnight tomorrow I may be the leader of this school. Why is it that I feel like I don't know what I'd really be getting into all of a sudden? I've been here for over a decade, how is it possible they're still keeping so much from me?

"Excuse me, I need Angela." The voice at the door draws my attention. It's not someone I recognize. This is a short man with a round stomach. He appears to be barefoot, which is really weird.

But Rolly seems to recognize him. He smiles. "Ah, this must be in preparation for the ceremony." He turns to me and winks. "Have fun at rehearsal, you are dismissed."

I get up and follow the short man through the hallways of the school. We don't speak. The sound of his bare feet slapping the linoleum is annoying, but I can't think of anything to say that may cover up the noise. He opens the door to the auditorium and steps out of the way so I can enter. The door shuts behind me, without him.

I look around.

The room has enough seats for everyone in the Magical community, graduates or students, to attend. All the seats are pointing at the stage, just like they would be on Broadway or something. This morning up on the stage the lights are all on. There are two chairs, situated in the center. Tanya is sitting in one, her legs delicately crossed at the ankles.

Standing before her is a tall man in a suit. As I walk up the aisles of seats I study him. The second man in one morning who I don't recognize. This one looks like the super villain of a hero movie. He's wearing all black, his black hair is slicked back with some kind of gel, and he looks like he has never smiled in his life. It's intimidating.

Having finally reached the stage, I take the empty chair. "Sorry if I kept you two waiting," I say.

Tanya, this close, looks nervous. Something is certainly wrong with her. She barely looks at me when I sit and she looks like she's been crying. I thought I heard a rumor that Logan dumped her, could that be what this is all about? Somehow, I doubt it.

"Let's get started," the man says. "Tonight at midnight we will have a ceremony on this very stage unlike any ceremony that has ever been held."

I hope that's true. I can't help thinking about that email I saw. Someone has a plan to eliminate one of us before the ceremony tonight. Someone is afraid of what will happen during this ceremony. I swallow that fear as best I can and attempt to focus on the man in front of me. Despite his appearance, he's not the enemy. The Magician, on the other hand, may just be.

"The words will be recited by both of you. Typically, at the end of the ceremony the person who said the lines somehow connects to the Magic sparks around the world. There is an obvious change in them and we welcome our new Magician. We expect, this year, that will still be the case. We expect that one of you will suddenly be given access to all the spark in the world. The other one will have to endure the entire speech and then watch the new Magician from here. It will not be pleasant. I cannot prepare you for that, so I will not try. Today we will merely have each of you practice the speech you are to give. You will practice alone and then together. Please review this paragraph." He waves his hand and a half sheet of paper appears just above each of our hands. We both catch it before it can flutter softly to the floor. "I will give you ten minutes." He turns and walks off to the wings of the stage.

"Are you okay?" I whisper to Tanya.

"Fine. Read."

I review the material in front of me.

I understand that Magic exists in the world. Some of us are born with the spark of bright Magic, filling us with light and the gift. The Academy seeks to cultivate this light and use it in the face of dark. Dark Magic can be born in this world. I pledge to seek out that dark Magic. I pledge to use my spark to control the spread of dark energy in the world and prevent the damages it can cause. I pledge to be the best Magician I can be for the Academy and for the world.

I read it twice. "Does this seem different to you?" I ask.

"The last line is new," she answers. "She didn't say that line at her ceremony."

"I wonder why. Why change a speech that's been used for hundreds of years?"

"I take it you've finished reading." Just like that the man is back. He walked so quietly that I didn't hear him. "Who wants to go first?"

I'm relieved when Tanya raises her hand lightly, volunteering. This isn't much to memorize and, honestly, I'm more worried about the fact that Chris and Steve weren't in class. Did she send them on another "field test"? If they're in trouble, I need to know. Sure, Tanya and I should be on full alert now too, in light of what I read in that email. But we are pretty safe right now, sitting in an auditorium.

The man starts directing Tanya where to stand and how to speak. Hopefully he won't notice if I duck out for just a second. I close my eyes and reach out to Chris. I feel the click of my conscious as it slips into his body. When I open my eyes, I'm outside. The sun is shining. I catch a glimpse of a perfectly blue sky.

Then, without warning, I'm shoved out.

It's not pleasant, it's not simple. It's violent. I feel it in my entire body like I was hit by a linebacker.

Suddenly, I'm falling.

December 31

Tanya

There's a crash behind me and the nicely dressed guy looks shocked. "What the hell?" he says. I turn around and see Angela, sprawled on the floor. She's beside the chair she was sitting in. If I had to guess, I'd say she fell out. She's just laying there, blinking up at the lights in utter confusion.

I rush over to her side, barely ahead of the instructor who looks annoyed. "What happened?" I whisper. "Are you all right?" Because something about this doesn't sit well with me.

"I'm fine." She stands up. "I fell, that's all."

She sure as hell doesn't look like that's all that happened. Her face is white and her eyes are wide. She looks afraid of something. Chris told me to trust Angela. He told me to let her in. I lean close to her ear. "Is it Chris?"

Her eyes widen even further, if that's possible. "How do you know --"

"All right, fainting lady. Let's give you a shot now. Get up here. Tanya, sit," the tall man commands.

Angela moves to the front of the stage. He tells her where to stand. He starts to talk about the dirt and salt rings. Suddenly getting to the bottom of whatever just happens seems more important than ever. I close my eyes and try to link to Angela. We're equals so I can't really take her over. But I can send her a message. "What happened with Chris?" I try to send. I think the same thought on repeat. Suddenly, I can tell one gets through. It feels different, somehow. Like I'm no longer repeating it to a void but like it actually delivered. This is hard to explain.

"He's missing." The thought fills my head like it was my own. Except it's not. "I tried to connect with him. He's outside somewhere, clear blue day. But then I got, like, shoved out. It hurt."

Shit. That can't be good. I know he tried to brush me off at our meeting. I know he acted like everything was fine. But the real truth is, if the Magician is on to us, he can get seriously hurt here. Angela may not know everything I know, but I can tell she is worried about him. Honestly, so am I.

I hear her launch into her speech. I try to ignore her. Instead, I reach for Chris.

It doesn't take Angela long to reach the end of the short speech. I wasn't able to reach Chris. Our connection isn't strong enough. I'm going to have to try something else. Something a bit more drastic.

"We should practice once with the two of you," the instructor says.

"Right after I use the restroom, it's an emergency," I say. I don't wait for him to argue, I just dash out. I need some privacy for this to work. Because what I'm about to do is really, really stupid. Like calling the cops ahead of time to tell them to watch the bank you're planning to rob the weekend before you rob it kind of stupid. Except that, in my analogy, I'm not planning to commit a crime.

I reach the bathroom and wait while the only person there washes her hands and leaves. I follow her out, shutting the door behind her. Then I turn around and lean on the door. I may not be close enough to Chris, but there's someone else who may be involved who I am close to. I shouldn't have any problem reaching her.

With my eyes closed I reach out for her subconscious. Like with Angela, this won't allow me to take over. But I may be able to read an idea or see a setting. Maybe. There's a big chance this will fail.

I feel it when it happens. Not a big drop, like clicking into someone with less of a spark than me. This is like softly bumping into a solid brick wall. It's there and it's stronger than me.

I push myself up against it as much as I can and open my eyes.

It's muted, like I'm viewing the world through heavy window tinting at night time. There are shapes, but they're hard to make out. I get one clear image before the brick wall shoves back and then I'm back in the restroom, gasping for air.

The Magician is in South Dakota and now she knows I'm looking for her.

Fall, Age 28

Emily

Tom and I pace nervously outside of the large room. We have been asked to come speak to the assemblage of leaders from around the world again. The topic of discussion is purported to be the school and our progress. Our statistics are strong, but I never like coming before large groups of people. For Tom, this is his first outing like this.

A man in a black suit and blue shirt opens the door and nods at us. "We're ready for you both," he says. Then he steps out of the way to allow us to squeeze past him into the chamber. Again the seats are full of important looking people behind placards that tell me their countries of origin. Many of them are wearing earpieces that will translate our spoken language into something they can understand.

Tom and I make our way across the stage and stop in front of the microphone. "Good morning," I greet them. "I am the

Magician at the Academy of Magic. This is my Container. You requested we be present today to answer some questions you have." I stand straight, watching the assembled people. No one makes any move to speak. Tom starts shifting behind me, betraying his nerves. Still, we wait.

Finally, a gentleman with a younger face than the rest in the crowd stands. "We've heard the statistics have improved since you took on this Container. We wondered if you could speak to why this has happened and whether, in your opinion, changes needed to be made to our contract."

I step back out of the way and nod my head toward the microphone. "You should take this one," I tell Tom in a quiet voice.

He steps up to the microphone. "I am the Container at the Academy of Magic. My position is new. It is our belief that this position was created because the World of Magic needed my skills. I was gifted with the ability to contain the darkness in the world without incurring any damage or changes to my own personality." He smiles a full, radiant smile for the audience. I notice that many cannot help but return the expression.

"With my position solidly in place and with me working side-by-side with the Magician we have been more successful at containing the darkness, therefore stopping it from spreading out into another soul to cause more chaos. Our success rate has doubled and the rate of crimes has decreased."

There is a smattering of applause. Tom nods. "Yes, this is something worth applauding. But you asked me here today to see if there was anything you could change. I'm sure I don't need to use Magic to tell me that this is because you are hoping to cut funding for our program. You are hoping that we can continue to do this job with less money, less support. Am I correct?"

Silence rings through the room. Tom grimaces as though he is offended by their inability to even voice the answer. "I am sure there are things you could spend this money on besides the Academy. But we are training the future generations in the skills we use. We are making sure that when the Magician and I retire, there will be more to take our place."

The thought makes me cringe. The scans show that sparks as large as mine and Tom's are rare indeed. While I trust in the World of Magic to give us what we need when we need it, there doesn't seem to be an influx of powerful Magic users waiting to take over our positions. Could the Academy survive without a Magician and a Container? It's something we've never considered.

Tom continues. "Without the Academy Magic users don't understand what they're capable of. It can result in experiments that are dangerous. It can result in abuse of our power. It can result in accidents and death. More important, I think, than our crime reduction statistics are our Magic user statistics." He slowly moves his head around the room, grabbing eye contact with various people in the audience. His public speaking skills will do him well with this powerful crowd, I know. "The suicide rate among 15-25 year old Magic users is down over 30% in the last ten years. The incarceration rate for accidental crimes influenced by

Magic is down over 75%." He lets the statistics ring out in the room for a beat.

"We are making a difference by teaching young Magic users their own strength and limits. We are giving them a safe space to learn their gift. Returning our society to what it was before the Academy in order to save money would only bring about chaos. It would bring about Magic users who have to hide in secret. It would likely invite someone to abuse their power and take advantage of those of you who have no Magic spark."

He opens his hands as if requesting a hug from the room. "Working together and keeping the agreement we have, as we always have, is the right solution. In this way, we remain a team."

There is applause and some nods all around the room.

I politely echo the applause but my stomach flips. When we talked about this, I used the same line: "we remain a team". But, somehow, hearing it delivered has me noticing one important thing.

To some people, that may sound like a threat.

December 31

Angela

"You have a second period to get to," the instructor barks at me. "Get out of my sight." I don't argue. He's not happy that Tanya never came back from her "emergency" trip to the restroom. I'm not happy that he wouldn't allow me to go track her down. I'm absolutely positive she's up to something, but I can't seem to link to her telepathically again. I'm acutely aware that likely means she's stronger than me, to be able to initiate that, but suddenly it doesn't seem as important as it would've seemed a few days ago.

God, tomorrow one of us will become the next Magician.

The thought is like a slap across my face, jarring and instant. It gives everything we're doing here a sudden sense of urgency. I rush out of the auditorium and point my feet toward the nearest bathroom. The hallways are really crowded today. With the pending ceremony everyone with any spark at all will be here. The campus will be filling up with alumni and dignitaries all day.

I feel a small pang of frustration and sadness. My own parents won't be here to see what could very well be the biggest moment of my life. Of course, if I don't figure out what is going on, there's a good chance Steve and Chris may not be here either. In fact, if that email is any indication, Tanya and I are going to have to really be on guard if we both plan on making it.

I force the feelings down into my stomach. I can't think about that right now. I have to find Chris. I have to find Tanya. What was that telepathic message, anyway? She knows something about Chris. But how could she? They're not even friends.

Are they?

I'm reaching for the bathroom door when something catches my eyes. It's Cheryl. But something is wrong. Her eyes are unfocused, staring straight ahead of her but looking down at the ground. Her hair is a mess of tangles wrapping like snakes around her face. Her overly pale face.

I step toward her. "Cheryl," I'm aware that I am speaking quietly like I'm afraid to spook her. "Are you all right?"

She looks up at me, technically. But it's creepy. In horror movies and books they'd say she's looking through me. But that's not it. It's more like she's standing there asleep on the inside. She's staring at nothing. I just happen to be in the path.

"Cheryl," I lay my hand on her shoulder. Even the lightest, gentlest touch I can manage shocks her. She jumps under my fingers. Her eyes skitter to me for a second, really coming to life. Then they flee back to flat.

"All wrong," she whispers.

At least, I think that's what she said. "What's wrong? Should we go see someone?" I ask. "The nurse? Mark?"

Her eyes come alive again, for longer this time. "No!" Then back to zombie. "I'm fine."

"You're not fine. I'm not fine. No one is fine." I look over my shoulder at the restroom. "Come in here."

I wrap my hand around her wrist and pull her into the bathroom. "Tanya?" I call out.

Silence.

Damn. I was really hoping to find her. I could use a little back up right now. I check the stalls. Empty. When I turn back around, Cheryl is standing exactly where I left her by the door. Her hands are up at her neckline fidgeting with something.

"Cheryl, I know you're not fine right now and I am here for you. I am just gonna check in on Chris and Steve really quick." Why do all my friends have to be in crisis at the same time?

I step back from Cheryl and grab my cell phone out of my pocket. I dial Steve's number and hold the phone up to my ear, eyes closed. "Hello." I don't wait for anything more, just reach out and latch onto his consciousness. Normally I would warn him, but I don't want to wait.

When I open my eyes I'm staring at the back of what I think is Chris. He's literally jogging down a street. Except it's not like an ordinary busy street. Wherever we are it looks like it's night time. Both sides of the road are littered with dry brush and lots of dirt. No cars, no people, no animals. Up on the left there's a small building, but it's pretty far away. Beyond that, nothing. My first thought is that this is not good, Chris doesn't really run. My second thought is that I probably should be catching him.

I take off and immediately notice that Steve is faster than I am. I catch Chris in no time at all, barely even out of breath. "Where are we going and why are we going so fast?" I ask.

He squints at me. "What?"

I'm an idiot. Steve would already know where they were headed. "I mean, do you remember where we're going?" I try. It's a lame cover-up. Chris isn't going to buy that.

He tips his chin up in the direction of that store off in the distance. "Right there."

"Of course, that makes sense," I whisper. Again, it's the only thing anywhere nearby. We keep our voices off as we continue the jog up to the store. It's strange, being inside of Steve's body for this long allows me to see what it's like to be him. Usually we're in and out quickly or for short bursts. This is a full on jog down a desert road at night. Steve is fit. I don't feel tired at all. His muscles are capable of handling this run like a champ. They know things my muscles absolutely don't know. I'm not breathing heavily. Of course, I also don't want to participate in a conversation, but it doesn't seem like I'm alone in that. Chris hasn't tried to get me to say anything.

I think I realize how wrong this all is the moment we slow our feet in the parking lot of the little store. It's closed. Lights off and not a single person in sight. So who exactly is playing host to the dark Magic we are supposedly here for?

December 31

Tanya

"**S**hit," I shout into the bathroom. It echoes around me as if accusing me of making an immensely stupid mistake, which of course I have. Still, I have information and I need to be using that information. The map she was staring at was a small narrow road inside of South Dakota. I close my eyes and imagine it again, just to be sure. I can see it. The state of South Dakota highlighted with a big yellow box on the left hand side of the screen. The right hand side of the screen zoomed into a long desert road of some kind and an abandoned market store.

This is so bad. Everything is coming to an end, right now. I'm suddenly so sure of it. I can't sit here and wait for something to get out of control. Chris is in danger. I don't have a choice. I have to do something drastic.

There's really only one thing I can think to do and it definitely fits under that heading of drastic. In fact, this idea also falls under the heading of stupid. But it's my only option. I really, really hope I remember enough details from that map to make this work. Teleporting myself to the wrong location would be unhelpful. Teleporting myself to a location that doesn't exist, one that I've only remembered in my mind … let's say I'm not sure what happens then but I'm pretty sure it wouldn't be good.

I decide to take a slightly safer route than teleporting. I'll open a portal. This will give me a glimpse of the destination before I end up there. Sure, it could still go wrong, but the odds have to be marginally better.

I wave my hands around in a circle on the wall across from me, keeping my back firmly against the bathroom door to hold it closed. I focus on everything I remember about the location, which isn't much. I'm relieved when the off-white bathroom wall starts to fade in front of my face. It's slowly being replaced with the watery image of what I saw when I tapped into the Magician's spark. I continue to work my hands in a slow circle, watching the image solidify until I've opened the portal before me completely.

I don't hesitate. I don't allow myself to stop and think about how this could go wrong. I don't analyze the situation further. I just let my feet lead me right through the portal and into what I hope is South Dakota.

I take a second to look around as the circle back to the bathroom closes in a watery reverse of what I saw when it opened. The building looks exactly like I expected. It's completely dark, made out of wood, and looks abandoned. There is a small parking lot, I guess you'd call it. Cracked asphalt lets weeds grow up into what may have been parking spaces at one time. There are no people around and the only soft light is coming from two lamp posts, casting their circles onto what may have been a bustling business once upon a time.

No people. I look up and down the road that seems to have been built expressly for the purpose of getting people into this business. No people. I expected to see Chris, at least. Maybe even the Magician herself. I'm not sure what she is up to, not really. But if I'm right about this being the beginning of the end, something should be happening.

I start to panic. What if I made a mistake? What if this is some imaginary land I just thrust myself into? Could I be inside my own head, somehow? Like this is some fantasy world and I brought myself there by accident? What would that even mean? Is that possible?

Just as my panic starts to make me feel like my chest is constricting, I notice dirt being kicked up from the surface of the likely unused road. I step closer to the road and squint. There are two people jogging up in this direction and getting closer.

I swallow my fear and plant myself under one light where they're sure to see me. This is happening.

My faith in myself wavers as I watch them draw closer. They're Solvers. What if this is real? Could I have been wrong about everything?

I look back over my shoulder at the building. No, I'm not wrong. There is no one here but me and I don't have a negative spark in my body.

My fear rushes out even further solidifying that I'm right about everything when the faces of Chris and his friend, Steve, come into view. They're not real Solvers. They haven't been promoted. That won't happen until tomorrow, after the ceremony.

That means my instincts were right.

They don't see me, not right away. No … correction. Steve doesn't. He's looking around the lot, trying to figure out what the call was for. He's looking for signs of this negative spark that would've been the reason they were out here. But Chris, he looks right at me. The sly way his lips curl up in a smile, the special smile Chris uses when he's up to something, solidifies it.

That's not Chris.

I step toward them, holding up my hands. "We need to talk," I say.

Steve looks shocked. "Tanya? What are you doing here?"

"She teleported," Chris answers. In reality I'm sure the voice belongs to Chris. But because of what I know I almost hear her voice, her cocky purr coming out of his mouth. "Which is a violation of Academy rules, I do believe."

"Really? We're going to talk about rules? Ok, how about this one? You have two underage Solvers here. There doesn't appear to be anything for them to be responding to." I gesture to the empty area around us. "And you have taken one of them over without his permission, at least that's what I would assume." I tilt my head to the side and squint. "How many rules did you break? I think I've lost count."

"You need to go home, Tanya. Now." The command sounds so much like her that I almost flinch.

"No." I take a step closer. "I can't let you do this. I know you think you need to keep control of the Academy. I know your deal all falls apart if one of us becomes the Magician. You're running out of time. I get it, I do. But this isn't the way to do it. You can't pin this all on innocents. These two boys, they didn't do anything."

"You don't know what you're talking about," Chris' voice spits the words at me.

"Then explain it to me." I have no interest in hearing her side of this, not really. But if I don't give her a chance, she may do something extreme. I look over Chris' shoulder and see Steve looking completely confused, poor guy. I don't have time, not to mention a method, to get him out of here safely. Not really. I kind of offer him a little shrug, as an apology. Then I turn my attention back to Chris. "Help me understand what is really going on, Francheska."

Steve makes an audible gasp at the use of the Magician's former name, the one we're not supposed to use. But it's the reaction from Chris that I'm paying attention to. She blinks his gorgeous eyes too rapidly, the name registered. She narrows his eyes at me and jabs a finger toward my chest. "What we are doing at the Academy is important. We are collecting dark sparks and getting them off the street. We cannot be shut down. We must continue to fight."

"Why would we be shut down?" I ask, although I have my suspicions.

She rubs the face she's occupying and then settles her arms across the chest. "The Senators oppose what we're doing. We have to have something big, something that shows them how important we are. Remind them what kinds of dangers we are preventing."

I think I understand what she's saying. I tilt my head to the right a little and say it, my voice questioning. "But if something bad happens then you didn't prevent it, which proves their point." I shake my head. "If you prevent it then you have no proof it would've happened without your intervention."

She nods. Despite hating this entire situation and fearing for my life right now, I still feel a flutter of pride at that little show of agreement. I hate myself for that. "You've found the problem exactly, Tanya," she says. "We need an obvious threat. A message left where everyone sees it. An obvious anger and proof of the power of the dark spark." Chris' body, powered by the Magician, takes a dangerous step closer to me. His eyes narrow menacingly. "If someone under the influence of a dark spark were to leave a message about a second crime along with the body of an Academy Solver, it would show how serious the threat was. Then, if we were to prevent the second crime, they would listen."

"But you're out of time," I say as I take a small step away from her. "You lose control of the Academy tomorrow." I have no idea how she plans to take out Chris. More importantly, I see absolutely no way of stopping her.

"Oh sweetie," she says. "It doesn't have to be Chris. You've given me a better idea." Reading my mind is new. It puts me off my game. I think that's why I don't notice the blade she has pulled from somewhere on Chris' clothing. I don't have time to wonder if she planted it on him or if he brought it along.

In fact, I only have time to draw a shaky breath before the blade sinks into my chest and everything goes black.

Winter, Age 30

Emily

I haven't seen much of Tom lately. We've been busy. Busier, even, than usual. I've been trying to catch him. We have something important to talk about. So today, when I let the Solver have control of his body back, I teleport myself to the location and wait. I watch as the Solver carries out my orders, separating the innocent from the darkness. I watch him take the innocent in for questioning, the newest requirement in our deal with countries like this one. I'm still sitting there on the sidewalk when Tom pops into existence in the middle of the street to collect the darkness.

He sees me. I can tell in the way he slows a little with his movements. His smile is small and crooked, but he doesn't have time for much more. He quickly gathers the darkness into the charcoal. I watch the pulsing I recognize as darkness until it disappears. Only then does Tom turn his entire body in my direction and wave. "What's up?"

I stand up and brush the dirt off the seat of my jeans. "Do you have a minute? We need to talk."

He jogs across the street to stand beside me. Although we're on a small side street and I haven't seen a single vehicle since we arrived, I notice he looks both ways before crossing. It makes me smile. When he gets close to me he bumps my arm with his elbow. "That sounds serious. Talk away. I'm listening."

"You heard about the new scans, right?" A few months ago we had a couple of students rescanned because they were showing aptitude for things that other students simply weren't capable of. The new scans revealed levels previously only seen in two people. The two people standing here on this quiet street corner having a conversation right now.

"Yes. I also heard their training is going remarkably well." He waggles his eyebrows. "Rumor has it one of them is actually a black spark. I was hoping you'd give me permission to start training them soon. Is that what this is?"

"Yes … "

Tom makes a fist and pumps it once in a celebratory gesture.

" … and no," I add.

He rolls his eyes and his expression grows serious. "All right, something is bothering you. Hit me with it."

"What if this is what we were waiting for? What if this is a sign that you and I are able to back out and retire? We can train these two and step back." I say all of it in a rush. It's not that I think Tom will argue with me. It's more that I'm worried he'll judge me. He may ask why I want to step away. He may think this is our responsibility. Basically, he may come at me with all of the things that I have been telling myself and I'm not sure I'm ready to face that.

"When was the last time you had a day off, Em?" he asks.

It's not what I was expecting him to say so it catches me off guard. I shake my head and give a little laugh. His face remains serious, clearly waiting for an answer. "Um," I wrack my brain trying to remember. "This isn't really a job that allows for a vacation." I shrug. Tom doesn't argue with me or agree with me. Instead, he widens his eyes and the ghost of a smile plays at the corners of his mouth. I roll my eyes, feeling defensive suddenly. What is he driving at? "Darkness doesn't take a break. You know that." I gesture around me. "You haven't taken one either."

He lays a hand on my shoulder and I feel myself deflate a little. "We've been at this a long time without a break. It's a tough job with a lot of expectations. I don't see any reason why we can't step into a more advisory role with the youngsters and allow them to take the day-to-day operations for a while."

I smile and sigh. "I thought you were going to argue with me," I admit.

"I'm exhausted. I have very little in the way of a social life and I would love a beer but I am always on the clock." He runs his hands through his hair, brushing it off his face. "You've been doing this longer than I have."

"Almost ten years," I admit.

"That's the magic number." He sighs. "We should put it in the rules. I bet you'll find that a new strong spark in black and a new strong spark in white will come along once every ten years."

I like the thought. It confirms the idea for me that has been brewing for a while. The idea that this is the right path. The idea that my time for leading the Academy has come to an end. The idea that the World of Magic is at the wheel here, and Tom and I are just passengers.

December 31

Angela

The scream I started in Steve's body finishes with an echo in the bathroom. Cheryl seems to come alive at the noise, turning her head from side-to-side as though trying to find out what I'm yelling about. "What…" her voice falters.

"We need someone. Anyone. Someone in charge. Right now. It's a matter of life or death," I say. I don't wait for her to answer. I push her out of the way of the door, swing it open, and stalk off down the hallway. I don't stop until I'm at Mark's door.

My knuckles dance across the surface in a sorry excuse for a knock before I turn the handle and open the door. Mark is seated behind a desk at the front of his room. His hands are positioned on his desk like he's about to push himself up. His eyes are locked on me. "What happened?" he asks.

The tears are pouring down my face, although I'm not sure when they started. "The Magician was using Chris and Steve for an assignment. I took over Steve so I could see what was happening. Tanya showed up, I think she teleported. She seemed to think the Magician was really Chris. They talked about a lot of things that don't really make sense to me right now. But it's not important. You have to find them." My voice is getting loud, too loud for the little room.

Mark stands up fully. I expect him to come to us so I'm shocked when he turns his back on us, facing the wall. "I was afraid of something like this. I will need to go. Someone may be in trouble. I'll scry for Tanya, you're sure she was there."

"Yes, but she's hurt. Chris, or the Magician or whoever was in there …" my voice breaks. "It was awful."

Mark turns and looks over his shoulder at us both. "It's time to tell her everything, Cheryl. We cannot wait to see which of them becomes the next Magician."

Beside me I'm aware of a small movement from Cheryl, possibly a nod. I watch as the wall becomes the scene I just left in South Dakota. He doesn't wait for me to give him more, he just steps into the circle.

Alone in the room, I turn to Cheryl. "Tell me what?"

"You better sit down," she commands. "This isn't going to be pleasant."

I do as she asks and drop into the nearest chair. Hastily, I swipe at the tears dotting my face. I'm not sure I understand what happened out there. I'm not sure I want to understand. But, if I'm supposed to take over at this place tomorrow, there are things I need to know. I keep silent and bring my eyes up to look at Cheryl's face.

Again, as I was this morning, I'm shocked by how much she's changed. Her eyes appear sunken and dark. She looks thinner than she did before, which is saying something. Even though she's more alert right now than she was before I took over Steve, something is clearly not right with her.

"Anyone can be born with a Magical spark," she begins. "Magical sparks are nature's way of marking you as a source for positive Magic. You can never develop a spark if you aren't born with one, but you can lose it."

"I know all that," I say. I'm frustrated. I'm scared. I don't want my time wasted.

She stops talking and fixes me with a glare that would make my mother proud. I decide to shut up and listen. I make it obvious that this is my new objective by shaking my head a little with my lips tightly squeezed together. "You can also be born with a dark spark," she says.

My resolve cracks. "What? That's not true. No, you can't."

This time, she smacks my knee. "Listen to me," she commands.

I grunt in frustration, but allow myself to be silenced.

"People born with the dark spark house dark Magic within themselves. It works exactly like the sparks you are used to with one huge exception. People with dark sparks have the ability to absorb darkness left out in the world without suffering from its influence."

She reaches up to her neck and frees the black necklace which I've seen before from under the collar of her plain white shirt. "People who have no spark inside them are susceptible to the rays of energy put off by a spark like yours. If you use Magic near or around them it sets loose an energy that is absorbed by a person and can be used. If, for example, you use your Magic to teleport yourself to the middle of a church to prevent some kind of massacre your Magic leaves a trace. That trace can go into a person and cause them to feel the need to help others, to rid the world of negativity, until the spark evaporates."

"But our business is in ridding the world of the dark sparks," I say.

"Yes." Cheryl leans down until our faces nearly touch. "If you were to use Magic while you are angry, hurt, or upset you put darkness out into the world. That can also linger and be absorbed by someone who has no spark. That is what we battle against."

She sits next to me and unclasps the necklace. She holds it in her cupped hands. "This is enchanted coal. When a Container goes to a scene they absorb all the dark energy into these stones." She holds them out to me.

Reluctantly, I cup my hands below hers and let her drop the necklace into my palms. Immediately I feel it. They're warm. They are almost pulsing with some kind of energy, practically vibrating along my skin. But the most obvious feeling is the instant anger that floods me. I drop the necklace. "What was that?" I ask, although I'm afraid I already know.

"The negative energy. It gets absorbed into these stones. You can usually feel it for a day or two before it would go back to feeling like coal again."

"But when I touched it, I felt it. Can't you feel it when you wear it?"

She takes her time answering. She picks up the necklace and slowly clips it back on. Then she smiles sadly at me. "It doesn't really affect me." She sighs. "I have a dark spark."

So many things bounce through my head at once; why didn't I know, how long has this been going on, when did this start, who else has this, what does it mean? Unfortunately, the thoughts are stuck and twisting like cold spaghetti in my head. I keep opening my mouth to let one loose and then snapping it shut again because I can't break one free.

Cheryl sighs. "It's not what you think. I'm not going to break into some massive crime spree." A little chuckle escapes her lips. "It means I am open to the darkness in the world. I can connect with it, feel it, tap into it." She sighs again, this one bigger and somehow more emotional. "It means I am one of the few people who can contain that darkness and really get it off the streets once and for all."

"Okay, wait." I finally grab hold of a question. I reach out and lay my hand gently on her arms as a way of proving to her, and maybe myself, that I know she isn't dangerous. "I thought dark sparks were responsible for crime and things. Isn't that how it works?"

"They are, in the wrong hands," she says.

"But you've always been dark?"

"Always."

"Did you know that? Like, before?"

"Not until Mark told us it was possible."

Us. The implication of that one world feels heavy in the room. "Frank is dark, too," I say.

Cheryl nods. "And Mark. That's why he's training us. Apparently every Container ever is dark. That makes us the only ones who can hold the collected sparks without it negatively impacting us. There's a new Container every ten years or so. This is the first time there has been two."

"Like us?" I ask, referring to Tanya and I.

Cheryl shrugs. "Except both of us can be allowed to keep ours. Mark thinks having two Containers is a response to the amount of dark in the world. There's more dark so we need more dark, if that makes sense."

"None of this makes sense." I say, shaking my head. "This is all ..." I swallow audibly. "Insane," I finish. It's not an adequate response. The word doesn't capture what I'm feeling. Everything the Academy has ever told us suddenly feels like a lie under the weight of the half truths we've been fed. "What does all this have to do with Chris?" I ask, remembering the awful scene I just witnessed.

"Well, that's what I'm not sure of. Like you, there are things no one tells me."

"How are we supposed to do this with incomplete information?"

"I don't know, Ang. But I have ideas about Chris." She drops her voice. "I think the Magician has been corrupted with dark sparks. I think she thought, because Mark can handle it and she's been told she's the most powerful Magic in the world, that she could handle anything he could handle. I think she exposed herself to the dark."

"Does that mean she has both sparks?" I ask.

"I think so. But she wasn't born dark, like I was. She was born light. She can't handle the darkness inside her. She'll be feeling that sick, heavy feeling you got a glimpse of when you touched my necklace. She's susceptible to its hatred. It's making her unstable and very, very dangerous."

December 31

Tanya

January 1, Age 30

Emily

I'm not in the room for the ceremony but I feel a difference the second it is complete. It's like someone spun a dimmer switch toward the off position on my own spark. I'm not empty, it's not gone. But I feel like I am no longer connected to everyone else with a spark. I take a deep breath and revel at my ability to relax for the first time in probably ten years.

Tom smiles at me. "You feel that?" he asks.

"What does it feel like?" my father sits up a little, dropping the relaxed posture he'd had up to this point.

"Like I just put down the barbell after doing an exhausting number of deadlifts," Tom answers.

"Freeing," I offer.

Dad shakes his head. "You two just gave the power of all the Magic in the world over to a couple of preteens who are barely able to control their own sparks." He reaches for his tumbler of amber liquid I suspect is alcohol and takes a swig, ice cubes tinkling against the class. "Don't sound so happy about it."

"This is a good thing," I tell him. I've told him this before. In fact, both Tom and I have told him countless times in the last week or so. "We are still planning on being right here on campus at all times. We both plan to be in the control room a lot, although admittedly not as often as we have been. Everything is going to be fine."

"Emily, with all due respect to the two of you and what you have done, you don't know that," Dad says. "Have you considered what could happen if these children cannot work together as well as the two of you have?"

I close my eyes to keep myself from rolling them and draw a slow breath through my nose. His worrying and concern is coming from a good place, I remind myself. He means well. "Yes, we have considered that. We believe that the World of Magic chose them because they can handle the position." I open my eyes and force a smile. "We will be there to guide them."

"We will watch them for signs that they cannot handle the pressure, cannot get along, don't want to continue to work with the government contracts, and to ensure that they remember the balance is always in the World of Magic and not in us," Tom offers. "We know the risks but we also know that we were both feeling burned out and that wasn't good for anyone."

"I understand," Dad answers. I hate that, for even a heartbeat, I let myself think he may only understand because Tom explained it. That's ridiculous, surely. Dad has always been trusting of me and my gift. This isn't about choosing Tom as a favorite over me. He's just heard it enough to finally understand what we're saying.

"Besides," Tom continues "Emily and I can always take back control if we feel like it would be in the best interests of Magic."

"Right," I say. But already I can tell them that will never happen. Now that I've taken off the weight I was carrying I know I would never willingly put it back on. I just have to do my best to keep things going smoothly.

Support. That is my new role.

January 1

Angela

I don't sleep that night at all. I stare at different parts of my ceiling, thinking about Tanya. I keep hoping my phone will ring with a call or a text message that updates me. Someone telling me that she's ok. Someone telling me what hospital she's been moved to. But nothing happens. No one calls.

Finally, at 5:28 I give up and get out of bed. I cross to the wall that is the most wide open, move a few things out of my way, and stare down the expanse. "Ok," I say out loud, "I've never done this before. Not really. I've seen it done and I've used a small portal to peek. But this is different. I'm going to try this." I look down at my hands like they are windows to my Magic spark. "Please work," I whisper.

Closing my eyes and focusing on Chris, I wave my hands in a circle on the wall before me. I feel a tingling in my palms, but I force myself not to focus on that. I think about Chris. Not just what he looks like, but what he sounds like. What he smells like. I remember the feeling of side hugs and handshakes, real tangible things that represent Chris.

My hands start to burn, but I don't move them away. Instead, I open my eyes.

Before me on the wall is an image that breaks my heart. I'm looking through the bars into a jail cell and Chris is sitting in an orange jumpsuit on a metal shelf along a brick wall opposite them. He looks exhausted, haggard. Exactly how I'm feeling myself, magnified.

I take a deep breath and step through the wall.

"Angela?" Chris says, startled.

I look back over my shoulder, watching the portal shrink closed. "I learned how to make a portal," I say. When I turn my eyes back to Chris, the tears are instant. "Oh my God, Chris. I think Tanya is dead."

Chris rubs his face with his hands. "That's why I'm here." As if that makes him remember, he shudders. Then he stands up. "You can't be here. There's bound to be cameras trained on this room. You have to go. They think I …" he closes his eyes.

"It wasn't you. I was there. I was watching. She took over your body. She was inside you."

"Who?"

"The Magician. At least that's what Tanya thought. I don't really have time to explain it. But I'll figure something out. You can't be held responsible for this." I take a small step closer to him. "I'll figure something out."

"Listen, Ang. You have to go. Seriously." His voice is urgent, fast. "But there's something you have to do for me. You need to go into Tanya's room and find a small flash drive. I have no idea where she would've hidden it. Take every single one you find in her room if you have to. She's got documents saved on there that prove something is going on at that school. We were planning to wait until she became the Magician and then release them."

There are more important things to worry about right now, so his words shouldn't sting. But they do. I feel like he slapped me right across the face. He was meeting with Tanya, making plans with Tanya? They were planning for what would happen when Tanya was the next Magician? The betrayal is strong but I have to swallow it and face the tasks at hand. I take a breath that rattles through my chest. "I can try to get in there. What kind of stuff are we talking about?"

Chris' head is already shaking before I can even get the question out. "Nothing I can explain. Not in here. Just find it, Ang. It's important. Please."

"I'll try."

His eyes are bloodshot and he looks as torn up about all this as I am. But knowing that Chris, who I thought of as an innocent victim in all of this, was really someone who had information before today feels like the ultimate betrayal.

"I should go," I say. I want to ask him if there's anyone in my life who wasn't hiding something from me. I want to ask if anyone thought I could actually handle the secrets they knew. But he's not the person to answer that. Obviously, he can't be trusted to tell the truth anyway.

Instead, I turn to a blank concrete wall on my right. This time, when I move my hands in a circle, the portal opens right away and I'm looking back into my bedroom at The Academy.

I step through without another word and let the portal close at my back. I will find that flash drive, I will get answers. Then, I'll take my post as the next Magician and keep learning. Enough is enough. I'm taking back The Academy.

JANUARY 1

ANGELA

My cell phone rings, startling me. I'm in the middle of Tanya's dorm room, where I've been for the last hour or so. She is surprisingly organized. Was surprisingly organized. Oh, man, I'll have to get used to that. Anyway, her stuff is all in neat little piles. That should be a good thing, but I can't find any flash drives. Not a single one.

I look down at my phone. The caller id has never been wrong before so I close my eyes as I bring the phone up to my ear, dreading this conversation. The Magician is calling me. That cannot be good. "Hello?" My voice comes out suspicious, doubtful.

"Angela, why are you not at rehearsal?" she asks.

"Oh, I lost track of time." I sigh out a breath. "I can be there in -- "

"Hang up your phone, please," she says. But the voice is not coming from my cell phone. I open my eyes to find myself on the stage with the Magician in front of me. "Let's begin, shall we?"

The same man from our previous rehearsal is standing center stage. Was that just yesterday? It's almost scary how much has happened since then. It doesn't seem possible that this little man is still standing there, ready to lead me through rehearsal like nothing has happened. But this time the Magician is standing beside him. Her shoulders are rolled back, her head is held high. If I had any doubt how much I hated her before this moment, I don't now. Everything inside me wants to rush at her, knock her off the stage. A good old-fashioned cat fight. If I thought, for one millisecond, that she'd fight fair, I'd do it.

Instead, I grind my teeth as I stare her down.

"Take your position, please," the man commands.

I do as he says, but I don't take my eyes off her. I recite the lines I've been told to say. I stand in all the right places. I want her to see me do this. I want her to watch me practice the ceremony that will give me all the power in the Academy.

I'm going to take it all away from her at midnight.

After the run-through, she does something that unnerves me. She smiles. "This will certainly be easier with only one of them," she says. Her voice is bubbly and light.

It has the opposite effect on me, making me feel like I'm being weighed down. Reality rushes back in. Tanya won't be here tonight. Tanya who knew she would win. Tanya who had some kind of information that could bring this whole organization crashing down. She's not here. She's never going to be here again.

"It certainly is different, yes," the man agrees. "More like the old days. Sad what happened to that girl though. She seemed nice enough yesterday. Odd, sure, but nice."

"Yes, none of us expected this from Chris. He was a loose cannon but I never suspected he was dangerous." Her eyes turn away from the old man and back to me, almost as if her final words are for me. "I guess we can never know what kind of danger lurks under a person's skin."

"Am I free to go?" I ask.

"Absolutely, my dear. The rehearsal was well done. You are ready," the man acknowledges with a small wave of his hand. "The ceremony begins at midnight. You'll need to be back here at 11:15, sharp. We will have people here to help you get into the right outfit and prepare yourself."

"I'll be here," I say. Then I click on my cell phone and glance at the time. I have just under eight hours to find that flash drive. It has to be enough time. I step off the stage into the darkened wing. Then, without asking for permission, I close my eyes and focus on Tanya's bedroom. I imagine myself being transported right back there. When I open my eyes, it's done. Already my spark is stronger. I don't know if it's because of the ceremony tonight or because of Tanya. Did her spark go back into the Magic community? Is that how this works?

Again a frustration builds in my chest. The entire point of dragging me away from my family for the last thirteen years of my life, making me attend school up here at the Academy, was to train me to be the next Magician. We are supposed to be learning how to control our spark, how to use our spark, how to keep people safe. But it seems like all I keep uncovering is secret after secret. I need answers.

That reminds me why I'm here. I have to focus on finding whatever this is that Tanya has hidden. "Why a flash drive?" I ask out loud. "Why an antiquated piece of technology when you're surrounded by Magic? Why not something newer?" As I question her decision, I turn myself in small circles at the center of the room. Looking for something, anything, that may hide the answers.

"Obviously you didn't want anyone to find it, which is why you couldn't put it in some cloud server. And, I assume, you didn't trust anything that was Academy owned or purchased. So the flash drive must have been bought while you were home." My eyes land on a couple of small bags hanging from the footboard of her bed. Could it be that simple?

The smaller bag hangs in front. It looks like a purse. Simple, black. I take everything out of the large compartment, which doesn't take me long. There's a small wallet, a cherry flavored chapstick, a mostly empty water bottle, and a pair of nail clippers. I open the wallet, also black, to find an ID card from Texas and a loyalty shopping card from a supermarket.

I run my hands along the inside of the bag, feeling for rips or bulges in the lining. I find a small pocket, zipped shut, along the side. I pull everything out of that pocket. Six gift cards to various restaurants, a nail file, medicated chapstick that smells like eucalyptus even with the cap on, and a small bottle of hand sanitizer. The pile of random things that are certainly not a flash drive is growing on the carpet of the floor.

Frustrated, I run my hands along the lining again, slower this time. I don't feel any other pockets, just a small hole at the bottom of the bag. I toss the bag out of my way, my eyes already falling on the backpack that was hanging behind it.

Something in the bag rustles.

I freeze, slowly turning my head back toward the black bag. I hold my breath, listening. Nothing. No noise at all. I reach for the bag and pull it back into my lap. This time I feel it and hear it. There is something rattling around in the purse. The empty purse.

I turn on the flashlight of my phone and shine it into the purse, confirming that it is empty. I shake it slowly, listening to the sound of something scraping along the bottom. Something small, like a flash drive.

I propel myself off the floor and toward the desk where I spotted scissors earlier. I don't spare a second worrying about the purse. I dig the end of the scissors into the soft black lining and shred it right up the middle. There, like a sleeping giant, is a single black and silver flash drive.

January 1

Angela

I consider the same safety precautions I thought about in Tanya's dorm room. I disconnect my laptop from the Academy network, going completely offline. Then I make sure my door is locked. I plug in the flash drive and click on the folder icon to open my options.

Inside the folder there is a video, two jpegs, and a document. I suppose I should start with the document. I click on it and wait for it to load all the way before I allow myself to start reading.

To Whom it May Concern,

As of this morning, I am the new Magician at the institution known as the Academy. In this capacity I have become privy to some information that, in my opinion, needs to be given to the public. Before today, you were left in the dark on many things. I will attempt to enlighten you to those secrets to the best of my ability.

[Insert plan for Academy moving forward as it is figured out by committee. Do not decide this alone.]

I read the little paragraph twice. Tanya's plan was to expose Magic to the world? Why? What am I missing?

I scroll down to the second page, hoping to find the answers there.

The purpose of the Academy, as we understood it as students, was to control the spread of dark Magic in the world. What we didn't know and couldn't have known was that the dark acts were being initiated by the head of our school.

"What?" My voice echoes in the empty room. I push the laptop away from me and cover my mouth. That is a big claim. That is a huge claim. If that were true …

I stop myself. Because is that really far outside of the possibilities? Is anything anymore? I would've told you using underage students in real situations wasn't happening here and look how wrong I was about that. I would have told you the head of Magic for the entire World would never murder someone and pin it on one of her students. And yet …

I pull the laptop back to me and keep reading.

On {DATE} the UN met to discuss the continuation of the Academy plan, to keep the school open and utilize the Magic users to keep the world safe. There was some disagreement about this being the best course for the UN at this time.

{Three days} after this open discourse there was a terrorist attack in a country that openly disputed the Academy. My mother, who was serving in the American Naval forces in that country, was killed during this attack. At the time it was suspected that the Magician knew about the attack beforehand, as was the

procedure at the Academy, but chose not to act. The truth, I must warn you, is worse.

[Show video 1]

My breath catches. I reduce the page and double click to open Video 1 from the flash drive. My screen fills with the image of the control room. I assume this is the real control room. The Magician is standing before the screens, her back to the camera. For half a second I want this to be someone else. I want someone to be impersonating her or manipulating her screens. But she turns her head to the right and that profile leaves no doubt.

She turns away from her screens and opens a portal on the right hand wall. But she doesn't step through. She conjures up a box of some kind, reaches her hand through the portal, and sets the box down on what looks like a street. Then she closes the portal and turns her attention to the screen.

On her screens she calls up a location. Then she dials a number on her cell phone. "I need a Solver on the ground." She gives an address and then waits as what I assume is Dispatch tells her how long it will take. "Unacceptable. Teleport someone to that location. Thank you." She hangs up. Then, as is procedure, a text message comes in with the information to connect her. She dials.

I listen as the Magician gives directions to bring the Solver to the location. If I hadn't watched her put that box there this would be an ordinary video of just another case. Then, on screen, something must go wrong. Instead of a successful solve, we watch as the entire screen lights up with fire.

The Magician continues to stare at it. She's not shocked, she's not worried, she doesn't cry. She just stands there, staring at the flames as though hypnotized.

The video ends. I'm a little confused. Sure, it seemed suspicious, but where did this video come from? Did she actually plant that box on the scene? Was that the box that detonated? I click back to the document and continue reading.

The crime scene reports from the local law enforcement officials say the device was a small bomb in a box, resembling a package not unlike the one we saw the Magician portalling to that location on the video. While this is not conclusive on its own, investigations reveal that the person responsible for the crime was also the Solver on the phone with the Magician in that video. At best, this means the person previously known as the Magician knowingly conspired with the Solver for the crime. This solution seems far fetched considering that Solver had to be teleported to that location. It is entirely more likely that the worse-case scenario, the Magician took over the body of that Solver for the crime, is what actually happened.

I lean back on the wall behind me and take a deep breath.

This can't be happening. This should be in the hands of the police or the government. Someone who can answer for what the Magician has done. Someone smarter than me.

January 1

Angela

As promised, I am not late. The flash drive is nestled in the safest place I can think of. A place I can't imagine anyone accidentally checking. It's in the left cup of my bra, nestled right up against my boob. There's just enough padding on my bra to make it impossible to spot, even if you are staring in the mirror looking for it. I checked.

I spend the entire wardrobe time stressed that someone will accidentally discover the flash drive. The makeup girl who is attempting to give me a face for the full audience of Magic users keeps making a strange, disapproving noise when she has to blot at my forehead with a tissue. Apparently sweating and makeup are not a good mix.

I manage to get through the entire process. It takes three women who are better at preparing for public appearances than I am, a whole lot of makeup, what feels like a full can of hairspray, a bucket full of pins for my hair, and one navy blue pants suit. Finally, I'm standing before a full length mirror admiring the work they've done. I look like I'm ready for all of this.

The Magician opens the door, wearing her customary black robe. A second robe is draped loosely over her arm. "I thought I'd bring you the accessory you'll spend the next ten years wearing for our cause," she says. The folded black garment quivers a little as if it knows she's talking about it. "Are you nervous?"

Nervous is not the word I would use. Angry. Frustrated. Scared. Those are more appropriate. "I'm ready," I say in lieu of correcting her. Ready to take the Academy away from her. Ready to understand what the files on this flash drive mean. Ready to find out what secret Tanya paid for with her life.

"Good." She drapes the black robe over the back of the makeup chair between us. "I'll see you out there. I'll be standing in the back of the auditorium, as is customary. Symbolically that places everyone in the Magical community between the two of us. I am passing them from my hands to yours." She traps my eyes with her hard gaze. "Take good care of them," she says.

Before I can find words to answer this command she pivots herself around and leaves the room. I sigh out a breath and follow.

The ceremony feels like it's happening to someone else, which is silly since I'm center stage. The bright lights are brutal, searing the memory of this moment into every exposed pore of skin it can find. I stand there, silently, as I was taught. A few people come out of the wings holding canisters. A circle of dirt is poured. "We root this apprentice to the earth," someone says. Someone else holds up a canister of salt. "We ward off disturbances." A circle of salt is poured on top of the soil.

Then it's my turn. Everyone backs off from the circles they've created, fading back into the wings of the stage. I'm alone under the bright lights. I know there are people out there. The Magician will be standing at the back of the room. I turn my gaze toward where she would be, if I could see anything other than bright white. I close my eyes against the blinding light. I take a centering breath and focus on saying the words loudly, projecting them to the entire room.

"I ask you to bear witness today as I take control of the Magic sparks around me. Magician is a title that commands respect and yet it is a title that reminds those who bear it that they are no longer individuals. Those with the title of Magician must stand for all who have given them sparks. When you give me control of your spark today, you will be entrusting me with your safety and security."

I open my eyes as I make the final promise. "I promise to use my power to control the spread of dark energy in the world and prevent the damages it can cause."

The feeling takes my breath away. It's like being knocked over by a huge wave in the ocean. Every spark in the building rushes at me at once. I see them all. I take a stumbling step backwards under their power and feel my head knock backwards until I'm staring up at the ceiling.

I feel them course through my veins. Each pulsating light brings a connection to a person in the room. If I were to focus on one of them I could access everything. Their memories, their emotions, their dreams, their hopes.

I right myself, standing up straight again, and look out over the audience. The lights must have dimmed a little because I can see everyone. My eyes rake over each one, my body automatically accessing their spark enough that I could name every single person in attendance. I realize, with a start, that I could take over their movements and their bodies with the blink of my eye or the flick of my wrist.

This power is intoxicating. It's shocking.

It's too much.

I am not supposed to say anything else. I am supposed to turn and leave the stage now. I hear the small girl from before making her way back onto the stage. I hear her announce me to the room. "Ladies and gentlemen, the Magician."

The applause starts but my voice stops it. "I promise not to abuse that which you have given me," I say.

My eyes fall on her at that moment and I don't stop the memories of the woman who is Francheska from pouring into me.

I take it all in.

Every last second.

January 2

Angela

Her memories are staggering. Shocking. I have so many answers but still so many questions. It's past midnight when I stumble off the stage and into the waiting arms of Mark. "You'll be all right," he whispers. "Just come with me." I let him wrap his arm around my shoulders and lead me out of the stage wings, down a corridor, and into a room. He sits me down on a desk and shuts the door behind us. The lights are already on but a quick glance around the room tells me it's empty. I throw my shoulders back and meet his intense gaze.

"There is a lot we were lied to about," I start. I can't think of a more intense word so I just repeat it. "A lot."

"Yes." He shoves his hands into the pockets of his jeans. "But you're in charge now. So you can change whatever you want. Including what we tell people and what they know."

I let that information roll around in my head a little. I can change whatever I want. I guess I didn't really think of that until right this second. I nod. "I plan to make changes. But there's one thing I don't fully understand. Why Chris? She targeted him, that's clear in her memories. She was afraid of him, I feel that. But I don't understand why."

"We'll need to see the scans." Mark takes his right hand out of his pocket and snaps his fingers. A small, unassuming black tablet appears in his hand. "First, yours." He clicks a button to turn on the tablet. He doesn't use Magic, perhaps because he wants me to know this is all real. He clicks on a search box at the top and types in my name.

There's a single image on the screen, a blank white human form that would normally be used for indicating a men's restroom. When he's done typing my name, the image changes. It's the same outline but now the black background is swirling with white smoke. "This is your Magic scan image. It's automatically set to fill with the color that is the highest contrast for your Magic, so black background is the computer's choice. The smoky things you're seeing are your spark. You have a lot of it." That's apparent by the fact that the entire image is filled with it.

He clicks on the search bar again. I'm expecting him to type in Chris' name so I'm a little surprised when he types in Cheryl Lasse. The image changes again. This time the background stays white but fills with black smoke. I gasp. "That's what she meant," I say.

"Cheryl is not the only one. You can search for Frank or myself and you'd find the same thing. We have a dark spark. This used to mean we were set to be Containers. Our power rivals yours." He's right. Cheryl's scan is completely full of black smoke like mine was full of white. Hardly any empty space. "Remember the smoke is what you're looking at. The background means nothing. Someone who has no spark at all appears a solid blue, actually. It's the color the developers chose so we could verify the scan had worked but no Magic is apparent in the system."

Now he clicks the search box and types in Chris Marshall.

The background is now green. But inside, that takes my breath away. "It's beautiful," I whisper. The white smoke dances lazily around the limbs of the figure. But around his heart and head the smoke is black. They dance and twist, caught in a waltz we don't understand. Mark powers off the tablet.

"Now you'll need to decide what to do with this information. The public doesn't know about Magic anymore. Governments all over the World have seen fit to keep people in the dark. Those that do know about it don't trust it. Even fewer people understand dark sparks. Now these abnormalities like Chris appear." He shakes the tablet. "You have to decide what we do with information like this. We're on new ground here. People appearing with both black and white sparks are unusual. You may not like how she handled that, and I don't blame you. But what will you do about it?"

January 2

Angela

The meeting with the new committee goes well.

MY new committee, I remind myself. It's strange to think of all this as mine now. My school, my control of Magic sparks, my assistants, my Container.

My mistakes. My consequences.

It's enough to take my breath away.

Cheryl taps my hand. "Are you all right?" she asks.

I nod. "I will be. This is good, everything we came up with today." I gesture around the conference room where we just sat making all the big decisions for the future of the Academy.

"It will be different," she says, grimacing. "People may not take it well."

I nod. "But it's the right thing to do and that is what matters."

An older man, a Magic user I just met who apparently bank rolls a lot of our operations here, stops on his way out to turn back to me and smile. "I'll have Mr. Marshall back here in time for the press conference," he says.

I nod at him, the best I can do. Something inside me believes him. It should be difficult to get someone out of jail. For the average person it would be. Yet something tells me it will not be difficult for this rich Magic user. Perhaps nothing truly is.

My eyes scan the crowd leaving through the door and fall on one man in all black slipping out into the hallway. "Where is Mark going?" I ask.

Cheryl shrugs. "He didn't say."

"I have a weird feeling about him," I tell her.

She tilts her head sideways. "Bad feeling in your gut or in your spark?"

I stop to ponder her question. It almost feels like my entire body is humming with the idea that I should be following him. "I think it might be in my spark," I tell her. "I think I should follow him." I push my chair back, intending to stand.

Cheryl puts pressure on my arm. "I have a better idea," she says. She gestures to the blank wall of the conference room on her right and a portal starts to form. "Let's just watch."

On the wall we watch the hallway of the school rush past. Wherever Mark is going, he's going in a hurry. He turns a corner and enters the room that has always been his office. Technically, Mark is no longer the Container. That's the role Cheryl officially took on at midnight. The office is full of boxes in the process of being packed up with everything personal Mark may have had in the office. He shuts the door behind him and crosses to the blank wall he's used before. He opens a portal, which gives Cheryl and I an odd sort of watery connection. We can still see it but it's not as clear as the one we're using.

We can tell Mark is rushing through a map quickly. This is a sure sign he is trying to scry for someone, zooming around places they have recently been. "Who is he looking for?" Cheryl asks.

I shouldn't know this answer but my spark provides it anyway. "Her," I say. Cheryl doesn't have to ask who I mean. "I just wish I knew why he wanted to find her."

"Let's wait and see," she offers. "We can always teleport there if something is going on."

Francheska, the former Magician, has been on the run from police since the moment I took office. I tried to reach out for her earlier, during the committee meeting. I can feel her presence, but not good enough to find her. I wonder if Mark will be more lucky. I also wonder why he didn't volunteer to do just that while we were in the meeting.

On the wall in front of Mark the zooming slows and then comes to a stop. Mark is looking at a cabin in the middle of the woods. "He got her," Cheryl says. "What do you think he'll do?"

Again, I should not know this answer. I have the distinct feeling it's somehow Magic that knows it, not simply me. "He's going to talk to her," I whisper.

Mark steps through the wall, which has become a portal. Our point of view switches, as if we are looking through a first person virtual reality game. We watch as he draws closer to the cabin and opens the front door. Francheska is seated on the floor, her back to the door. "Hello Mark," she calls. "I wondered when you'd come."

"Are they working together?" Cheryl says.

"I seriously hope not," I answer.

Mark crosses the room and looks down at Francheska's face. "There's a lot of people looking for you," he says. "What's your endgame here?"

She sighs. "Would you believe I never had one? I never thought that far in advance. My entire goal was to keep that school open, to get the government to keep our funding in place."

"The things they're saying you did," Mark begins. He shakes his head as if finishing the thought pains him. "I didn't know how bad it was."

"If that's true it's only because you didn't want to know," she says, waving her hand. "I could see and feel everything you did from the moment we took office. We were completely connected, a perfect pair. If you didn't know what I was doing you have only yourself to blame."

He shakes his head. "I'll do plenty of blaming myself for the next few years. Make no mistake about that." He takes a step closer to Francheska and points down at her, his expression darkening. "But this is all on you. You made a decision that costs people their lives. You put the kids we were responsible for at risk. You might have killed Tanya."

"I visited her," she whispers.

My breath catches in my throat. "Is Tanya still alive?" I whisper.

"I can't feel her," Cheryl says. "I thought that meant --" she lets her voice trail off. It's clear what she thought. I thought the same thing.

I shrug. "A group of people left to visit her in the hospital. I thought maybe they were, you know, being cautious and erasing memories if necessary. Now I'm wondering if they may have been stripping her of her spark." It's funny, having all this control. It's like Magic somehow knows these answers. As if being connected to all these other Magic users has given me the answers, I just have to trust Magic to lead me. Knowing all that, I really don't understand how Francheska let herself get so out of control.

"Why?" Mark asks Francheska. "Why visit her? Why risk that?"

"She needed to have a mind wipe. Do you know what she knows? I can't let that be out there in the world."

Mark laughs, the sound bouncing off the walls of the cabin. "Angela knows everything."

She nods and somehow the gesture looks sad. "She wasn't ready, that girl."

I scoff and resist the urge to call her a foul name.

"They're going to change everything, aren't they?" she asks.

Mark nods. "They're putting things right. Everything you messed with, everything your ancestors messed with. It's been wrong up there for a long time. This group is going to fix it. It's on their shoulders now."

"And what will you do?"

Mark sighs, long and deep. I feel his sadness reverberate inside me like an echo. "You've condemned me to a life of guilt and second guessing. I don't belong in that world anymore. Not after what I allowed you to do. You should turn yourself in."

"That's not going to happen," she whispers.

"I figured as much." He runs his hands through his hair. "I can feel how damaged you are. Something you did caused damage to your spark."

I reach for her and suddenly I can feel what he is feeling. He's right. The reason I couldn't reach her before is that something has damaged her. She is a shell of what she once was. It's like looking for a match that was once giving off bright light in the darkness of a cave but now it's been blown out. The heat is there, but it cannot give light anymore.

"I dabbled in your dark spark and when Angela took control, I lost a lot of my own. I'm nothing like I was. There's hardly anything left."

"You know I have to take even that," he says. He kneels down before her and she smiles at him, their faces now closer. "I cannot leave you with anything you can use to the detriment of what is left."

"I've done enough," she agrees. "It's time."

Cheryl and I watch and Mark holds his hands out to Francheska. She slips her hands into his, their palms touching. She closes her eyes. Because I am so in tune with the Magic inside Mark I can feel that he is interfering. It's as if he's wrapping his hands around the spark inside Francheska, holding her spark inside of his. Then, I feel him squeeze until there's a small pop.

Francheska sighs. Her eyes open.

"It is done," Mark says.

"I am free," she answers. "It is more than I deserved."

"No one else in the world will be as kind if they are to find you," he says.

"After today, there is no part of me they will be able to reach for."

Cheryl lays her hand on my shoulder. "Do you want to teleport there now, get her under arrest? If he leaves, we'll never find her again."

I shake my head. "She is not Magic. She is not our domain any longer. Perhaps the police will find her." I swipe my hand along the wall, turning off the portal. "I also suspect we will never see Mark again."

"Perhaps that's for the best," Cheryl says. Still, she sounds as sad as I feel. Things will never be the same again.

Fall, Age 12

Tanya

I drop the newspaper with the shocking headline about the explosion on the base from all those years ago on the table between my father and I. "We need to talk about this," I say. I see his eyes flit to it and immediately back to me. Already I can tell he's going to say no. "I found someone at school who could investigate it. He's rich. His family has a lot of money. His Dad died that day too and they hired someone to look into it."

"Let it go, Tanya." He sounds tired.

"I can't. They already looked." I pull the little black and silver flash drive out of the pocket of my skinny jeans. "I want you to watch this video they found."

"No." He stands up. "Asking questions can absolutely get you in trouble. Your mother isn't going to come back because you find out why she died. Things happen, Tanya." He shakes his head. "Please, let it go."

My eyes fill with tears. I want nothing more than to be able to let this go. Because what I've learned changes everything. What I've learned means the lady who's been entrusted with running the school I'm supposed to keep hidden, the lady I'm supposed to be looking up to, is dangerous. "You don't understand," I whine. "It's so much worse than just an accident."

He's already turning around, walking away from me. "I'm sorry, Tanya. I don't have time for these crazy theories. I have to get to work."

I call Chris as soon as my father is out of the room. "What is your mother going to do with the file?" I ask, hoping for something better than what I just heard.

The sigh gives away his answer before he has to tell me. "Nothing. She said it doesn't prove anything, it was probably illegally obtained, and she wants to move on."

"This is on us," I say. Part of me knows we're too young for all this. But a bigger part of me knows everyone else will be afraid to take her on. We have no choice.

"I'm with you, T," Chris agrees. "Whatever it takes."

Spring, Age 83

Emily

I am dying. I've had a good life, I suppose. I got to live through more adventure than most people. I got to experience Magic. I opened a school. I had a part in training thousands of Magic users in how to use their spark appropriately. I spoke in front of world leaders on more than one occasion. I fell in love, I had children, I have grandchildren. I traveled the world. I have fears and I've made mistakes. But I have no regrets. Not really.

My daughter stands up when someone knocks on the hospital door. "Come in," she calls. She squeezes my hand. "I'm going to go down and get a coffee. I'll be right back." She's being polite, I'm sure. Leaving me to say goodbye to whomever this is that has come calling in my final hours. She could Magically pop coffee into existence, we both know that. But she won't.

I turn my eyes to the doorway in time to watch my daughter squeeze by Tom, who is coming in. "Hey there," he says to her. "How are you?"

She spares a quick glance back at me. "I'm all right, thank you for asking," she says.

He drops into the chair my daughter vacated with a sigh. He grabs my hand, automatically squeezing. "Em, how are you feeling? Are you in any pain?"

"Not today," I tell him. "They've put me on some pain killers and Magic took the rest of the edge off." I don't have long. The doctors say it could be weeks but something tells me it's more like days, hours maybe. "Thanks for coming."

"Of course." He raises my hand to his lips and kisses the back of my hand. "Whatever you need."

"I want to talk about the Academy," I tell him.

He shakes his head. "No. Let's not talk about work."

"It's important, please."

He nods. "Make it quick."

"We need to talk about my granddaughter." He closes his eyes as if pained by my choice of topic. "It's time for the truth, Tom." It's not a question, but I wait for him to nod. "I'm sure you remember the reason why she wasn't allowed to become the Magician," I begin.

"There was an accident," Tom says. "I remember. But wasn't it your daughter's call, ultimately?"

"Sort of." I squeeze his hand. My daughter, the one who just left the room, spent ten years as the Magician when she was around twenty. After her time there she started a family. Then, her own daughter presented with a strong spark. She was taken to the Academy and trained as the next Magician. But there was a second girl with a spark that was almost as strong. Three months before my granddaughter was supposed to take over as Magician there was an accident. "There were three students on the scene the night of the accident," I remind Tom. I know the memories of that night will not be burned into his brain like they are on my own. "My granddaughter, the boy named Shawn, and a girl named Sonia."

"All right," Tom says.

"They were not supposed to be there. No one from the Academy knows why they decided to open a portal that brought them to Mexico. None of the students knew anyone in Mexico and there didn't appear to be a crime at that location at the time," I continue. I know that, since that day, the Academy has agreed to stop teaching students how to open a portal, for their safety.

"I think I remember these details," Tom says.

"Right. The part we decided to keep quiet comes next." I see the hurt cross his face. He has always suspected that I kept secrets about the Academy from him, I think. But this is proof. It's a good thing, I suppose, that I don't have long left. Because it pains me to see how much I have hurt him. "One of the three of them was putting out some disturbance at that time, creating a darkness that was picked up on the scanner. The Magician sent a Solver to the location. It took a few minutes before one arrived on the scene."

"Darkness is a common problem among children of that age with sparks, Em," he says as though trying to reassure me. It's a habit, I assume. Because we both know he'll keep listening as long as I am telling him a story I find important. Deathbed confessions are a cliche for a reason.

"But the Solver arrived in time to see what ultimately happened. My granddaughter was sitting on the curb beside the building when the fire started. She wasn't indoors."

Tom startles. "I thought she never became the Magician because she injured her spark in the fire."

I hold his eyes. "We took her spark from her."

Tom's eyes widen in surprise. "Why?"

"The Solver ran to the building when the fire started, as they're trained to run into danger. There was a young girl, Sonia, who made it out safely. The boy, as you know, did not. But the Solver said there was an argument between the two girls."

"Argument? What did they argue about?"

"He didn't know. So when I saw her, I had to find out what she was hiding."

"She was a candidate for Magician but you were still stronger than she was." He doesn't say it like a question. He knows how all of this works as well as I do.

"My daughter and I made the decision to combine our Magic to strip her of her spark when we learned she had gone to that location ahead of the other two. She had set that trap for them. She lured them there. It was not an accident. She intended them both to die."

Tom's face is a mask of horror. I can almost see the same questions and doubts I had all those years ago play out on his face. It takes him a few heartbeats to get his thoughts organized. "Why them? Why did she set up those two specifically?" he asks quietly.

"Sonia was the second most powerful white Magic at school and Shawn was the largest dark. He would've been her Container. My granddaughter saw them as competition and she was unwilling to let them best her." It hurts to say the words. I had to tap into my own granddaughter to read the emotions and this is what I have learned. I hate that I have to tell this secret, but Tom needs to know.

"You should've told me all of this," Tom says as if he read my mind.

"I know. You would've helped." I feel my eyes well up with tears. "But we were afraid of the judgement. We were afraid for that poor boy's family. The damage had already been done and stripping her of her Magic was the least we could do." The shuddering breath that rips through my lungs hurts, but I deserve it. "I'm sorry."

"Why now?" he asks. He runs his hands down his face and lets out a deep sigh. "There's more, isn't there? More than you telling me she killed a student. More than the regulations that have come since, forcing us to hide the Academy and Magic from the public." Tom pushes back from my bed just a little, putting space between us. Space for his anger, for his frustration. "Emily, I'm not going to like this, am I?"

"No," I answer honestly. "She grew up, got married, and had a child. Her daughter, my great granddaughter, Francheska, has presented with a spark."

Tom traps his face, lined with age, between his hands. "How strong?" he asks.

"Strong."

"White or dark?"

"White." I sigh. "Just like her mother."

He pushes himself out of the chair and starts pacing the small room. "I get what you're afraid of. I get that you're afraid being raised by her mother the desire for power might become overwhelming. But she's also white like you were. White like her grandmother was. There's a chance that the Academy is the right place for her. That she can be raised to be strong and good."

"Take her away from her mother," I say. "Please."

He stops at the foot of my bed and turns to face me. "What?"

"That can be a change. One I'm sure the world leaders will get behind. Instead of letting families know but keeping Magic a secret from everyone else, we should start keeping it a secret from anyone who doesn't have the spark. My granddaughter no longer has the spark. Francheska is young, she's only six. You can wipe her memory, wipe her mother's memory. Take her to the Academy. I don't know how the details will work, Tom. But my granddaughter was willing to kill people in order to be the strongest Magic user on that campus. She will influence her daughter, I just know it."

He shakes his head. "I can't do that, Em. I can't make that kind of promise." He crosses back to the chair, dropping heavily into it. "I will watch out for Francheska. I promise. I will make sure that she's influenced by the best people."

"And if she shows signs of being power hungry?" I ask. I know what I want him to say. I know what I would do.

He sighs. "If that happens, I'll take her spark." He grabs my hand, squeezes. "I promise."

I believe him. I can see in his gentle eyes that he means well. I offer him a smile. "Thank you."

"I wish you had told me sooner. But I'm glad you told me at all." He leans down and kisses me on the cheek. "I'll keep my eye on Francheska for you. We won't let her ruin everything we've built. You have my word."

January 2

Angela

"**M**y name is Angela Terra. As of midnight I am the Magician, keeper of the white Magic at the institution known as the Academy of Magic. I have had a chance to review the knowledge and memories associated with the position I am now holding, and have made some decisions. Please bear with me as I explain those. I will take questions at the end if time allows." I offer a small smile to the assembled reporters. Then I roll my shoulders back and continue.

"It has come to my attention that the public's knowledge of Magic has been severely redacted. In my opinion, the time has come to explain Magic to the general public. This is not a decision that makes me popular. But it is time nonetheless. At the time of birth, some people are born with a Magic spark. This spark, as it turns out, can be either white or black on a scan. Because of the nature of mythology, people at the Academy believed this to mean the person was capable of either good or bad Magic. This, I know for a fact, is incorrect." I clear my throat. No one moves at all. I take this as a sign that they are listening and continue.

"In previous years the Academy has invited students with a spark to our campus to train them in the ways of Magic. They were brought up to identify dark sparks in the world and eradicate them for the safety of everyone. At least, that's what those students were told.

"In reality, the students were releasing innocents from the spark, sending the dark Magic into the air. A person known as a Container, a mysterious profession even among the learned in our Magic community, would then absorb that darkness into themselves. The practice is dangerous, unstable, and unadvisable." I am sure the reporters in front of me will question the danger. I decide to wait on that explanation until they ask. There are other things I need to say.

"Recently, it has come to my attention that there is also a new breed of spark. Scans have revealed these new sparks began showing themselves about nine years ago, although we are not yet sure why. This spark presents as a swirl of both black and white. We are calling this the grey spark.

"I had a meeting with my small council of advisors this morning, and we have reached a few important conclusions. The Magic that was practiced at the Academy takes children away from their families while they complete their training. More importantly, what the students are learning at the Academy is often woefully incomplete knowledge based on incomplete assumptions. For this reason, effective immediately, the Academy as we know it will be closed." I pause for a second, in which I imagine that every Magic person who is watching this live on their television screens will have a moment of shock or outrage. I narrow my eyes at the camera, trying to show that I mean business.

"The Academy will become a training ground. Beginning at the end of this press conference we will be accepting applications for those adults with the spark to come learn more about the truth behind our abilities. They will begin developing new methods of containing loose Magic. They will learn about white and dark sparks, truly develop an understanding, and help my team revise the programs accordingly.

"The underage children with sparks will be returned to their family homes to attend traditional schools. They will each be given a mentor. Those pairings will be our first priority and will be made within the next week. I will personally oversee all mentors to ensure that the student's training is in line with our new direction and information that comes in from the Academy Research team."

I put my hands out to the sides of me to indicate the people who have been beside me the entire conference, silent. "This will no longer be an individual effort. In addition to my own knowledge and memories unlocked by the position I hold, we also have a few shining stars leading the way." I turn my head to the right, indicating whom I am introducing. "Cheryl Lasse,

Container, keeper of the dark Magic at the Academy." Then I turn my head to the left. "Chris Marshall, Solver, keeper of the grey Magic at the Academy."

I face the reporters again. "We will now take questions."

"Is the public in any immediate danger?" a man in a brown suit asks.

"No, we do not believe so. In fact, we believe that much of the danger that you were told about was actually the fault of the previous leader of the school."

"What is being done with her?" a woman in a power suit calls.

"We have reason to believe her Magic spark has been removed from her. She is currently being sought after by the police. As for the part the school can play, we are unsealing all Academy documents and cooperating fully with the investigation."

"Wasn't this man," the reporter points to Chris, "recently charged with a crime?"

I step back from the microphone a little and indicate Chris. "Perhaps he would like to speak for himself?" I ask.

Chris nods and I move aside to let him take the microphone. He looks amazingly handsome in his pressed black suit and white tie. I have never seen him dressed so adult before. He smiles a loose, friendly smile at the assembled guests before speaking. "Good afternoon. As Angela told you, my name is Chris. Recently, you are likely aware, I was apprehended at the scene of a violent crime where a fellow Magic user was injured. I want to make this very clear. I was not in full use of my body or mind at that time. I was being used by someone with a stronger Magical spark than mine.

"That seems like a convenient excuse, but Angela is now privileged to have access to the memories of the person who used my body as a vessel, meaning we now have the proof we need to clear my name for those charges." A few people in the audience smile at Chris. He's charming. He's winning them over, for sure. "More importantly, we now have proof that we have been dancing around for years. Many people in the Magic community have claimed similar incidents have happened to them over the years. Not just Solvers, who expected to be used for solving crime and stopping the spread of dark Magic. People have claimed to have been taken over for no obvious reason and used for purposes they are not aware of. We now have proof that is possible and probable." He sighs as if the information pains him, which I know it does.

"We hear you. We believe you." He leans on the podium in front of him and peers into the camera as if speaking directly to the Magical community watching at home. "We make these changes not to scare you or make you feel alone. We make these changes because it has been done wrong for too long and it's time someone stepped up to make it right." He straightens back up. "Thank you."

He turns to leave the podium again but someone shouts a question. "Are you a carrier of this grey spark Angela spoke of?"

He leans back to the microphone. "As far as we know I am the first person to be born with the spark that appears both black and white under scans. I was the only person in the Academy files with this spark. It is our belief that others exist and we aim to find them." This time, when he straightens up, he also walks away from the podium.

I step back to the microphone. "We will take two more questions and then we need to get back to work."

"How can you be sure the black spark is safe?"

I look at Cheryl. "Black sparks have been found in quite a few of the students who formerly resided at the Academy. Some of them have held positions of power and influence in the areas of Research and Dispatch as well as being made into Containers. Our research indicates that approximately 35 percent of the Magical community is actually a carrier of the black spark. Some of them were likely unaware of this. In addition to that, Cheryl is one of the strongest Magic users I know and one of the best people I know. She also happens to have a black spark within her." I smile. "At this time we believe there is no real difference between the three sparks that we have any reason to fear. We will continue to conduct more research into the topic to be sure of this."

A man in the back of the room holds up his hand like a child in school. I point at him and he speaks in a loud, booming voice. "Will you continue to keep the public informed now that you have made us aware that Magic exists?"

I smile at him, thinking how perfect a closing question that is. Then, I nod. "We plan to do just that. Thank you for your time."

January 2

Tanya

Dad uses the remote control to mute the television as the press conference comes to an end. "How about that," he says, "Magic in the real world." He raises his eyebrows in my direction. "Can you believe that?"

I try to shift myself a little on the bed. I've recently been moved back to my house after a short stay at the hospital. I don't remember much of anything. The doctors say that I likely won't remember much. One woman looked very familiar to me when I woke up. I thought she was my mother, which drove my father to tears. He hated having to remind me that my mother was dead. He said it was like living it all over again. He didn't know who the woman was. He said she worked for the hospital and had been trying to help me regain consciousness.

The girl at the press conference looked familiar too. Angela, I think her name was. But that's not possible. Why would a girl from Texas know a powerful Magician who is on TV holding a live press conference? "I can't believe it," I answer him. "Magic isn't real."

He laughs a little. "I guess we'll believe it when we see it, hey pumpkin?" He pats my leg just as there's a knock at the front door. "That'll be the nurse," he says. "I'll just go let her in."

I nod. Part of the agreement to my being allowed to come home was that we have a nurse visit at least twice a week. She's supposed to provide physical therapy and make sure my dressings are all clean. I push myself up a little more in the bed, trying to find a comfortable position. The TV is showing clips that are apparently related to the press conference story. I want to hear what they're saying, I find this all fascinating.

The little mute symbol mocks me from the bottom corner of the screen. I try to reach for the remote Dad left, but it's beyond arm's length. Frustrated, I turn back to the screen and watch the images flash.

Then the woman from the hospital's face fills the screen.

I gasp. Why is she being shown? I squint as if that will make the volume turn up.

Where is he? What is taking so long? I just want to hear the TV.

The volume cuts in, shocking me. " *... the former Magician, responsible for the ...*"

The mute symbol is gone from the corner and the reporter is talking again. But I'm not focused on that. My heart is pounding. How did that just turn itself back on?

Dad enters the room, the nurse trailing behind him. He crosses to the TV and flicks it off. "All right, I'll just leave you two to it." He kisses me on the forehead and leaves the room again.

I try to ignore it. It's not important. It was an accident.

I'm sure I didn't just do Magic.

About the Author

Tabatha Shipley is an author, avid reader, and book addict from Arizona. She has an amazing husband, two remarkable children, and one really quirky dog. She can often be found on social media raving about whatever book she is most recently obsessed with. Find her to join in on the obsession and add to her TBR with your favorite titles.

tabathashipleybooks.com